MW00476017

ORA ET LABORA

VOLUME I

First Printing, 2021
ISBN 978-0645103908
Ordo Templi Orientis
GPO Box 1193
Canberra, ACT 2601
AUSTRALIA

Every effort has been made to determine the ownership of all photos and secure proper permissions. If any errors have inadvertently occurred, we apologise and will correct such in subsequent printings.

www.otoaustralia.org.au
ora-et-labora.site

Editor: Brendan Walls
Cover Design: Ben Hay (honeyrogue.com)
Layout: Padraig Maclain

ORA ET LABORA

AN OTO RESEARCH JOURNAL

MARCH MMXXI E.V

VOLUME I

GRAND LODGE OF AUSTRALIA

ORDO TEMPLI ORIENTIS

IN PERPETUITY PUBLISHING

For

J.W.

CONTENTS

PREFACE

Do what thou wilt shall be the whole of the Law.

Since the foundation of the Oriental Templar Order
(OTO), our 'Academia Masonica' has voluminously
published its research, typically covering its traditional
curricula in the hermetic sciences and related disciplines
such as magic, the yogas, neo-gnosticism and
theosophical masonry. If anything, this process was
democratised with the Order's acceptance of the Law of
Thelema, with more and more members writing about
the new Law and OTO's constitutional alignment to it,
in efforts of promulgation. Today, the Order boasts a
worldwide community of scholar-practitioners looking
into the theory, practice, worship, antecedents, ethics
and morality of Thelema, together with OTO
constitutional design, as well as its ecclesiastical and
magical practice. Together they celebrate and inculcate
the Order's transformation from masonic to magical
Order. The pedagogy behind this research academy
and social laboratory I have called "Social Scientific
Illuminism." The Oriental Templar universe of
discourse is diverse, with research interests and methods
not always expressed in the formal conventions of the
Academy, or finding acceptance in the often contrived
and compromised academic invention of 'western
esoteric' studies. There is no readily definable
"Thelemic scholarship," or an OTO one. What we
have though, around the globe, is something really

exciting going on. The authors in these two volumes of *Ora et Labora* are a snapshot of this new OTO thought leadership. In this case they are the friends and colleagues who answered my private call for papers when the idea for this journal – something agile, rapid, and low resolution – was born. They are people who just get on with it – giving, collegial and unassuming. *Ora et Labora* may well be the first OTO journal ever with such an international scope of contributors, a glimpse of the depth and breadth of the Order's universe of ideas – a timely reminder there is serious commentary and analysis beyond the frivolities of memes and social media brain farts.

Gottfried Heuer has written about a scholarship that is a "trans-temporal, trans-generational and trans-personal approach to the past as an intersubjective web of ideas and concepts." I would add trans-national. For Heuer, this "arcs backwards to the past with the intention to contribute to healing present and future. This orientation equalises meaning and fact and contains a redemptive and numinous dimension – numinous in the sense in which intimate interrelating, conditional for healing, invokes the presence of the holy." At this time of global pandemic, socio-economic disruption, cancel culture, woke-dopery, and a rise in extremism, populism, and weird-ass conspiracy theories, invoking the presence of the holy is in dire need. It is time for an OTO enlightenment heralding forth an Oriental Templar renaissance – a new and revitalising exchange of ideas and reorientation to our landmarks – let us call it intimate interrelating: that might do its bit to see superstition, tyranny and oppression trumped by the traditional OTO values of Peace, Tolerance and Truth, and our pillars of Light, Life, Love and Liberty – Thelema – a beacon and banner in dark times.

Love is the law, love under will.

Shiva X°

National Grand Master General

Ordo Templi Orientis (Australia)

EDITORIAL

Do what thou wilt shall be the whole of the Law.

The idea for *Ora et Labora* came to the Australian Grand Master Shiva X° in the midst of the global pandemic of 2020 e.v. and it came fully formed. For the team who worked on this, it was simply a matter of execution. People were contacted and essays came in almost immediately. The project from inception to completion has taken a handful of months. It seems borne of necessity and has manifested itself without friction and under its own power.

As Grand Secretary General of the Order here in Australia, I was tasked with editing the two volumes you have in your hands. "Editor" is probably a stretch. It was a lighting fast turn-around, again, borne of its own necessity. The essays arrived in great shape, there were a few corrections, but largely you are reading exactly what the authors want you to read. I take responsibility for any mistakes, oversights or errors.

If there was an editorial principle at work it was from the words of the Grand Master who said to me "think of this as a profess house of scholar-practitioners".

These volumes were never intended to adhere to a classical academic approach; rather, they are the collected insights of Order members who have lived the work of the Order for many decades, recorded those experiences and now seek to feed that learning back into the living temple we have all sworn to build. This is the *profess* process, hinted at by the Grand Master, to "avow" "before all, publicly"[1]. These personal research essays constitute living testimonies of the experiences of people who have put theory into practice for the benefit of all. Like much of our work, these are intimations, on-the-move commentaries from the living stream of the unfolding of the New Aeon.

My approach to editing, collecting and ordering the essays was this:

> "The first principle of the growth of the Order as of all living things is modulation or variation; uniformity is to be detested as a symbol of death."[2]

With the exception of Frater O.I.P.'s ground-breaking study of Baphomet, which he generously trusted me to assist with, I have not sought to standardize textual references, style, idiosyncrasies of phrase, sentence or paragraph structure.

I'd like to express my sincerest gratitude to all of the contributors to these journals. I have learned so much from each of you: the professors of this profess house.

---

[1] Skeat's *Etymological Dictionary of the English Language* p. 477.

[2] Liber CXXIV *Of Eden and the Sacred Oak*, Verse 2.

Thank you to Troy MacKellar, Ian Drummond, Federica Tagliabue, Peter Holmes, Daniel Corish & Lisa Campbell-Smith for proofreading, and to Padraig MacIain for hyper-speed layout and design work. Kick out the jams!

In the words of Our Gnostic Saint Friedrich Nietzsche "Nothing succeeds in which high spirits play no part."

Love is the law, love under will.

Brendan Walls

Grand Secretary General

OTO Grand Lodge of Australia

ANNO VVI ☉ 5° ♒ : ☽ 27° ♉

IN THE WEAVES OF THE ORDER

FR. ΦANHΣ X°

In October 2014 e.v. the Grand Lodge of Italy hosted a series of lectures of Br. Shiva X° in Florence, Italy, to celebrate the 100 years of the Paris Working[1]. Unknown to the audience, the Supreme & Holy Kings of the OTO had gathered to officially elect the OHO according to the provisions of the International Bylaws of the Order[2]. Over the same weekend I delivered a lecture on the concept of Authority in the two great schools of initiation in this Aeon, the A∴A∴ and the OTO.

This article is a way to revamp this topic of great initiatic importance. My aim is to show how a symbolic tripartite template informs the concept of Authority in both thelemic Orders[3]. Much can be gleaned from the doctrinal and historical sources available. It is my hope

---

[1] See 'Liber CDXV. Opus Lutetianum, The Paris Working', in 'The Equinox' IV:2.

[2] See http://oto.org/news1014.html

[3] While my lecture was based upon personal research, I had been deeply inspired by J. Daniel Gunther's own presentation 'The Order that hath No Name among Men', and Fr. Shiva's seminal lecture 'Aspiring to the Holy Order'.

that this short overview of the Offices in both schools will trigger further research and magical imagination.[4]

It may be fitting to begin this discussion on authority mentioning what etymology tells us: the Latin verb *augeo* (to exalt, praise, enrich, augment) informed the noun *auctor*, indicating one who promotes, causes, creates new things through its own ingenium. This in turn gave birth to the concept of *auctoritas* (meaning influence, prestige, authority). Among the ancient Romans, the *auctoritas* was originally the intangible power to give meaning to things, to generate a direction and exert influence (rather than command) by virtue of a link to the numinous, divine sphere[5]. It could be held by individuals or connected to offices or institutions alike.

Within the Great Order of the A∴A∴, Authority lies in the Supreme College or Third Order. These Chiefs delegate their Authority to the Adepts of the Inner Order who have forged the proper Link. They in turn supervise the operations of the Outer College or First Order. This is recounted in 'Liber X Porta Lucis', 'Liber

---

[4] It may also help to avert some misunderstanding or worse, confusion generated by fraudulent claims as in the case of self-styled OTO groups or A∴A∴ 'lineages'.

[5] *Auctoritas* was also a technical term of haruspicy, and became connected to the priesthood; a foremost example of *auctoritas* was the office of *Pontifex Maximus* For a general overview, see Cicero's 'De Legibus' ('On the Laws').

LXV vel Causae' and 'One Star in Sight'[6]. It should be underlined that this template resonates with the Tree of Life of the Qabalah; and this structural design was used at the end of the XIXth century to formulate the Hermetic Order of the Golden Dawn.[7]

And so we find the Inner College being governed by the *Praemonstrator* or Teaching Adept, the *Imperator* or Commanding Adept, and the *Cancellarius* or Recording Adept. Their Latin origins are worth mentioning. The first title comes from the Latin *praemonstrare*, *prae* (before) and *monstrare* (to show), a verb meaning to teach, to guide, to predict or to reveal. The second title comes from the Latin *imperare*, a verb signifying to command, to rule, to order. The third title comes from the Latin noun *cancellus*, which means a railing, and therefore gate. As GH Brother Hymenaeus Beta once told me, functions of these Adepti should be investigated in light of Dumezil's studies on the Capitoline Triad in the ancient Roman pantheon[8], and in connection with the three traditional functions of Prophet, Priest and Prince (King).

In the A∴A∴, these three functions have a different latitude compared to ancient Rome or the Medieval

---

[6] See 'The Holy Books of Thelema' (being 'The Equinox' III:9) and 'Magick', Appendix II.

[7] See the Golden Dawn paper 'Z1: The Enterer of the Threshold'.

[8] See Georges Dumezil, 'Archaic Roman Religion'.

times. For the sake of inspiration, I will use the image of the Arrow from 'Liber 418' (5th Aethyr) to describe these in order. In relation to the Chiefs of the Third Order, the Prophet represents the blooming Understanding of the Scarlet Woman; the Priest represents the burning Wisdom of The Beast; the Prince receives the Authority on the middle pillar from the beaming Crown of Aiwass. Taking the paraphrase a step further: Love waits: Life works: Light watches. One Eye in the Triangle.

Another way to observe the archetype of the number 3 at work in connection with the Qabalah is constituted by the corresponding Wands and Robes of the Officers[9]. The blue of Mercy is connected to the Praemonstrator, who bears the Caduceus Wand. The scarlet red of Strength is used for the Phoenix Wand of the Imperator. We find the yellow of Beauty for the Lotus Wand of the Cancellarius.[10]

These colors also appear within the context of the OTO. The most evident example, and by no means unique, is of course found in the Gnostic Mass, the central ritual of the Order. Any Student who has already identified the initiatic logic of the A∴A∴

---

[9] The colors follow the Queen Scale table of correspondences; see 'Liber 777' and 'Magick'.

[10] See 'Liber VII', ch.7 and the Suit of Wands in 'The Book of Thoth'.

underlining the entire structure of Liber XV will know that this is no coincidence.

I would describe the blue of the Virgin as concealing the nakedness of Nuit: adoring Her unveils the Heart of Blood of the Priestess, bare and rejoicing in honor to the blue-lidded daughter of Sunset. The scarlet or brilliant red is the color of the sun-flaming robe of the Priest called to administer the Virtues to the Brethren; it is also the color of the Beast as described in Revelations (17:3). The yellow adorns the Deacon, the minister who acts both as guardian of the Temple in admitting the Congregation and as messenger and mediator while leading the People[11]. For this reason I consider our Mass to be a Carmen of the duplex Alliance between the two Orders, and to constitute – in essence, and beyond any official *imprimatur* – a duplex Class D paper par excellence like 'Liber Resh vel Helios'.

Interestingly, the tripartite pattern is also noticeable in the OTO's structure, although the source derives mainly from our Masonic ancestors. While the pattern is not intentionally connected to the Tree of Life, some resonances may be found when examining the traditional literature of the OTO issued under Past

---

[11] IV° members of the OTO Lodge of Perfection should devote a special effort in studying the Mass in light of 'Magick', Part III, ch. XX and the Temple symbolism of this Degree. It will provide a relevant preparation for the Priestly Recognition when they will reach the dignity of Dame or Knight of the East & West.

OHO Br. Merlin Peregrinus (Gnostic Saint Doctor T. Reuss). According to it, the Order's affairs are administered by an Executive Committee of Three also called the Supreme Council. In the 1917 OTO Constitution one can see the following titles of the three principal Officers of the Headquarters: *Caput Ordinis* or (Outer) Head of the Order; *Quaestor Ordinis* or Treasurer General, and *Cancellarius Ordinis* or Secretary General.

The 'Outer Head of the Order', or *Frater/Soror Superior* is mentioned in the Constitution as *Caput Ordinis*. The Latin word *caput* means head or top; originally it did not mean 'leader' among the Romans, yet today's words like chief, chef, chapter, capital, cap all derive from *caput*. *Ordinis* comes from the Latin nominative noun *ordo*, meaning row, line, originally row of threads in a loom, and connected to *ordiri*, to begin to weave[12]. Later it was used to indicate the lines, and therefore the ranks, of soldiers in battle.

As Commander in Chief he or she is the 'Head of OTO with ultimate responsibility for the government, welfare, continued international growth and expansion and overall management of OTO worldwide.' (cf. 'OTO International Bylaws'). The Office of OHO passed to Br. Baphomet (Gnostic Saint Sir Aleister Crowley) in 1923 e.v and was confirmed by the other

---

[12] See in connection 'Liber CXCIV OTO An Intimation with Reference to the Constitution of the Order', last paragraph.

Grand Masters in 1925ev. As OHO Crowley took the name Phoenix and the cartouche of Ankh-f-n-Khonsu as his own OTO Ring of Authority.[13] Since Crowley's tenure as Frater Superior, the symbolical thread leading to the A∴A∴ Office of Imperator has become doctrinally striking, as stated elsewhere.[14]

The word *Quaestor* derives from the Latin verb *quaerere*, which means to seek, to inquire. During the Roman Empire, the title was given to magistrates, usually indicating a financial administrator in charge of the state funds and goods, like a treasury officer. One Quaestor was a high ranking court officer and custodian of the Temple of Saturn, housing the keys of the state treasury in ancient Rome.

Within the OTO the Quaestor or Treasurer General has charge and custody of all funds and securities of OTO; he or she administer the finances, that is, part of the nourishment of the Order. Initiation into the OTO is granted when the Application is accepted, counter-signed by two witnessing sponsors and the payment of the dues & fees. The money collected goes in part to the Treasury of the OTO. The traditional aspect of Saturn as agricultural God, linked to Mother Earth

---

[13] It is since then the OHO's Ring of Marriage and as such should be hold sacred and never worn by any other member of the Order.

[14] See my paper 'Gathered in their Fold', published in 'Success Is Thy Proof'; relevant portions can be found in Keith Readdy's book 'One Truth. One Spirit'.

(*Saturnia Tellus!*) makes the symbol of the Coin or Disk within this context worthy of further considerations[15].

As we have seen, the word *Cancellarius* comes from the Latin word *cancellus*, meaning gate. Originally, the Cancellarius was the title of the custodian of the gates of a tribunal; later it became the name of the official in charge of the registration of the judge's official acts, that is a secretary or clerk. During medieval times, the Cancellarius was the title of the keeper of the Imperial Seals.

According to the OTO Bylaws, the Cancellarius or Secretary General records the minutes, proceedings and is the custodian of the records of the OTO, as well as of the Golden Book in which are recorded the amendments to the Constitution and the appointments of all officials. Being also the chairman of the Publications Committee of OTO and with

---

[15] See also the Vow of Poverty embodied in the degree structure of the Lover Triad, and in connection to the Grand Treasurer General's office in the context of a National Grand Lodge. (Cf. 'Liber CXCIV', 30-31, 33-34). Such Vow finds its historical antecedent in the solemn promise made by members of religious orders to renounce to the right of individual property or to the free enjoyment of one's own goods, subordinating wealth to a higher purpose. In the OTO we find the concept of poverty interwoven with those of renunciation and service. See also 'Liber CI OTO An Open Letter' and 'Liber CLXI OTO Concerning the Law of Thelema' for inspiration and meditation on the same.

responsibility for intra-Order communication in general, this office has a distinct mercurial quality[16].

These duties are in turn partially delegated to appointed officers of National Sections when a Grand Lodge is being chartered to operate in a country; the Executive of a Supreme Grand Council (of a national Grand Lodge) is modeled upon the Executive of the Supreme Council (of OTO International Headquarters). In 'Liber LII – Manifesto of the OTO' we read: 'The National Grand Master General *ad vitam* is assisted by two principal officers, the Grand Treasurer General and the Grand Secretary General' (point 7); and: 'All communications should be addressed to the Grand Secretary General, and all cheques in favour of the Grand Treasurer General' (point 15).

The model is replicated on smaller scale in Chapters, Lodges and Oases (OTO local bodies), the administrative structure reflecting the initiatic one, as known by our members.[17] While the ceremonial roles of the officers shouldn't be in anyway discussed outside the guarded borders of our Encampments, these deserve attentive meditation, in connection to the Temple's

---

[16] It should be underlined that the element attributed to Mercury is Air, whose weapon is the Sword or Dagger (Cf. 'Magick', Part II, ch.VIII).

[17] The topic of devolution within the structure of the OTO System should be studied in Shiva's 'Aurora Australis: Topological Reflections on the modern MMM in Australia', in 'Best of OZ'.

setting & furniture, and to the Rites' wordings & actions.

So we see that the two main schools of Thelema, despite their distinct structures and historical origins, share a symbolical similitude in relation to their Authority, which is ultimately connected to 'The Book of the Law'[18]. The distinction may be further analyzed in light of the complementary duplex model of Initiation used – one in the Natural World, the other in the Spiritual World.[19]

Yet I consider the purpose of Authority in both Orders to be ultimately the same: to serve the Candidate, the *prima materia*, the free and starry human, that he may become the weaving author of his godly Existence.

---

[18] See 'The New Comment' to The Book of the Law, Ch. II:28

[19] See again J. Daniel Gunther's lectures 'The Order that hath No Name among Men', and Fr. Shiva's 'Aspiring to the Holy Order', as well as the Editorial in 'The Equinox' III (1)

TYPOLOGY OF WILL

in the Writings of Aleister Crowley, Meister Eckhart and Carl Gustav Jung

KRZYSZTOF AZAREWICZ

True and Untrue Will

The concept of Will is a key element of Aleister Crowley's religio-magical philosophy. He emphasized the necessity of finding and then doing the "True Will"[1], a task identified with the accomplishment of the Great Work. Analysis of Crowley's writings demonstrates that he had definite views regarding the components of Will, which can be divided and attributed to the various stages of the Great Work.

For example, in 'Liber CL, De Lege Libellum' he distinguished finite and infinite Will:

> The great bond of all bonds is ignorance. How shall a man be free to act if he know not his own purpose? You must therefore first of all discover which star of all the stars you are, your relation to the other stars about

---

[1] The term "True Will" doesn't appear in *The Book of the Law*. Ultimately, "each man and woman has the same True Will – to regain its original Mother [i.e., Nuit]. See Crowley's comment to 'Liber LXV' III:54 in *The Equinox* IV(1), p. 127.

you, and your relation to, and identity with, the
Whole.

In our Holy Books are given sundry means of making
this discovery, and each must make it for himself,
attaining absolute conviction by direct experience, not
merely reasoning and calculating what is probable.
And to each will come the knowledge of his finite
will, whereby one is a poet, one prophet, one worker
in steel, another in jade. But also to each be the
knowledge of his infinite Will, his destiny to perform
the Great Work, the realisation of his True Self.[2]

Here a "finite Will" refers to the discovery of our life
mission on the material plane, whereas an "infinite
Will" to realisation on the spiritual plane.

Logic suggests that if there is a "True Will", there is
also an "untrue" or "false Will". Crowley doesn't use the
adjective "untrue" in this context, however he refers to
other types of Will quite often. For example, in chapter
66 of *Liber Aleph* he talks about "a false or a
superannuated Will" and in chapter 77 on "Wills
diseased [and] perverse".[3]

Those "negative" aspects of Will also play an important
role in the Great Work; they may serve as a catalyst

---

[2] Crowley, *The Equinox* III(10), p. 63

[3] See Crowley, *Liber Aleph vel CXI. The Book of Wisdom or Folly*.

allowing us to undertake our life's task and to begin a process of transmutation of the base metal into living gold.[4]

Finding one's own true Will may be experienced as the "Knowledge and Conversation of the Holy Guardian Angel", but what about the "untrue" Will?

Crowley seems to address the matter in his commentary to the holy book 'Liber LXV' IV:34:

> Spirit may manifest either as the Holy Guardian Angel or as the Evil Persona, the Dweller on the Threshold, portrayed sensationally for trade by Sir Edward Bulwer-Lytton in his romance *Zanoni*. The doctrine is also frequently found in folklore, where man is represented as attended by both a good and an evil genius. The horror of the latter is intensified by his function as the alternative to the Holy Guardian Angel. No other evil intelligence can compare with this either as subjectively terrible and loathsome or as objectively hostile. For the evil genius is no less a possibility of Attainment than the Holy Guardian Angel.[5]

Although this doctrine may be seen as pertaining only to the ordeals of the A∴A∴, in my opinion it also

---

[4] For the psychological interpretation, see Marlan, *The Black Sun. The Alchemy and Art of Darkness.*

[5] *The Equinox* (IV)1, pp. 152-153.

resonates with the system of O.T.O. and moreover, with the life of every Aspirant who *must* experience various ordeals regardless of his or her affiliation. For example, premature awakening of the *cakras* associated with the Man of Earth degrees, uncontrolled opening of the *nāḍīs* or channels of energy in the subtle bodies – both could result in various types of personality disorders (resulting in e.g. addiction to power, abuse of authority) expressed metaphorically by the term "Evil Persona". In such case an Aspirant is unable to maintain indifference to events, nor is he or she able to "act and react with perfect elasticity":

> The vilest weeds spring up; cruelty, narrow-mindedness, arrogance – everything mean and horrible flowers in those who "mortify the flesh." Incidentally, such ideas spawn the "Black Brother." The complete lack of humour, the egomaniac conceit, self-satisfaction, absence of all sympathy for others, the craving to pass their miseries on to more sensible people by persecuting them: these traits are symptomatic.[6]

An exegesis of Crowley's *Liber Aleph* shall indicate other types of Will but before we look into concepts presented in that book, let us examine a typology suggested by the man whose epistolary style may have

---

[6] Crowley, *Magick Without Tears*, p. 319.

inspired Master Therion to compose *Liber Aleph* – Meister Eckhart.

We know that Crowley read at least some of Eckhart's Sermons. He wrote a short review of them in *The Equinox* and knowing how fierce he could be as a critic, his opinion – although a bit sarcastic – is quite positive: "Too pedantic and theological to please me, though I daresay he means well."[7]

Three Wills of Meister Eckhart

Eckhart von Hochheim (c. 1260-c. 1328), commonly known as Meister Eckhart, was a German philosopher, mystic and a member of the Dominican Order who taught theology at the Universities of Paris and Cologne. In later life, he was accused of heresy and treated as a heretic by Pope John XXII in the latter's 1329 bull *In agro dominico*.

Eckhart preached a "religion of heart" in which man could achieve union with God by direct contemplation of his own soul. He also spoke of passing *beyond* God to a "simple ground," a "still desert" out of which all things were created – a concept strikingly similar to the Tao of Lao Tzu. In his Sermons he discussed the psychological transformation of man and the creative power inherent in detachment:

---

[7] Crowley, *The Equinox* I(2), p. 389.

When I preach it is my wont to speak about
detachment, and of how man should rid himself of self
and all things. Secondly, that man should be in-formed
back into the simple good which is God. Thirdly, that
we should remember the great nobility God has put
into the soul, so that man may come miraculously to
God. Fourthly, of the purity of the divine nature, for
the splendor of God's nature is unspeakable. God is a
word, an unspoken word.[8]

He would take one sentence from the New Testament
and write a comment on its metaphorical content and
ethical meaning. He hoped to deliver a practical
message that could be implemented by the common
man in his effort to become a better person. In other
words, Eckhart was interested in teaching how to
ennoble the human character.

He influenced Paracelsus, Jakub Boehme, Arthur
Schopenhauer, Erich Fromm, Carl Gustav Jung and
inspired modern syncretic spirituality. There are many
studies discussing parallels between Eckhart's
soteriology and Eastern thought.

In his Sermons Eckhart used the term 'Will' quite often.
For him Will was one of the most important factors,
not only responsible for human conduct, but also as a
dynamic force of the universe. It wasn't a mere faculty

---

[8] Eckhart, *The Complete Mystical Works*, Sermon Twenty-Two, p.
152.

of the mind which selects the strongest desire; it wasn't just a cognitive process by which we decide on a particular course of action; it was the Will of Nature, the Will of God manifesting itself as the Process, a progressively unfolding desire of the Finite and Infinite to become *One*; and, since he called God "Nothing" – to become *None*.[9]

In Sermon Seventeen[10] Eckhart discusses the condition of man, his relation with nature and the divine. He doesn't refer directly to the concept of Will, but nevertheless he seems to allude to it in a threefold fashion. A careful examination of the content suggests the following types of Will manifesting in those relations:

- Sensual (Instinctive) Will[11] which we may associate with drives, everyday needs and desires. In its positive manifestation, it is closely related to Mother Nature and the natural law of necessity. In its negative aspect, it is associated with the Father as Logos, resulting in a distancing from Nature and its regulations

---

[9] Cf. *Liber AL vel Legis* I:45 in Crowley, *The Holy Books of Thelema*.

[10] Eckhart, *The Complete Mystical Works*, pp. 129-132.

[11] Eckhart writes how on that level Nature creates "form, image and material being".

towards destructive sexual deviations, crimes, damaging asceticism and the like.

- Rational (Intellectual) Will[12] which we may associate with realisation in life, the attainment of the unity of thoughts, words and actions. It is the highest level of the Ego's development, in which – in Jungian terms – Persona and Shadow are unified. This matter will be addressed later on.

- Eternal Will[13] which we may associate with the experience of the union of the Will of an individual with the Will of God. Here all sufferings and joys, pains and exaltations appear as clouds; they come and go, and the only thing which remains is a direct insight into the I AM. For Eckhart, God was born from the soul of man.

Concept of Will in Crowley's *Liber Aleph*

In chapter 27 of *Liber Aleph* ("On the Silent Will"), Master Therion also enumerates three types of Will:

- Subliminal Will which is expressed by Dreams, Phantasies, and Gestures. It is a link between the

---

[12] According to Eckhart, God creates a Soul.

[13] In Eckhart's words, "it is a strange and desert place, and is rather nameless than possessed of a name, and is more unknown than it is known."

Unconscious and the Conscious. It has its own physical part and if it remains unsatisfied, "its Utterance will predominate in all these automatic Expressions."

- Silent Will which is associated with conscious thoughts, words, and acts. Why is it described as "silent"? We will try to find the answer later.

- Hidden Will which is "the Vector of the Magical Self".

In my opinion such typology resonates well with the concept of Meister Eckhart. By way of demonstration, I would like to briefly analyse Crowley's tripartite division in the light of *Liber Aleph* and his other writings.

Subliminal Will

In the second chapter of *Liber Aleph* ("On the Qabalistic Art") Crowley mentions the tendencies of the mind which "lie deeper far than any Thought, for they are the Conditions and the Laws of Thought".

Those tendencies are called *saṃskāra*s or mental impressions, psychological imprints, lasting traces of our everyday actions which are hidden deep in the unconscious. Those traces – although seemingly latent – are not passive; they have a dynamic nature which manifests itself in the human *psyche*.[14] Most of the time,

---

[14] Feuerstein, *The Encyclopedia of Yoga and Tantra*, p. 314.

we are not aware of such tendencies. We don't control them and moreover, they decide for us in which direction we go through life and as such they are "barriers upon the Path; they are modifications of the Ego, and therefore those things which bar it from the absolute."[15]

In the third chapter of *Liber Aleph* ("On Correcting Life"), Therion describes them as passions, hindrances that are not part of the True Will. They are "diseased Appetites, manifest in us through false early Training."

In the same chapter we read: "Either the Force of Repression carries it, and creates Neuroses and Insanities; or the Revolt against that Force, breaking forth with Violence, involves Excesses and Extravagances. All these Things are Disorders, and against Nature."

I think Crowley refers here to the shift from dependency on Mother Nature towards the Father, the Logos. In other words, a subject is trapped in the dialectics of instinct and reason, or using kabalistic phraseology, of Nephesh and Ruach.

In chapter 30 ("On the Way of Liberty"), we find further comment on that matter. True Will is surrounded by:

---

[15] Crowley *The Book of Lies*, commentary to the chapter 46 where he prefers Pali term *saṅkhāra*. See also chapter 47.

... false and perverted Wills, monstrous Growths, Parasites, Vermin are they, adherent to thee by Vice of Heredity, or of Environment or of evil Training. And of all these Things the subtlest and most terrible, Enemies without Pity, destructive to thy will, and a Menace and Tyranny even to thy self, are the Ideals and Standards of the Slave-gods, false Religion, false Ethics, even false Science.

In the language of psychology, *saṃskāra*s are dispositions hidden in the unconscious. In order to achieve the final emancipation, they must be burned down or – as Crowley puts it in *Liber Aleph* – "brought to Nought".[16]

Part of our work is to introduce permanent change in the consciousness; to reprogram ourselves. This is why Master Therion devoted so much space in *Liber Aleph* to discussing dreams which are expressions of the Subliminal Will. The content of dreams change with the reduction of *saṃskāra*s .

Thelema offers a whole range of techniques for reducing the imprints, however this is beyond the scope of this essay. Crowley sums up the matter in the chapter 44 of *Liber Aleph* ("On Wisdom in Sexual Matters"): "the Problem is ever to bring the Appetite into right Relation with the Will."

---

[16] See chapter 2.

When the Aspirant harmonises his or her Appetite and
Will, the focus of consciousness moves from the
Subliminal Will to the Silent Will.

Silent Will

It must be emphasized that in the Thelemic ethos there
is nothing wrong with Subliminal or Instinctive Will.
'Liber Libræ' encourages us to strengthen the animal
passions, *but* at the same time to control them.[17]
Shifting the focus to the Silent Will requires discipline
of our emotions and the reason.

In other words, we need to regulate the machinery of
sephira Netzach which is associated with emotions and
feelings and of sephira Hod which is associated with the
intellect. The machinery of the lower mind must work
without friction and unnecessary drone. In letter 14 of
Magick Without Tears, Crowley writes that the greatest
obstacle to human progress is noise.[18]

In chapter 130 of *Liber Aleph* ("On Reason, the Minister
of the Will"), we read:

> O my Son, do thou lay this Word beneath thine
> Heart, that the Mind hath no Will, nor Right thereto,
> so the Usurpation bringeth forth a fatal Conflict in
> thyself. For the Mind is sensitive, unstable as Air, and
> may be led foolishly in Leash by a stronger Mind that

---

[17] Crowley, *The Equinox* III(10), p. 84.

[18] Crowley, *Magick Without Tears*, p. 125.

worketh as the cunning Tool of a Will. Therefore thy Safety and Defence is to hold thy Mind to his right Function, a faithful Minister to thine own True Will, that is King of that Star whose Name is Thy Self, by Election of Nature.

To paraphrase 'Liber Libræ', at this level we should not only "act passionately" but also "think rationally". Such thinking has nothing to do with materialism, nor with rejection of the Great Unknown. It rather implies sharpening the blade of the intellect and training of the reason. As we read in 'Liber Libræ':

> To obtain Magical Power, learn to control thought; admit only those ideas that are in harmony with the end desired, and not every stray and contradictory Idea that presents itself.

> Fixed thought is a means to an end. Therefore pay attention to the power of **silent** thought and meditation. The material act is but the outward expression of thy thought ... Thought is the commencement of action, and if a chance thought can produce much effect, what cannot fixed thought do?[19]

The world seen through the eye of the focused mind is harmonious and beautiful; thoughts become precise and crystal clear. To such a mind, even apparently chaotic

---

[19] Crowley, *The Equinox* III(10), p. 84. My emphasis.

and destructive manifestations have their own place in the Great Plan: "For the Aspirant, there must be Nothing, however mean, insignificant, vile and loathsome, that is not the Voice of the Most High, music and beauty to the Neshamah. Then, not before, your Ruach may construct (by means of its machinery) a mortal intellectual image of the truth you have won".[20]

Now Will becomes "silent" as it doesn't experience any frictions, noises or random thoughts. Through the contemplation and harmonisation of emotions and intellect the Aspirant achieves a state of union with himself. As Crowley wrote in his comment to Liber LXV I:18 "Perfect union is silent".[21]

Hidden Will

It is very difficult to grasp with the rational mind things that are "hidden". The laws governing the Hidden Will are those of paradox; and here freedom means bondage. The Hidden Will – to quote chapter 8 of *Liber Aleph* – is "true Motion of thine inmost Being". And that "inmost being" is our True Self. It is much greater than we can imagine.

In his essay 'Duty' Crowley wrote:

---

[20] Crowley to Frieda Harris, Dec. 17th, 1940(?), Yorke Collection NS 117.

[21] Crowley, *The Equinox* IV(1), p. 91.

You must accept everything exactly as it is in itself, as one of the factors which go to make up your True Self. This True Self thus ultimately includes all things soever; its discovery is Initiation (the travelling inwards) and as its Nature is to move continually, it must be understood not as static, but as dynamic, not as a Noun but as a Verb.[22]

Here lies the key to the Law of Thelema. Success in the Great Work requires our ability to adjust ourselves to the environment around us, to accept it so that we can fully develop and use our potential without unnecessary frictions with the outside world. We can't escape the influence of the society, culture and family we were brought up in. Those factors should be seen as the utterance of the Hidden Will.

Let us contemplate what Master Therion writes in chapter 142 of *Liber Aleph* ("On the Harmony of Will and Destiny"): "it is thine own self, omniscient and omnipotent, sublime in eternity, that first didst order the course of thine orbit, so that the which befalleth thee by fate is indeed the necessary effect of thine own will."

Further comment on the matter can be found in chapter 57 ("On the Necessity of Will"):

---

[22] Crowley, *The Revival of Magick and Other Essays*, p. 135.

> Learn also that all Action is in some sense Magick, being an essential Part of that Great Magical Work which we call Nature. Then thou hast no Free Will? Verily, thou hast said. Yet never the less it is thy necessary Destiny to act with that Free Will. Thou canst do nothing save in accordance with that true Nature of thine and of all Things.

And indeed, "there is no law, beyond do what thou wilt."[23] It seems that Will and Destiny are the same concepts, and the silent, hidden Self is a resounding voice of the world around. All conditions are only a field for the manifestation of Will and we are not "Its master, but the vehicle of It."[24]

In some sense the Hidden Will must always be hidden: its complete discovery would mean an end of the journey. We can grasp only temporarily its particular facets, and such moments of contact help us to integrate what is hidden with our Rational or Silent Will through the above-mentioned intellectual machinery of Ruach. An allusion to that process is found in the Holy Book Liber VII 1:7: "Let the work be accomplished in

---

[23] *Liber AL vel Legis* I:42.

[24] Crowley, *The Book of Lies*, chapter 18. The problem of free will and obedience to the "higher forces" is discussed by Mahatma Guru Sri Paramahansa Shivaji in his *Eight Lectures on Yoga*. See the third lecture for Yellowbellies, in particular paragraphs 4,5 and 6. This matter is relevant especially to the members of O.T.O.

silence."[25] To paraphrase: "Let the work be accomplished in the Silent Will".

Three Aspects of Will and Carl Gustav Jung

Swiss psychiatrist and founder of analytical psychology, Carl Gustav Jung, suggested that the process of fulfilment of the individual ("an Individuation") requires a confrontation with three seemingly independent parts of personality:

- **Shadow** which is the animal nature of man, responsible for the emergence of negative feelings, thoughts and actions. It's instinctive, irrational and responsible for a mechanism of projection.

- **Ego** which is expressed through the conscious mind: thoughts, memories and feelings. The ego is responsible for the sense of identity and integrity.

- **Self** which is the unification of the conscious with the unconscious, male with female. Its totality is the final result of the individuation.

Will of the Shadow

It can be argued that the Shadow is the dark side of the human personality and the birthplace of Original Sin. Shadow can be projected on to another person so that

---

[25] Crowley, *The Holy Books of Thelema*, p. 11.

we don't see negative aspects in ourselves, but only in others. If properly integrated, it can become the best teacher as it shows our weaknesses, deficiencies and sources of obsessions:

> Dr. Jung has pointed out that the shadow cast by the conscious mind of the individual contains the hidden, repressed, and unfavorable (or nefarious) aspects of the personality. But this darkness is not just the simple converse of the conscious ego. Just as the ego contains unfavorable and destructive attitudes, so the shadow has good qualities – normal instincts and creative impulses. Ego and shadow, indeed, although separate, are inextricably linked together in much the same way that thought and feeling are related to each other.[26]

I will revisit this aspect below.

Will of the Ego

Ego helps us organise thoughts through the synthesis of information and through the ability to judge them. It is worth noticing that although consciousness resides in the Ego, not all the Ego's activities are conscious. It is in close contact with the Subliminal Will and any friction between these two centers result in the creation of all sorts of defense mechanisms, guilt, inferiority complex, anxiety and the like.

---

[26] Joseph L. Henderson, 'Ancient Myth and Modern Man' in C.G. Jung, *Man and His Symbols*, p. 118

In the Kabalistic interpretation, the Shadow and the Ego are connected to each other in the sephira Yesod. In *Liber 777*, this sephira (together with Malkuth) is attributed to the lowest *cakra* called *Mūlādhāra*.[27] However, at the same time, Yesod functions as the lowest level of the intellectual sphere of Ruach, which obviously is the seat of the Ego.

Quite often spiritual literature perceives the Ego as the source of evil which should be completely annihilated. Personally, I disagree with this notion: the Ego should be disciplined and set in the right proportions in relation to other centers. Even if during the process of initiation, the Ego must be disintegrated, it needs to be reintegrated on the higher plane of the Eternal Will of the Self.

Will of the Self

Jung postulated that once we have secured the needs and security of the Ego, which takes place in the first half of life, it is time to focus on the conscious discovery of our totality, or the Self.

Why is the Will of the Self called the Hidden Will? Although the Ego serves as the vehicle for manifestation of the Self, the Self is much greater than the Ego. We can grasp it only for very short periods of time, but we will not understand it, we will not reveal its mystery completely. Constant experience of the

---

[27] Crowley, *Liber 777*, col. CXVIII, p. 22.

depth of the Self would mean losing contact with Ruach and phenomenal reality.[28]

The journey itself, the journey towards what is hidden, is the most beautiful reward, because reaching the goal would bring rest, stagnation and finally death. As we read in *The Book of Lies*: "The weary pilgrim struggles on; the satiated pilgrim stops."[29]

Tripartite Will and the Gnostic Mass

Eckhart's and Jung's typologies of Will resonate with the mysteries of Thelema. Let's take as an example the formula of "Three in One". It is impossible for one of three Wills to be dormant. They may experience some serious disharmony and chaos, however we inherit them all and they constantly operate in various proportions.[30]

---

[28] One may argue that for Crowley, his Self was manifesting to him as V.V.V.V.V. He was able to establish contact with it/him only occasionally.

[29] Crowley, *The Book of Lies*, chapter 46. Also see *Liber AL vel Legis* I:44: "For pure will, unassuaged of purpose, delivered from the lust of result, is every way perfect."

[30] They are like three *gunas* and zoomorphic totems revolving on Atu X, The Fortune. The secret root of our existence, the Khabs, is the solar axis of the wheel. It is the true and total I AM. The three Wills are represented by the three wheels on the card: the first of which serves as the axis with the star, the second which serves as the rim and the third, often overlooked, placed horizontally, slightly behind and above the Sphinx. They formulate a principle

The Gnostic Mass,[31] in which Thelemites glorify the "eternal Sun" who is "One in Three, Three in One", can be perceived as the journey of the hero (the Priest), who goes through various initiatory stages towards his Self. Other officers represent functions of his persona:[32] the Priestess is the higher intuition of the hero, the Deacon represents the faculty of reasoning and the Children are his four senses.[33] In this context the Mass plays an illustrative or educational role for the members of the congregation who can contemplate the unfolding the mystery of the Individuation.

The temple is divided into three parts which are separated from each other by the veils.

- In the West there is a Tomb with a veil which is pulled down by the Priestess' sword.

- In the middle there is a font, a small black square altar, of superimposed cubes and three steps leading to the second veil.

---

which in the Gnostic Mass is called "triform Mysterious Energy".

[31] Cf., 'Liber XV O.T.O. Ecclesiæ Gnosticæ Catholicæ Canon Missæ' in *The Equinox* III(10), pp. 123-138.

[32] As we read in 'Liber XV': they are "part of the Priest himself."

[33] The four senses are symbolised by Children's weapons: a cellar of salt (Touch), a pitcher of water (Taste), a casket of perfume (Smell), a censer of fire (Sight). The fifth sense (Spirit) is represented by the strike of the Bell. See Crowley, *Liber 777*, col. LV and *The Book of Lies*, chapter 62.

- In the East, behind the great veil, which is parted by the Priest's lance, there is a shrine and pillars.

The three areas of the temple correspond to the Subliminal, Silent and Hidden Will. In my personal opinion, they also reflect the work of the three triads of O.T.O.: the Man of Earth, the Lover and the Hermit.

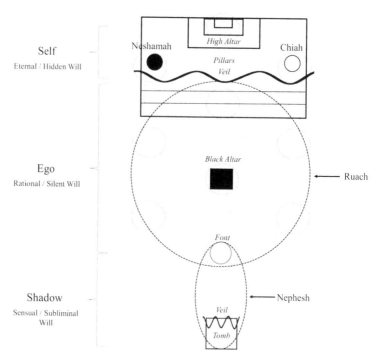

Subliminal Will and the Gnostic Mass

The Subliminal Will, associated with the senses, instincts and the Shadow, manifests itself in the tomb.

Work related to this stage is very personal. The basic tools for mastering it are given during the progressive initiations of the Man of Earth.

The Priest, leaving the tomb, the land of the shadow of the Man of Earth, gives three regular steps and signs. He demonstrates that he is a Master Magician[34] who experienced Lustration, Consecration and Devotion corresponding to his past, present and future. In other words, he knows where he comes from, who he is and where he is going. Those three questions play an extremely important role in the full integrity of the Ego and the conscious formulation of them is a very important step in the progression of the Aspirant whose goal is to know himself.

By implementing the tools given to him at his initiations, the Priest is able to experience the first miracle: the awakening of the divine intuition, Neshama, which is represented by the Priestess.

The Third Degree is associated with *Svādhiṣṭhāna cakra*. *Swa* means "one's own", whereas *adhisthana* means "dwelling place". This *cakra* is associated with the genital area and with the unconscious which stores *saṃskāras*. The awakening of *Svādhiṣṭhāna* confers liberation from inner enemies such as lust, hatred, greed

---

[34] Technically, the Priest's ordination takes place at the degree of the Knight of the East and West. This doesn't contradict the fact that after leaving the tomb he takes three steps and signs referring to the three first degrees.

and the like. Now, the Master Magician may become a *Paśupati* or "a master of animal instincts"[35]: "before the ego can triumph, it must master and assimilate the shadow."[36]

The Priestess enters the temple as if to respond to the recitation of the Creed by the congregation. The recitation takes place after the Deacon proclaims "the Law of Light, Life, Love and Liberty", and urges people to take the first step on the path represented by the step and sign of the Man and Brother. It is the Deacon, as an integral part of the Priest, who awakens Neshama. In other words, the Aspirant fulfilled the degree work of the Man of Earth and now is focused on the implementation and promulgation of the Law of Thelema and its four pillars (Light, Life, Love and Liberty) within and without. Divine Inspiration is a direct answer to his Aspiration and Neshama descends to the tomb in the form of the "mortal intellectual image of the truth he has won."

Silent Will

After pulling down the veil of the tomb, the Priestess makes three crosses with her sword, as if to emphasize the need to awaken the three Wills. Similarly (but this time with an open hand), she makes three signs during

---

[35] Cf. Saraswati, *Kundalini Tantra*, p. 148.

[36] Joseph L. Henderson, 'Ancient Myth and Modern Man', in Jung, *Man and his Symbols*, p. 121.

the purification and another three during the Priest's consecration. Crosses are drawn "over his forehead, breast, and body" which allows us to identify the three Wills with corresponding parts of the body. Note that there are a total of nine crosses, and the number nine corresponds to Yesod. Thus, the aspirant enters the lower space of Ruach, into the world of Silent or Rational Will which is governed by the laws of the Ego.

In theory, the further progression of the ceremony seems to be very fast and before we realise it, the Priest is already facing another veil. Nevertheless, in the temple between both veils a huge number of events take place: namely, the aforementioned purification and consecration of the Priest, his clothing and crowning, the elevation of the Priestess, the Priest's circumambulation, the orations in front of the great veil and recitation of the Collects.

All these elements should be analysed and reflected on. They are not just symbolic; they form *yama* and *niyama* which have a strong impact on formulating and later, mastering the Aspirant's Ego.

Hidden Will and the Gnostic Mass

The same can be said about the Hidden Will. The voice of intuition in the Priest makes him realise that "There is no law beyond do what thou wilt". It is only due to this realisation that he is able to open the great veil to see the world as it really is.

The Priest exclaims: "Iô iô iô iaô sabaô, Kurie Abrasax Kurie Meithras Kurie Phalle. Io Pan. Io Pan Pan". To quote the "Prologue of the Unborn" from 'Liber VII', his "tongue breaks forth into a weird and monstrous speech", and "the sixth interior sense aflame with the inmost self of Him." The experience is overwhelming, it "flung [him] down the precipice of being", "even to the abyss, annihilation".[37]

The Priest is not only able to experience such a powerful insight but also to show others the essential elements leading to it. He turns to the congregation with the host and the wine, which represent his body and blood transformed into the body and blood of God. *Deus Est Homo.* Sharing that experience in the form of the Eucharist has enormous importance and cannot be underestimated. It becomes a "story" passed by the older generation to the younger so that the flame of Gnosis is kept alive.

The experience is so powerful that it is impossible to remain constantly on such a level of consciousness. Hence the Priest returns to the tomb, the world of the Shadow, where nourished by the memory of the experience, he may continue the never-ending Work of perfecting himself.[38]

---

[37] Crowley, *The Holy Books of Thelema*, p. 9.

[38] The return to earth is important for another reason: the Priest attends to the "welfare of mankind". See Crowley's comment to 'Liber LXV' I:47–48 in *The Equinox* IV(1), p. 94.

Gnostic Mass as the Monomyth

In *Magick Without Tears*, Crowley compared the process of initiation to "a celebration of the Adventures of the God whom it is intended to invoke."[39] The adventures are experienced during an aspirational journey portrayed symbolically in the Gnostic Mass, where the Priest assimilates various parts of the *psyche* on his quest to self-discovery.

Joseph Campbell describes as many as 17 stages of the Hero's Journey.[40] Those stages may be organised in a number of ways, including division into three "acts" of the narrative:[41]

- Departure (also called a Separation)

- Initiation

- Return

In the departure part, the hero lives in the ordinary world, symbolised by the tomb in the Mass, the world of 'dark stars' or people who are not initiates, those who constantly sleep and who are conditioned. The hero receives a call to go on an adventure. Initially, he is reluctant to follow the call, but is helped by a mentor, in the Mass represented by the Priestess who – on one

---

[39] Crowley, *Magick Without Tears*, p. 123.

[40] Campbell, *The Hero with a Thousand Faces*, p. 227.

[41] Ibid., pp. 47-226.

level of the interpretation – symbolises his divine intuition.

Quite often when the call is given, the future hero first refuses to answer it. This may result from fear, insecurity or any other reasons that hold a person in his or her current circumstances. In the Gnostic Mass the future Priest says: "I'm a man among men". He doesn't feel worthy.

The initiation section begins with the hero traversing the threshold to the unknown or "different world", where he faces various ordeals. In the Mass those ordeals are apparently absent; this is because of the special emphasis placed in Thelemic training on the conduct and attitude of the hero. During the course of the ceremony there is no time to analyse traps waiting for us on the path. One simply follows the instruction and by repetition the acts become habits and then the new *saṃskāras* are volitionally planted in the unconscious. Thelema, as the formula of going, is dynamic, not static. Thus, the hero reconditions himself.

In other words, it seems that the Mass presents an idealised process of positive reintegration. Hence, there are no negative energies in it. In the monomyth of the Priest there are no dangers and we can only speculate that he has integrated all his personal demons in the tomb, during the Man of Earth training. What remains is to constantly repeat the formula, to invoke often and to enflame one's own being with prayer.

The hero must then return to the ordinary world with his reward, very often presented as the Elixir of Life, which may now be used for the benefit of others. The essence of life and joy of the earth are within him.

There, hidden again in the shadow of the earth, under the wings of dark night, he doesn't sleep anymore. He is awake. In the contemplative tranquility he experiences the moment of truly being him-Self, and he is free from all wants, from I and No-I. The Will of the Self is an agreement for all to occur because it *occurs*. The Will of the Self flourishes in a minute fraction of time beyond time, where we don't want anything, and we don't reject anything, because everything is exactly where it should be. And then, hidden again behind the veil, he shall hear the Voice of the Master: "all ways are alike, being endless, eternally coiling in curves of ineffable wonder."[42]

I would like to thank Ania Orzech and Frater 515 for helpful comments and proof reading.

---

[42] Crowley, *The Heart of the Master*, p. 39.

Meister Eckhart	Master Therion	C.G. Jung	O.T.O.	Liber Librae 10	Liber Librae 12
Sensual (Instinctive) Will	Subliminal Will	Shadow	Man of Earth	Strengthen and control the animal passions	Act passionately
Rational (Intellectual) Will	Silent Will	Ego	Lover	Discipline the emotions and the reason	Think rationally
Eternal Will	Hidden Will	Self	Hermit	Nourish the Higher Aspirations	Be Thyself

AN ANALYSIS OF *LIBER LIBRAE*

FRATER V.I.A.

Liber Librae sub figura (under the figure of) *XXX*, also called *The Book of the Balance*, was the second book to appear in the first volume and number of *The Equinox*, the Official Organ of the A∴A∴ in the Spring of 1909 e.v. The A∴A∴, which is the name of the Third and Supernal Order, as well as the name of the system as a whole, had been reconstituted just two years previous in 1907. *Liber Librae*, in part, announced this newly formulated Order, and at the same time drew from the ashes of its predecessor, the Golden Dawn, which in turn was the name of its first Order or Outer College.

The Praemonstrance (from the word praemonstrare, to show, or show beforehand) of the book lists Frater D.D.S., the Inner College motto of George Cecil Jones, as the first Premonstrator (see Praemonstrance) or instructor of the A∴A∴; Frater O. S. V., the initials for Ol Sonuf Vaoresagi (Enochian; ol sonf uorsg, 'I reign over you'), is the motto of Aleister Crowley, the first Imperator or governor of the A∴A∴; and Frater Non Sine Fulmine (Lat., 'not without a thunderbolt'), is the motto of J.F.C. Fuller, the first Cancellarius or secretary/scribe of the Great Order. All three of these officers play a significant role in what follows.

A ∴ A ∴ Publication in Class B.
Issued by order :
D.D.S. $7° = 4°$ Premonstrator
O.S.V. $6° = 5°$ Imperator
N.S.F. $5° = 6°$ Cancellarius

According to *Liber CCVII, A Syllabus of the Official Instructions of the A∴A∴*, first published in *The Equinox* I: X (1913), Class B books consist 'of books or essays which are the result of ordinary scholarship, enlightened and earnest.' For an example, two recently published Class B A∴A∴ books, which will be referenced, are *Initiation in the Aeon of the Child* and *The Angel and the Abyss* by J. Daniel Gunther.

A photograph that precedes the text of *Liber Librae* is called 'The Silent Watcher.' This is also the first appearance of what became the border for A∴A∴ books or Libri, noting in particular the double crown of truth (worn by Egyptian gods such as Min) at the top of the pillars on each side. This crown and its association to the formula of Truth will reoccur. Absent at this time are the stylized hieroglyphs from the *Stele of Revealing*, which came to inform the base of the pillars.

Regarding the robe of this figure, Hymenaeus Beta notes in *Book IV* (pg. 725): 'The first volume of *The Equinox* has many photographs showing a Second

Order robe, which has a characteristic cross on the breast; Crowley's red Adeptus Major robe survives, which is probably the robe in these photographs.' The Grade of Adeptus Major is attributed to the Sephira Geburah (Strength) and to Yetziratic Mars. Here we have a connection to the title of the book in that Geburah is connected to Tiphareth (Yetziratic Sol), through the path of Lamed (Yetziratic Libra).

The figure itself is giving the gesture called the Sign of Silence or Harpocrates, as taught in another book published in the next number of *The Equinox*, *Liber O vel Manus et Sagittae* ('hands and arrows'). *Liber O* specifically references this image and describes it as such: 'place the right forefinger upon the lips, so that you are in the characteristic position of the God Harpocrates.' According to a description of the old Neophyte ritual (Z1), also published in *The Equinox* I: II, Harpocrates is situated in the central path of Samekh ('arrow') on the Tree of Life, between two figures: the 'Evil Triad' (the 'Tempter, Accuser and Punisher of the Brethren') at Yesod, and the Hegemon, who is at the intersection of Samekh and Pe;' 'the Balance at the equilibrium of the Scales of Justice...' Additionally, the latter has two forms, signified by her mitre, which in turn suggests the double-crown of Truth. One of her forms as the Goddess Thmaist is identified with Themis, who Gunther identifies with the Egyptian goddess Ma'at. Harpocrates is described as the 'Lotus-throned Lord of Silence, even that Great God Harpocrates, the younger brother of Horus.'

In *The Equinox* I: I, preceding the book *John St. John*, is the compliment to the Sign of Silence – the Sign of the Enterer or Horus. The photograph is titled 'Blind Force,' which is a designation for an undirected energy (see Book I of the Z2 in *The Temple of Solomon the King*, in *The Equinox* I: III), and may allude to the title of the Hiereus: 'Horus in the City of Blindness.' Note that the two signs in the photographs appear opposite of how they are given in practice with the active sign of the Enterer (with a wand) followed by the defending sign of Silence. Regarding this arrangement, consider the 'function' of the Third Order or A∴A∴ in *Liber Tau*: 'Silence in Speech'; 'Construction.'

Initially, both of these signs were attributed to the
Neophyte 1°=10□ Grade associated to the sephira
Malkuth and earth in the old G.D. Order (which
became under the A∴A∴, the Outer Order grades of
Neophyte through Philosophus). However, with the
addition of the Probationer Grade, the Signs of Horus
and Harpocrates became attributed to the Grade of
Probationer, residing in the Qliphoth below Malkuth
(see pg. 206 of *Initiation in the Aeon of the Child*), and
outside the Outer Order of the G.D. Perhaps not
surprisingly, *Liber Librae* is one of the books assigned
for study by the Probationer. Note also that Horus is
'at the borders of the Qliphoth' in the old G.D.
Neophyte temple, whereas the robe of the Probationer
'showeth Ra-Hoor-Khuit <the perfected Horus>
openly upon the breast…' (*Liber VIII*).

The editorial of *The Equinox* I: I states: 'In this first
number are published three little books; the first an
account of Their character and purpose, restored from
the writings of von Eckartshausen <*An Account of
A∴A∴, Liber XXXIII*>; the second an ethical essay
restored from the Cipher MSS. Of the G∴D∴. (of
which MSS. A complete account will later be given);
these two books chiefly for the benefit of those who
will understand wrongly or not at all the motto 'THE
METHOD OF SCIENCE – THE AIM OF
RELIGION,' in which (if rightly interpreted) all is
expressed….' Emblazoned on the cover of *The Equinox*
is this motto, which also shows an image of a woman

with a sword and balances (i.e. an image of Justice and Libra, the sign of the Fall Equinox). Additionally, both *An Account of A∴A∴* and *Liber Librae* are also similar in that they are 'restored' versions by Crowley of other documents.

In the 'Official Instructions of the A∴A∴,' first published in *Magick in Theory and Practice* in 1929, *Liber Librae* is labeled an 'ethical essay' and described as 'An elementary course of morality suitable for the average man.' Note again that the book is in Class B, indicating 'ordinary scholarship' and that 'average' is a synonym for 'ordinary.' Additionally, in *Book IV* part 1, 'ethical questions' are also referred to *Liber Librae*. Ethics, based on moral principles, which in turn inform conduct, are addressed by Crowley in other places – oftentimes within an OTO context. For example, *Liber LXXVII* or *Liber OZ*, is described as 'the OTO plan in words of one syllable,' which contains five sections, the first of which pertains specifically to 'Morality.' There is also the OTO text *Duty*, which deals with 'the chief rules of practical conduct to be observed by those who accept the Law of Thelema.' Additionally, there are a number of chapters in *Liber Aleph* (96, 186, etc.), that touch upon morality, as well as a number of letters in *Magick Without Tears* ('Morality' parts 1 and 2, 'Thelemic Morality,' 'Sex Morality,' etc.). In a document titled 'Obligations,' written around 1913, Crowley also notes that the OTO gives a complete moral system based on the Law of Thelema.

Consider also this statement from *One Star in Sight* regarding Members of the A∴A∴: 'They must accept the Book of the Law as the Word and the Letter of Truth, and the sole Rule of Life.' Compare this to the declaration given in the Vth degree 'obligation of allegiance' in respect to *Liber CCXX*: 'I declare it to be the Letter and the Word of Truth and the Supreme Rule of Life' (Starr, p. 54). As Crowley explains in the

'System of the OTO' in *Magick Without Tears*: 'We, however, are concerned mostly with the very varied experiences of Life.'

There is also a note to the number assigned to the book: '30 is the letter lamed [which means an Ox-goad or spiked stick used for driving cattle], which is "Justice" [renamed Adjustment in *The Book of Thoth*] in the Tarot, referred to Libra.' Libra is the 6th of the 12 signs of the Zodiac – it is in the center, or the place of balance. From Crowley's description of Justice (1915):

> … At the entrance of the Sun into Libra, the days and nights are again equal, and this card is a fitting complement to 'The Emperor' who presides over Aries. This is the moment of the crucifixion of the Sun who now descends beneath the equator for the remaining six months of the year. Libra is ruled by Venus, but Saturn is exalted in the sign, and this indicates, with reference to the life of man, the sorrow and burden of the woman. It will be noticed that the sceptre in the hand of the Emperor, the symbol of creation and construction, is replaced by the sword which destroys. It is this woman who executes the fiat of the Almighty, who has appointed that every rise shall be equilibrated by a fall. (pg. 39 in *The General Principles of Astrology*)

The 'sorrow and burden of the woman' has it's origins in *Genesis* 3:16 (KJV): 'Unto the woman he said, I will greatly multiply thy sorrow and thy conception; in sorrow thou shalt bring forth children; and thy desire *shall be* to thy husband, and he shall rule over thee.' According to Gunther, the Scarlet Woman is 'a technical name for the Master of the Temple,' a grade which is attributed to the planet Saturn, which is again exalted in the sign of Libra. Moreover, the trigram attributed to the Master of the Temple in *Liber XXVII* has the Yetziratic attribution of Libra in *The Angel and the Abyss*.

The 'life of man,' including 'the sorrow and burden of the mother' described above also suggests the progression of the aspirant. According to Gunther: 'Beginning as one dead, the first goal of the seeker is resurrection from a death which the world calls life, thereby reversing the Wheel in order to become the Child and reenter the womb of the Mother.'

The sun's movement into Libra is also 'the moment of the crucifixion of the Sun.' In the image 'The Crucifixion of Frater P,' Frater D.D.S. - who resembled traditional conceptions of Jesus Christ according to Crowley and who wears the double-crown of Truth - presides over the crucifixion of Frater Perdurabo (Crowley's Neophyte motto).

THE CRUCIFIXION OF FRA. P.

As mentioned previously, Libra is the path connecting the Sephira Geburah (Yetziratic Mars – 5) on the Pillar of Severity, with the Sephira Tiphareth (Yetziratic Sol – 6). Note that 6 (Sol) x 5 (Mars) = 30, the number of Lamed. Also, the Tarot association to Lamed, without the switch with Leo, is Atu or Key XI – the number of Magick (5 + 6 = 11).

In reference to *The Gnostic Mass*, note that the diagonal path of Virgo, the Virgin, is opposite the diagonal path of Libra on the Tree of Life. Additionally, the traditional figure of Justice is of a woman bearing a sword and scales, and the color of Libra in the Queen Scale of Color – the paths 'as they are found in Nature,' is blue (the principal color designating the Priestess).

Although initially designated the Virgin in the ritual and described as '*virgo intacta*,' the Priestess, enters *The Gnostic Mass* temple with a sword and two children (i.e. the scales), and halts at the center of the temple (the place of balance). The Priestess of *The Gnostic Mass* is also 'specially dedicated to the service of the Great Order,' or the A∴A∴.

Consider further the significance of the woman in Crowley's description of Libra, and that the other path leading to Geburah (6°=5°) or Mars is the Hanged Man ('The Brothers of A∴A∴ are Women: the Aspirants to A∴A∴ are Men.'). As noted with the 'technical name' of the Scarlet Woman above, Gunther similarly attributes the 'true' Hanged Man to the Master of the Temple (pg. 121 of *The Angel and the Abyss*) - who is shown suspended from an averse ankh representative of Venus, which rules Libra.

The 1986 publication of *The Equinox* III: X, included the second appearance of *Liber Librae*. The Introduction reads:

> We have collected virtually all of the OTO's founding documents for this number...the purpose of this collection is twofold: first, to provide a ready compendium of the essential OTO material as a guidebook during the renaissance the Order presently enjoys, and secondly, to make plain to the public exactly what the Order is, and is not.

Additionally, *Liber Librae* is listed in Section 1 of the *OTO Curriculum* which includes 'Official publications of the A∴A∴ that are cited or quoted in published and unpublished OTO literature, or which contain significant discussion of OTO doctrine....' So, how is *Liber Librae* connected to the OTO?

The OTO makes an initial appearance in *The Equinox* I: VIII, published in Autumn 1912, with this note: 'The Premonstrator [who governs] of the A∴A∴ permits it to be known that there is not at present any necessary incompatibility between the A∴A∴ and the OTO and M∴M∴M∴, and allows membership of the same as a valuable preliminary training.' Restating, the OTO and its British Section at the time, the M∴M∴M∴, was considered 'valuable preliminary training' for aspirants to the A∴A∴. While the OTO came to take on an increased and broadened significance for Crowley, particularly in the light of his 1915 $9°=2^{\square}$ (Magus) initiation, these initial remarks were never rebuffed or amended. Consider also Charles Stansfeld Jones' *The Alpha and Omega of Initiation*, where the 'preliminary' or Alpha part of the text relates to the OTO, and the Omega portion addresses the Great Order. Perhaps, not surprisingly, the letters Alpha and Omega are being weighed on the scales of Atu VIII, Adjustment.

Crowley's drawing of a lamen, with a more polished version composed by J.F.C. Fuller, first appeared on the cover of *The Star in the West* in 1907, and shows a sword and balances. The balances contain the letters

Alpha and Omega (see above) and place the black scale on the right and the white scale on the left (which for a comparison, see the 'countercharged' pillars and Children arrangement in *Liber XV*). Additionally, the initials V.V.V.V.V. are in the center.

In the book paired with *Liber Librae* in the Editorial of *The Equinox* I: I, *An Account of A∴A∴*, V.V.V.V.V. is described: 'This society is in the communion of those who have most capacity for light; they are united in truth, and their Chief is the Light of the World himself, V.V.V.V.V., the One Anointed in Light, the single teacher for the human race, the Way, the Truth, and the Life.' In regards to the 'One Anointed in Light,' Crowley wrote to C.S. Jones in 1916: 'With OTO you only become a magician, and a priest of the Holy One – a very fine and balanced $6°=5^\square$ [Major Adept], but no more.' Interestingly, *Liber XV* begins its Creed with: 'I believe in one secret and Ineffable LORD.' Consider also Crowley's October 9, 1906 diary entry published in *The Equinox* I: VIII: 'I did get rid of everything but the Holy Exalted One, and must have held Him for a minute or two.' Additionally, as Gunther has noted, Crowley's revision of parts of *The Cloud of the Sanctuary* that compose *An Account of A∴A∴* replaces all instances of Jesus Christ with V.V.V.V.V.

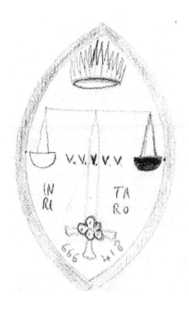

Furthermore, *Liber LXI vel Causae* verse 29 ascribes an A∴A∴ grade to V.V.V.V.V.: 'Also one V.V.V.V.V. arose, an exalted [note this word in Crowley's vision above] adept of the rank of Master of the Temple (or this much He disclosed to the Exempt Adepts) and His utterance is enshrined in the Sacred Writings' (i.e. the Holy Books of Thelema). Additionally, according to chapter 41 of *The Book of Lies*, V.V.V.V.V. chooses 'to manifest' 'in one' (i.e. the Praemonstrator, representative of the grade of Exempt Adept; see above), and 'It is he [V.V.V.V.V.] who is responsible for the whole of the development of the A∴A∴ movement which has been associated with the publication of THE EQUINOX...'

V.V.V.V.V., as the motto of a Master of the Temple, is associated to the Sephira Binah, Understanding, within the Supernals, on the Tree of Life.   Similarly, the principal figure of Atu VIII, Adjustment, according to *The Book of Thoth* is the Goddess MAAT. 'she bears upon her nemyss the ostrich feathers of the Twofold Truth.' ' This all takes place within the diamond formed by the figure which is the concealed Vesica Piscis through which this sublimated and adjusted experience passes to its next manifestation.' From verse 7 of the Holy Book, *Liber A'Ash vel Capricorni Pneumatici*:

> 'For two things are done and a third thing is begun. Isis and Osiris are given over to incest and adultery. Horus leaps up thrice armed from the womb of his mother. Harpocrates his twin is hidden within him. Set is his holy covenant, that he shall display in the great day of M.A.A.T., that is being interpreted the Master of the Temple of A∴A∴, whose name is Truth.'

The lamen of V.V.V.V.V., which is within a vesica, faces the text of *Liber Librae* in *The Equinox* III:X – an Equinox specific to the foundation of a revitalized OTO, as *The Equinox* I:I initiated the reconstitution of the Great Order.   As with *Liber Librae*'s initial appearance, the double Crown of Truth (the 'name' of the Master of the Temple) crowns each pillar. Chap. 177 of *Liber Aleph* ties much of this symbolism together: 'Now this Ox is the Letter Aleph, and is that

Atu of Thoth whose Number is Zero, and whose Name
is Maat, Truth, or Maut, the Vulture, the All-Mother,
being an Image of Our Lady Nuit, but also it is called
the Fool...Also, he is Harpocrates, the Child Horus,
walking (as with Daood, the Badawi that became King,
in his Psalms), upon the Lion and the Dragon; that is,
he is in Unity with his own Secret Nature, as I have
shewn thee in my Word concerning the Sphinx.'

Another connection between the OTO and *Liber
Librae* is found in *Liber LII*. This document was
originally called *The Manifesto of M∴M∴M∴*, privately
published in 1912/1913, and was later published in *The
Equinox* III: I (1919) as *Manifesto of the OTO*.

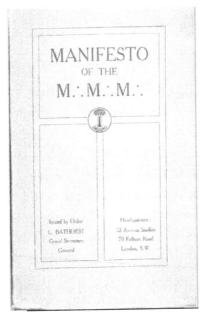

Originally, the text of *Liber Librae* was adapted from an earlier Golden Dawn Lecture at the Practicus or 3°=8° grade entitled *Lecture on the General Guidance and Purification of the Soul*. In the *Manifesto of M∴M∴M∴*, it is stated that: '1. The OTO is a body of initiates in whose hands are concentrated the wisdom and knowledge of the following bodies...' Concluding this list of groups was 'The Hermetic Order of the Golden Dawn,' which was omitted in the 1919 publication.

> 20. The Hermetic Order of the Golden Dawn, and many other orders of equal merit, if of less fame.
> It does not include the A∴A∴ with which august Body it is, however, in close alliance.

The word Practicus is from the ancient Greek word πρακτικός , *praktikós*, 'of or pertaining to action, concerned with action or business, active, practical,' from πράσσω, *prásso*, 'I do.' Taken at face value, it pertains to action. As point 5 of *Liber CLXXXV* makes clear: 'Let him remember that the word Practicus is no idle term, but that Action is the equilibrium of him that is in the House of Mercury, who is the Lord of Intelligence.'

So why was a book attributed to the Practicus grade assigned to Libra? Perhaps it is because VIII (Atu VIII is the number attributed to Adjustment) is the number of Mercury, and the Grade of Practicus is attributed to Hod, which is ruled by Mercury, the planet that rules The Magus or The Magician (the title of the Grade attributed to Life in the OTO). The image of Justice is concealed or masked (the magical power of Binah being in part 'The Outer Robe of Concealment') whereas in *The Rite of Venus* (the planet ruling Libra), it is Taurus that conceals Mercury. Similarly, in the Rite of Sol, it is Scorpio who becomes Venus, clothed in green (Libra in the King Scale of Color).

A Brief Textual Comparison

The text of the *Lecture on the General Guidance and Purification of the Soul* that I consulted was copied by hand by J.F.C. Fuller from Allan Bennet's Golden Dawn notebooks.

The Equinox I:I editorial notes that the text was 'from the Cipher MSS. of the G∴D∴' and the cover page of Fuller's copy similarly has 'from the Ancient Cypher M.S.S.' This note does not appear in any of the Isis-Urania or Stella Matutina published versions of this text. Having access to the cipher manuscript that composed the G.D. grades – which Crowley valued and sought access to based on his correspondence with W. Wynn Westcott, there is no mention of this lecture in the G.D. cipher manuscript – the closest thing being the listing of the Parts of the Soul.

As far as the title of the document, it bears some similarity to 'The Spiritual **Guide** which Disentangles the **Soul…**' by Miguel de Molinos (Saint of E.G.C.), a text of 'Christian Mysticism' in both the A∴A∴ and OTO Curriculums. Also, note that the G.D. document is a 'Lecture,' meaning that it intended to be heard aloud.

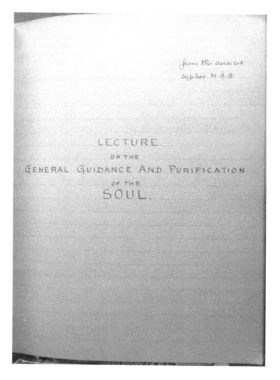

One noticeable difference is that there is no versification of the text in the G.D. paper. *Liber Librae* contains verses from 0-21. Regarding this numeration, it is curious that in the cipher manuscript pertaining to the Practicus Grade, the Yetziratic attributions connecting the Tarot to the Hebrew Letters occurs (0-21). Additionally, note that the reoccurring formula of Truth (AMTh), which in part formulates the first name of the Hegemon, is the multiplication of 21.

Going forward, I will provide the *Lecture on the General Guidance and Purification of the Soul* as transcribed by J.F.C. Fuller, and pair this with *Liber Librae* where significant differences occur. I will further draw attention to these changes, and comment on these, as well as on parts of the text generally. However, being an 'ethical essay,' much of the instruction is unambiguous:

> Learn first; Oh! Practicus of our ancient Order that true Equilibrium is the basis of the soul. If thou thyself has not a sure foundation, where on wilt thou stand to direct the forces of Nature?

> 0. **Learn first – Oh thou who aspirest unto our ancient Order!—that Equilibrium is the basis of the Work. If thou thyself hast not a sure foundation, whereon wilt thou stand to direct the forces of Nature?**

What Order is one aspiring to? Despite later connections that were made in respect to the OTO, the answer to this question should be clear. As Crowley wrote to Frater Progradior in 1916: 'Please distinguish carefully between A∴A∴ and OTO. The latter is a practical organization devoted to the establishment of the work of the former.' Also, as chapter 3 of *Liber CCCXXXIII* makes clear, 'the Aspirants to the A∴A∴ are Men.' Within an OTO context, consider that one is made a 'man' (Aspirant or 'adherent') upon entering the Man of Earth Triad.

In *The Book of Thoth*, Crowley notes that in Atu VIII, Adjustment, the 'equilibrium of all things is hereby symbolized.' The principal figure of this card forms the 'concealed *Vesica Piscis*' which in turn indicates the yoni a veil of the negative in the 'Triangle of the Universe' described in *Liber CMLXIII* –although in her connection to the formula of AL, she 'represents Manifestation...'

The 'forces of Nature' may be indicative of the Tetragrammaton, represented by the four elemental weapons, before which the Magus stands; 'the arrangement of the weapons on the Altar must be such that they *look* balanced.' The word 'juggler,' which is an older title of the Magician, is etymologically connected to the word jest and joke, and it may in turn indicate a magician and conjurer.

The overall message of the text is specific to an individual who wills to 'direct the forces of Nature'; i.e. a magician. As the *Goetia* notes: 'Whence magicians are profound and diligent searchers into Nature; they, because of their skill, know how to anticipate an effect, the which to the vulgar shall seem a miracle.'

> Know then that as man is born into this world amidst the Darkness of Matter, and the strife of contending forces; so must his first endeavor be to seek the Light through their reconciliation.

Besides the versification, there are no significant differences between the two documents.

It is the Hegemon that directs the Aspirant to 'enter into the Path of Darkness' in the old Neophyte ritual. 'Strife' is a title for the five of Wands, which 'represents all this tameless irrational energy and disturbance,' that derives from the 'feminine.' 'Contending forces' may suggest the twins of god, Thaumiel of the order of the Qliphoth, indicating duplicity - the denial of the singularity of the Crown; see also the first verse of *Liber Ararita* chapter II.

Also, chapter VIII (i.e. Libra) of *Book IV* begins: 'Before there was equilibrium, countenance beheld not countenance…One countenance here spoke of is the Macrocosm, the other the Microcosm.' The robe of the Probationer has the general symbol for the Microcosm (pentagram) on the breast, and the Macrocosm (hexagram) on the reverse. However, consider the reversal of these two forms in the description of the crown in *Book IV* chapter XI, as well as the elevation of the Host and Cup in Part VI of *Liber XV* (noting that V.V.V.V.V. is also represented by a pentagram, for which see the note to the 20th Aethyr in *Liber CDXVIII*, and *Liber CCXXXI*).

The 'Reconciler between the Light and the Darkness' is a function of the Hegemon. And after noting the 'good' and 'evil' paths confronting the Neophyte in *Konx Om Pax*, Crowley concludes in part that 'a consistent equilibration of all imaginable opposites will suggest to us a world in which they are truly one; whence to that world itself is but the shortest step.'

Thou then who hast trials and troubles of this life, rejoice because of them, for in them is strength, and by their means is a pathway opened unto that Light Divine.

2. Thou then who hast trials and troubles, rejoice because of them, for in them is Strength, and by their means is a pathway opened unto that Light.

In the old Neophyte grade and elsewhere, there is an emphasis on the descending of the 'Light Divine' from above. *Liber Librae* omits the word 'Divine:' 'The Kingdom of Heaven is within you' (*Luke* 17:21).

3. How should it be otherwise, O Man, whose life is but a Day in Eternity, a drop in the Ocean of Time, how, were thy trials not many, couldst thou purge thy soul from the dross of earth?

So is but now that the higher life is beset with dangers and difficulties; hath it not ever been so with the Sages and hierophants of the past? They have been persecuted and reviled, they have been tormented of men; yet through this also has their Glory increased.

There are no significant differences between the two documents. The text describes the environment of the aspirant as one of struggle, recalling that the Sephiroth beneath the Supernals are at war (*Liber CCCXXXIII,* Chap. 5)

Rejoice therefore, O initiate, for the greater thy trial the greater thy triumph. When men shall revile thee, and speak against thee falsely, hath not the Master said: "Blessed art Thou!"

4. Rejoice therefore, O Initiate, for the greater thy trial the greater thy Triumph. When men shall revile thee, and speak against thee falsely, hath not the Master said, "Blessed art Thou!"?

Who is the Master referenced here? The Editor's notes to *Book IV* references *Matthew* 5:11 (KJV): 'Blessed are ye, when *men* shall revile you, and persecute *you*, and shall say all manner of evil against you falsely, for my sake.'

Another connection to this Master or Magister is indicated on the back of the Rose Cross lamen of the old Golden Dawn in the 2nd Order of the Roseae Rubeae et Aureae Crucis, 'Red Rose and Golden Cross.'

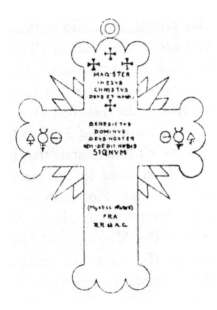

Note the words 'Majester Jesus Christus' (Master Jesus
Christ) under three crosses (see *Liber XV* part VI). It is
perhaps noteworthy that 'Jesus' is one of seven
'prophets' listed who have 'attained unto the Grade of
Magus' ($9°=2^{\square}$) in the 6th Aethyr of *Liber CDXVIII*.
Additionally, under the title of Master is written 'Deus
et Homo' or 'God and Man,' beneath which is a single
cross (ibid., part VIII). A similar Latin formulation
'Deus est Homo' or 'God is Man' accompanies the
OTO lamen (compare the placement of the dove to the
name in the center of the lamen above), which may
have been first published as such in *The Equinox* III:I
(1919). However, note that the arrangement with the
lamen suggests a descending triangle (ibid., 'He closes
his hands, kisses the PRIESTESS between the breasts,

and makes three great crosses over the Paten, the Cup, and himself').

An older version of the back of the Rose Cross lamen occurs in the 16th/17th century text *Secret Symbols of the Rosicrucians*, translated by Franz Hartman (one of the co-founders of OTO) which is in both the A∴A∴ and OTO Curriculums. Both crosses also contain in the center the Latin words (called by Frater I.A., 'Mighty Words') 'Benedictus Dominus Deus Noster Qui dedit nobis signum,' a rough translation of which is 'Blessed Lord our God gave me a sign.' Perhaps Crowley's December 9th, 1906 vision could qualify as a ' sign.'

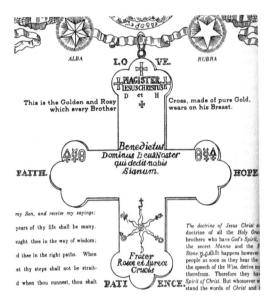

Yet, O Practicus, let thy victories bring thee not Vanity, for with increase of Knowledge should come increase of Wisdom. He who knoweth little, thinketh he knoweth much; but he who knoweth much hath learned his own ignorance? There is more hope of a fool than of him.

5. Yet, oh aspirant, let thy victories bring thee not Vanity, for with increase of Knowledge should come increase of Wisdom. He who knoweth little, thinketh he knoweth much; but he who knoweth much has learned his own ignorance. Seest thou a man wise in his own conceit? There is more hope of a fool, than of him.

In *Liber Librae*, there is no question as to whether or not a man 'who knoweth much hath learned his own ignorance.' Unlike the Lecture, Crowley includes the entirety of *Proverbs* 26:12.

> Be not hasty to condemn others' sin; how knowest thou that in their place, thou couldst have resisted the temptation? And even where it so, why shouldst thou despise one who is weaker than thyself?

> **6. Be not hasty to condemn others; how knowest thou that in their place, thou couldst have resisted the temptation? And even were it so, why shouldst thou despise one who is weaker than thyself?**

Crowley removes a behavior and moral qualifier here ('sin'). The injunction in *Liber Librae* is to not be quick to condemn people as they are (noun), whereas the Lecture condemns specific actions (verb).

> Be thou well sure of this: that in slander and self-righteousness is sin; the Master condemned not the adulterous woman, but neither did he encourage her to repeat her sin; for she had no beauty, that he should desire her.

This part is omitted from *Liber Librae*. However, the incident with 'the adulterous Woman' is found in *John* 8:3-11 (KJV):

3. And the scribes and Pharisees brought unto him a woman taken in adultery; and when they had set her in the midst,

4. They say unto him, Master, this woman was taken in adultery, in the very act.

5. Now Moses in the law commanded us, that such should be stoned: but what sayest thou?

6. This they said, tempting him, that they might have to accuse him. But Jesus stooped down, and with *his* finger wrote on the ground, *as though he heard them not.*

7. So when they continued asking him, he lifted up himself, and said unto them, He that is without sin among you, let him first cast a stone at her.

8. And again he stooped down, and wrote on the ground.

9. And they which heard *it*, being convicted by *their own* conscience, went out one by one, beginning at the eldest, *even* unto the last: and Jesus was left alone, and the woman standing in the midst.

10. When Jesus had lifted up himself, and saw none but the woman, he said unto her, Woman, where are those thine accusers? hath no man condemned thee?

11. She said, No man, Lord. And Jesus said unto her, Neither do I condemn thee: go, and sin no more.

Interestingly, although this story is contained in some of the earliest manuscripts of the Bible, these verses are frequently omitted in that they vary, and are not consistently found in the same area of the text.

'Slander' is a synonym for a false accusation, which connects the act to the Qlipoth of Hod. The statement that the woman 'had no beauty,' may be explained by Mather's description of Lilith (associated to Malkuth, 'The Woman of Night') in a paper he wrote on the Qlipoth: 'the appearance is that of a woman at first beautiful, but afterwards changing to a black monkey-like demon.' Jesus quietly writing on the ground with his finger after the accusation was made (and pretending to not pay attention) and following his own response, suggests a magical action.

> Thou therefore who desirest Magical Gifts, be sure that thy soul is firm and steadfast; for it is by flattering thy weakness that the Evil Ones will gain power over thee. Humble thyself before thy God, yet fear neither man nor Spirit. Fear is failure & the forerunner of failure; and courage is the beginning of Virtue.

> **7. Thou therefore who desirest Magical Gifts, be sure that thy soul is firm and steadfast; for it is by flattering thy weaknesses that the Weak Ones will gain power over thee. Humble thyself before thy Self, yet fear neither man nor spirit. Fear is failure, and the forerunner of failure: and courage is the beginning of virtue.**

'Evil Ones,' is replaced by 'Weak Ones.' Similarly, 'thy God' is replaced by trust in one's 'Self' noting that 'The Self' is attributed to Yechidah – 'The highest principal of the Soul, attributed to Kether.' 'Virtue' is initiated with 'courage' and 'strength,' the antithesis of weakness.

In the old G.D. Neophyte ritual, the Hiereus (Horus) points the sword at the breast of the candidate and proclaims: 'Child of Earth, fear is failure: be therefore without fear! for in the heart of the coward Virtue abideth not!' As Horus was attributed to Geburah in the old G.D., consider that 'Fear' or 'Terror' in Hebrew (PChD), is a name of Geburah. Compare this sentiment to that of *Proverbs* 9:10.

> Therefore fear not the Spirits, but be firm and courteous with them, for thou hast no right either to despise or revile them; and this too may lead thee into sin; command and banish the Evil ones, curse them by the Great Names of God if need be; but neither mock nor revile them, for so assuredly wilt thou be held in error.

> 8. Therefore fear not the Spirits, but be firm and courteous with them; for thou hast no right to despise or revile them; and this too may lead thee astray. Command and banish them, curse them by the Great Names if need be; but neither mock nor revile them, for so assuredly wilt thou be led into error.

'Sin' is replaced in *Liber Librae* with that which may lead the aspirant from the path. Instead of commanding and banishing specifically 'the Evil ones,' the 'Spirits' generally have the potential to lead the aspirant astray – both the evil as well as the good.

> A man is what he maketh himself within the limits fixed by his inherited destiny; he is a part of mankind, his actions affect not himself only, but also those with whom he is brought into contact, either for good or for Evil.

9. A man is what he maketh himself within the limits fixed by his inherited destiny; he is a part of mankind; his actions affect not only what he calleth himself, but also the whole universe.

What one 'calleth' oneself may parallel the previous verse in addressing the Spirits by commands, banishments, etc. The Lecture presupposes an awareness that only extends as far as one's neighbor, whereas *Liber Librae* includes 'the whole universe.'

> Neither worship nor neglect the physical body which is the temporary connection with the outer and material world. Therefore let thy mental equilibrium be above disturbance by material events, repress the animal passions nourish the Higher Aspirations; the emotions are purified by suffering.

10. Worship, and neglect not, the physical body which is thy temporary connection with the outer

and material world. Therefore let thy mental Equilibrium be above disturbance by material events; strengthen and control the animal passions, discipline the emotions and the reason, nourish the Higher Aspirations.

The 'animal passions' are not denied in *Liber Librae*, but controlled, and more notably, strengthened. Again, there is an emphasis and positive value place on strength, which is reminiscent of Blake's 'Argument' in his *Marriage of Heaven and Hell*: 'Evil is the active springing from Energy.'

The 'reason' is not addressed in the Lecture, whereas 'the emotions and the reason' are paired and disciplined, with no mention of purification 'by suffering' in *Liber Librae*. 'Suffering' may suggest the 'Cup and Cross of Suffering' attributed to the Hanged Man, which Crowley specifies in his notes to *Liber 777* as pertaining to the 'now superseded formula of Osiris.' *Liber Librae* also employs an order of significance ('animal passions,' 'emotions,' 'reason,"Higher Aspirations') that is absent in the Lecture, mirroring to some extent the Parts of the Soul.

> Do good unto others for God's sake, not for reward, not for gratitude from them, not for sympathy. If thou art generous, thou wilt not long for thine ears to be tickled by expressions of gratitude.

A noteworthy difference with verse 11 is the initial statement to 'Do good unto others for its own sake.' In *Liber Librae*, an authenticity is indicated when doing something – i.e. acting – outside and apart from a mandate from a divine agency, which we are instructed to neither 'fear' in verses 7 and 8, nor slavishly follow.

> Remember that unbalanced force is evil; that unbalanced severity is but cruelty and oppression; but that also unbalanced mercy is but weakness which would allow and abet Evil.

In this instance, *Liber Librae* departs from the text and concludes verse 12 with the admonition to: 'Act passionately; think rationally; be Thyself.' This may represent in part a three-fold division of the Parts of the Soul: (1) Nephesh (2) Ruach (3) Yechidah (including Neshamah and Chiah).

> True prayer is as much action as word; it is will.

Verse 13 gives 'True ritual' instead of 'True prayer,' which might be considered somewhat synonymous. Consider, for example, the chapter on Invocation in *Book IV*, 'the whole secret' of invocation summarized as: 'Enflame thyself in praying.' However, ritual is more specific to the passionate pairing of action and speech, which when combined equally (the text suggesting that perhaps speech has been valued over action), 'is will.' In the old Neophyte temple, when the Hierophant moves from the throne of the East, he is Arouerist, the elder Horus. In the New Aeon, the actions of the Hierophant are 'established or manifest by being "let down into the Animal Soul of things," which is the Nephesh of the world.'(*Initiation in the Aeon of the Child* pg. 177). It is by employing the first two parts of Dialectical Motion that the third and final phase ('will') is obtained.

> The Gods will not do for man, what his higher powers can do for himself, if he cultivate will and wisdom.

This sentence is omitted from *Liber Librae*. While Crowley emphasizes the primacy of 'Self' in contrast to self, he considered the words 'higher self,' or in this instance, 'powers' to be in many respects misleading. The angel 'is not a mere abstraction, a selection from, and exaltation of, one's own favourite qualities, as the "Higher Self" seems to be'. 'It is ruin to that Work if one deceives oneself by mistaking one's own "energized enthusiasm"' for communion with the angel (*Magick Without Tears*, 'This "Self" Introversion').

> Remember that this Earth is but an atom in the universe, & that thou thyself art but an atom thereon, & that even couldst thou become the God of this Earth whereon thou crawlest and grovelest, that thou wouldst, even then, be but an atom & one amongst many.

There are no significant differences between the two documents.

> Nevertheless have the greatest self-respect and to that end sin not against thyself. The sin which is unpardonable is knowingly and willfully to reject spiritual truth. But every sin and act has its effect.

> **15. Nevertheless have the greatest self-respect, and to that end sin not against thyself. The sin which is unpardonable is knowingly and willfully to reject truth, to fear knowledge lest that knowledge pander not to thy prejudices.**

Putting the motivations of any individual or group ahead of one's own sense of 'self respect' and individual sovereignty, despite one's best intentions (or the intentions of those who wish to swerve you), is a disservice for all involved. Practically speaking, if you cannot respect yourself, it should not come as a surprise if others ('the forces of Nature') don't respect you in turn.

Liber Librae does not qualify the type of 'truth' that is rejected. It could be 'spiritual' truth, or no. This may reflect a mystical disposition to *Liber Librae*, in that 'spiritual truth' may extend outside or beyond the confines of what one might perceive as 'spiritual' (one's church, or temple, etc.). *Liber Librae* expands upon the 'sin which is unpardonable,' by adding an additional admonition against the 'fear' of any 'knowledge' that is at loggerheads with our personal biases. One need not flatter one's own weaknesses (verse 7) in order to allow for a new 'knowledge' that may call into question one's current understanding. On the other hand, the Lecture significantly diminishes its statement regarding the rejection of 'spiritual truth' by equating that 'sin' with the 'effect' of 'every sin' and 'act.'

> To obtain Magical Power learn to control Thought; admit only ideas that are in harmony with the end desired, and not every stray and contradictory idea that presents itself.

There are no significant differences between the two documents.

> Fixed thought is a means to an end. Therefore pay attention to the power of silent thought and meditation. The material act is but the outward expression of the thought, and therefore hath it been said that the thought of foolishness is sin – Thought therefore is the commencement of action, and if a chance thought can produce much effect, what cannot fixed thought do?

There are no significant differences between the two documents. From *Proverbs* 24:9 (KJV): 'The thought of foolishness is sin: and the scorner is an abomination to men.'

> Therefore as hath already been said, Establish thy-self
> firmly in the equilibrium of forces, in the centre of the
> cross of the elements, that cross from whose centre the
> creative word issued in the birth of the Dawning
> Universe.

There are no significant differences between the two
documents. The beginning of this verse appears to refer
back to verse 1. In the chapter on 'Magical Equilibrium'
in *Dogma and Ritual of Magic* (which is specified in the
A∴A∴ *Curriculum*; all of Eliphas Levi's works
pertaining to the *OTO Curriculum*) Levi notes that 'the
Equilibrium of Forces is power'.

Crowley's diary entry for June 3rd, 1923 reads: 'The
creative word, the word of the poet, is divine, not
devilish, because its substance has no importance. Its
value consists in the effect that it produces on the
human mind. Notice the terrific power of a word like
Thelema…'

> As it was said to thee in the 2=9 grade of Theoricus:
> "Be thou therefore prompt and active as the Sylphs,
> but avoid ferocity and caprice; be energetic and strong
> like the Salamanders, but avoid irritability and ferocity;
> be flexible & attentive to images like the Undines, but
> avoid idleness & changeability; be laborious and
> patient like the Gnomes, but avoid grossness and
> avarice.

There are no significant differences between the two documents, although for the Sylphs, 'ferocity' should be 'frivolity' – Fuller mistakenly gives ferocity twice. According to a comment attributed to S.R.M.D.:

> This paragraph must not be taken to mean that the Sylphs themselves are necessarily frivolous and capricious; that the Salamanders are irritable and ferocious; the Undines idle and changeable; the Gnomes gross and avaricious; but that contact with these Races without due preparation and self-control might easily tend to increase and foster such defects in ourselves to an undesirable extent.

> **So shalt thou gradually develop the powers of thy soul, & fit thyself to command the Spirits of the Elements.**

The Theoricus Grade referenced in the equivalent part of verse 19, concludes in verse 20. The relevant portion from this grade follows:

> The Fan, Lamp, Cup and Salt represent the four elements themselves, whose inhabitants are the Sylphs, Salamanders, Undines and Gnomes. Be thou therefore prompt and active as the sylphs, but avoid frivolity and caprice; be energetic and strong like the salamanders but avoid irritability and ferocity; be flexible and attentive to images like the undines, but avoid idleness and changeability; be laborious and patient like the

gnomes but avoid grossness and avarice. So shalt thou
gradually develop the powers of thy soul, and fit
thyself to command the Spirits of the elements.

This section is in turn adapted from Levi's 'Conjuration
of the Four' in his *Dogma and Ritual of Magic*:

But it is necessary to be as prompt and active as the
sylphs; as flexible and attentive to images as the
undines. As energetic and strong as the Salamanders; as
laborious and patient as the gnomes; in a word, we
must conquer them in their strength, without ever
allowing ourselves to be enthralled by their
weaknesses. When we shall be well fixed in this
disposition, the entire world will be at the service of
the wise operator. He will go out during the storm
and the rain will not touch his head; the wind will not
derange even a single fold of his garments; he will go
through fire without being burned; he will walk on
the water, and will behold the diamonds through the
crust of the earth. These promises which may seem
hyperbolical are only so in the minds of the vulgar; for
though the sage does not do materially and precisely
the things which these words express, he will do many
greater and more wonderful. In the meantime it is not
to be doubted that individuals can direct the elements
by the will to a certain extent, and change or really
stop their effects.

The attributes of the elemental spirits are addressed in detail by Levi, with corresponding Hymns to each spirit. The grouping of these four spirits has its origins in the 16th century writings of the alchemist Paracelsus.

In 'Notes for an Astral Atlas' in *Book IV*, Crowley designates the grouping of 'various types of earth-spirits as gnomes' under a synthesized 'set of symbols, obtaining a more general form.' He also considered the elemental sections of 'The Bornless Ritual,' (which became *Liber Samekh*, and which he considered in practice an invocation of IAO), to pertain to each of the elemental spirits. For example, he invoked Air (Section B of *Liber DCCC*) and attributed this to the Sylphs. From 'The Book of Results': 'March 16...I invoke IAO. Intuition to continue ritual day and night for a week.' 'Fra. P. tells us that this was done by the ritual of the 'Bornless One,' identical with the 'Preliminary Invocation' in the *Goetia*, merely to amuse his wife by showing her the Sylphs.' As a result of this ritual Rose became 'inspired.' Additionally, Section 2 of the A∴A∴ *Curriculum* also lists the fictional work *Undine*, by de la Motte-Fouque, as 'Valuable for its account of elementals.'

For wert thou to summon the Gnomes to pander to thine avarice, thou wouldst no longer command them but they would command thee. Wouldst thou abuse the pure creatures of God's creation to fill thy coffers & satisfy thy lust of Gold? Wouldst thou debase the spirits of Living Fire to serve thy wrath & hatred? Wouldst thou violate the purity of the Souls of the Waters to pander to thy lust and debauchery? Wouldst thou force the Spirits of the Evening Breeze to minister to thy folly & caprice? Know that with such desires thou canst but attract the Evil, not the Good, and in that case the Evil will have power over thee.

Instead of pure creatures of God's creation, *Liber Librae* replaces 'God' once more with 'the pure beings of the woods and mountains.' As with verse 7, the word 'Evil' is again replaced with 'Weak.' However, the word 'Strong' replaces the word 'Good' as well, which is again reminiscent of Blake's tranvaluation of values, wherein energy, vitality, and strength are virtuous.

> In true religion there is no sect, therefore take heed that thou blaspheme not the-name by which another knoweth his God; for if thou do this thing in Jupiter thou wilt blaspheme YHVH and in Osiris YHShVH. "Ask of God, & ye shall have! "Seek & ye shall find." "Knock and it shall be opened unto You!" +

Lastly, one is taught tolerance with respect to how another may know his or her god. *Liber LXV* V:19 appears to address this approach in respect to Crowley's case:

> Accept the worship of the foolish people, whom thou hatest. The Fire is not defiled by the altars of the

Ghebers, nor is the Moon contaminated by the incense of them that adore the Queen of Night.

The connection of Osiris (the Greek form of the Egyptian Asar) to YHShVH (the Pentagrammaton created by Johann Reuchlin) is reminiscent of the connection made in *Liber AL* III:49 regarding Asar and Isa. Finally, the quote concluding the book is from *Matthew* 7: 7 or *Luke* 11:9, and *Liber Librae* removes 'of God,' which is also absent from the King James Version of the text.

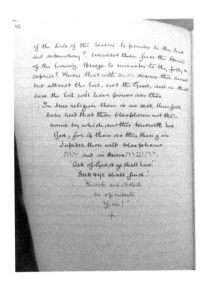

WHEN MEDITATION GOES BAD

CYNTHIA CROSSE

'Go to a 10-day Vipassana retreat,' they told me, 'they're wonderful.'

I did. It was the worst 10 days of my life.

Vipassana retreats are silent and involve 11 hours each day of sitting cross-legged in meditation, beginning at 4am! Each evening there is a video of the founder, S.N. Goenka, talking about what you are likely to have experienced during the day. I can tell you what I experienced on my first day ... terror! This was accompanied by a deep sense of failure and shame. How could I, who have been meditating on-and-off for years and involved in all sorts of magickal practice, find this so difficult – I needed to escape and fast.

I tried to in fact, but we were literally chained in at the gate. My anxiety turned to panic. My chest was constricted, and I could hardly breathe. What did this mean for me whose life had been dedicated to the Great Work? Was I a damned and lost soul? It certainly felt like it.

In Goenkaji's discourse, he explained that the first day was analogous to 'a surgical operation with the knife going in deeply.' Those are the actual words he uses in these recordings … what the hell did day two have in store?!

I was only able to complete the excruciating 10 days because I was too scared to leave – how would I cope with the failure?! I heard later that a woman had committed suicide after one of these retreats – I understand her headspace.

Looking back over the experience, I concluded that it is entirely irresponsible for people who teach meditation, not to forewarn about, and accommodate for, the mental health issues that can be an inherent part of it. The same may be said of teachers of magick and mysticism.

I think how much easier my Vipassana experience might have been if, at the beginning of the day, I had heard:

> You may experience all sorts of extremes of the mind that may cause you to feel you are going mad – relax! These are 'normal' experiences and just about everyone in the class will feel the same. You are not alone; you will not go mad; and you will come out the other side to great benefit.

We hear endlessly about the advantages of meditation; in his book *Mastering the Core Teachings of the Buddha*, Arahat, Dan Ingram, is one of the few who warns of the *risks* of meditation:

'These side effects are no fantasy,' he explains. 'When they show up, they are as real and powerful as if some dangerous drug had seriously skewed your neurochemistry, and I often wonder if that might be something like what happens. Thus, it seems only fair to have the same standards that we apply with such pronounced zeal and fervent litigation to drug companies and doctors also applied to meditation teachers and dharma books.'[1]

'… not telling practitioners about this territory from the beginning so as to give them a heads up to what might happen is so extremely irresponsible and negligent that I just want to spit and scream at those who perpetuate this warped culture of secrecy.'

In their 2015 book, *The Buddha Pill: Can Meditation Change You?*, Oxford psychologists Dr Miguel Farias and Catherine Wikholm devote an entire chapter to 'The Dark Side of Meditation.' It in, they site that up to 7% of people can suffer profoundly adverse effects from meditation, even experienced meditators.

Examining half a century worth of clinical studies, the researchers conclude that consumers should be wary of the hyperbole that surrounds the practices. Rather, they also warn that people using meditation techniques

---

[1] Page 262-3

should be properly prepared for both the positive and negative thoughts that will inevitably arise.

> 'Meditation wasn't designed to make us happier or more relaxed,' says Dr Wikholm. 'So perhaps we shouldn't be surprised if negative issues do come up... It doesn't mean it's not worthwhile, but there is a need to increase awareness that meditation and mindfulness may not be the smooth ride that media stories about it might suggest.'

Farias and Wikholm also point to the concerning lack of regulation for teachers. Invariably, they say, teachers lack mental health experience and are unable to deal with issues as they arise.

In his book, *A Path with Heart*,[2] Jack Kornfield too speaks of the need to put the brakes on when the going gets tough:

> At times in intensive spiritual practice or in extreme or accidental circumstances, powerful altered states and energetic processes can open too rapidly for us to work with them skillfully. At these times, the degree of energy, the power of the experiences, or the level of release goes beyond our capacity to handle or hold it in a balanced or wise way. With a teacher and within ourselves, we must be able to acknowledge these limits

---

[2] p. 130

and have the compassion to respond to them wisely. At this point, we must then find a way to slow down the process, to ground ourselves, to put on the brake.

Kornfield tells the story of a young karate student who over-zealously sat down to meditate for an entire day and night. 'If one does this long enough,' says Kornfield, 'the pain and fire become so powerful that consciousness becomes disassociated and catapulted out of the body.'

When the boy rose after 24 hours of meditating, he strode into the filled dining room and 'began to yell and practice his karate maneuvers at triple speed.' The retreat managers stopped him from meditating, got him doing physical work in the garden for a few days, and he came right.

In *The Dark Side of Being Full of Light* writer Robin Lee weighs in:

> The process of being led to the light, of *waking up* as so many of us like to say, is not simply [about] becoming more luminous. I'd love to see that idea detonate. It is also the process of getting very intimate with the dark, ravenous, insatiable heaviness inside of you.

> The more we practice, ... the more we let the light in, the more the darkness will arrive, exist, and grow to bring contrast. Denying it, causes a lot of mania.

> When we continually push it away, judge it, or
> believe it to not be aligned with our path (who we
> think we are) it only grows in power and presence....
> What happens when we ignore the parts of us that we
> are afraid to look at, is that we become slaves to that
> master... It grows and grows, and becomes fear, guilt,
> shame, terror, anxiety. The pangs of which you may
> not wish on your worst enemy.

The comment could be a cut and paste from Crowley's
writings!

In fact, it is something that J. Daniel Gunther discusses
in *Initiation in the Aeon of the Child*:

> The formula of LVX ... although efficacious,
> represents an incomplete perception of the universe.
> ... Analytical psychology has taught us that the dark
> aspects of the human psyche cannot be ignored
> without danger – for a gross imbalance invites the
> intrusion of adverse elements – threatening to practice
> Magick and ignore this counsel is flirting with
> disaster.[3]

So, with these otherwise strewn pieces of wisdom, let
us not be surprised when the practice we do to lead us

---

[3] p. 34

to the extremes, leads us to both extraordinary and extraordinarily painful places. It keeps us authentic.

As Robin Lee says:

> You can sort of sense it, when you meet someone authentic… they recognize that darkness is part of being human, and they are okay with baring their humanity to the world.

HEALTH IN THELEMA

The Stone of the Wise & The Holy Guardian Angel[1]

SHAWN GRAY

Introduction

'Peace, Tolerance, Truth; Salutation on All Points of the Triangle; Respect to the Order. To All Whom It May Concern: Greeting and Health'[2] These words form the opening of the *Manifesto* of Ordo Templi Orientis, an international fraternal organization centred on *Thelema*, a religion founded by English occultist Aleister Crowley (1875-1947). Although the word 'health' does not occur in the primary text of Thelema, *Liber AL vel Legis* (The Book of the Law), the subject of health does find mention elsewhere in the Thelemic corpus. There has been a notable lack of attention to the topic of health in the academic discussion of Thelema, however. The aim of this essay is to help fill this void by providing a brief overview of health as understood in Thelemic esotericism, with health being

---

[1] Presented at ESSWE 4. The 4th Conference of the European Society for the Study of Western Esotericism, 28 June 2013, University of Gothenburg, Sweden

[2] Crowley, *The Equinox III:10*, 153

here defined as, 'the general condition of the body or mind with reference to soundness and vigour; freedom from disease or ailment; vitality'. This overview of health in Thelema will be accomplished first by examining the role of Eucharistic ritual in the two primary Thelemic Orders, Ordo Templi Orientis and A∴A∴. Discussion of the OTO's central rite, the Gnostic Mass, will shed light on the understanding of well being in the context of the Thelemic OTO (from the time of Crowley onward). Several eucharistic rituals of the A∴A∴, a magical Order formed by Crowley in 1907, will be noted for their implications in relation to the primary spiritual attainment of the A∴A∴, known as the 'Knowledge and Conversation of the Holy Guardian Angel'. The nature of this spiritual attainment will be discussed in terms of psychology, which will serve to shed light on the understanding of psychological health in the Thelemic context.

Health in Ordo Templi Orientis: The Stone of the Wise

A brief examination of the health-related interests of the founders of the pre-Thelemic OTO will serve as a useful backdrop to discussion of the understanding of health in the OTO following its transformation into a Thelemic Order under the leadership of Aleister Crowley. We will therefore begin this section with a short historical examination of the ideas of Dr. Franz Hartmann (1838-1912), Dr. Carl Kellner (1850-1905) and Theodor Reuss (1855-1923).

Health Interests of OTO Founders

The son of a medical doctor, Franz Hartmann was born in Bavaria in 1838 into a family that claimed quite a number of mysterious, paranormal experiences. In 1860, Hartmann began his studies in pharmacy and medicine at the University of Munich.[3] Having completed his education by 1865, Dr. Hartmann moved to the U.S., where he established a medical practise in Colorado. Much of his work involved treatment of injuries of mine workers, and he included in his list of specialities the treatment of chronic conditions and ear and eye diseases. (It is said that he was the first oculist in Colorado to have performed a cornea transplant.) During this time, he also contributed to the *Medical Brief*, a St. Louis medical journal that claimed the largest circulation of any medical journal in the world.[4]

Hartmann was very interested in Spiritualism and the occult, which led to his discovery of the Theosophical Society. In 1883, he left the U.S. for India to represent the Theosophical Societies of America at the eighth anniversary of the Theosophical Society in Adyar.[5] After returning to Europe in 1888, he became active in local Rosicrucian and theosophical circles, which led to

---

[3] Kaczynski, *Forgotten Templars*, 49–50

[4] Ibid., 52

[5] Ibid., 57

his meeting with Dr. Carl Kellner in Hallein, Vienna the following year.

Carl Kellner was born in Vienna in 1850 and rose to prominence as a wealthy industrialist. Far from being interested only in mundane business affairs, however, Kellner had built his lucrative career in chemical engineering out of his interest in alchemy, and gained a glowing reputation as a great inventor, world-renowned electro-chemist and inventor of chemical paper-pulp and electric soda-manufacturing, and as a great mystic, occultist, and student of alchemy.[6] In 1901, Kellner presented to Vienna's Academy of Science (*Akademie der Wissenschafter*) a paper expounding his theory of alchemical transmutation, but unfortunately this paper is not known to have survived. One of his writings that did survive is a booklet on yoga, entitled *Yoga. Eine Skizze über den psycho-physiologischen Teil der alten indischen Yogalehre* ('Yoga. A Sketch on the psycho-physiological aspects of the ancient Indian teaching of Yoga').[7]

Exactly how Hartmann and Kellner met is unknown, but they were both involved in theosophical and Rosicrucian circles in Vienna at the time, and it is known that Hartmann also shared an interest in yoga. In 1893, Hartmann's observations of Kellner's chemical

---

[6] Ibid., 71

[7] Ibid., 68

processes for treating wood pulp resulted in a joint venture between the two men, in which they developed a treatment for respiratory diseases including pulmonary tuberculosis, leading to commercial production of *Dr. Hartmann's Lignosulphite* and the opening of an 'inhalatorium' the following year.[8]

It was through overlapping relationships in Theosophy and Freemasonry that Hartmann and Kellner came into contact with Theodor Reuss. Reuss was born in 1855, educated in Augsburg, Germany, and moved to London, where he became a Freemason – he took his three Craft degree initiations in London between 1876 and 1878.[9] He later moved back to Germany, where he continued his involvement with Freemasonry and became involved in the Theosophical Society as well.

After some time, Kellner, Hartmann, and Reuss began to discuss the founding of their own Order, which was eventually made possible through charters issued by Freemasonry Grand Master John Yarker (1833-1913). This allowed the new Order to operate as a completely independent Masonic system, and Reuss began publication of *The Oriflamme*, a Masonic journal, in 1902. Reuss and Kellner together prepared a brief manifesto for their Order in 1903, which was published in the *Oriflamme* in 1904. After Kellner's death in 1905,

---

[8] Ibid., 72

[9] Ibid., 33

Reuss assumed full control of the OTO and prepared a
constitution for the Order the following year.[10] In the
same year, 1906, Reuss penned an essay entitled *Mystic
Anatomy*, which was published in *The Oriflamme* in
1913. This essay demonstrates Reuss' adoption of some
of Kellner's ideas regarding Hermetic Science. Reuss
introduces the essay by stressing the importance of
knowledge of the physical medical sciences as a
prerequisite for Hermetic Science.

> Any student who desires to study Hermetic Science
> must have, not only, a thorough knowledge of
> ordinary Anatomy, he must also be able to apply his
> knowledge of ordinary medical science to the
> requirements of Hermetic Physiology in order to
> understand the Finer Forces of Nature which alone
> will enable him to realise what Mystic Anatomy is.[11]

This statement indicates an emphasis on the importance
of physical health as a basis for esoteric practise, an
approach Reuss had in common with Kellner and
Hartmann, whose educational backgrounds and
professional careers were anchored in the natural and
medical sciences.

Although the ideas of the original founders of the OTO
cannot be said to represent *Thelemic* views as such, they

---

[10] Sabazius, *History*

[11] Reuss, '*Mystic Anatomy*', 8

do demonstrate that the OTO was, from its very inception, led by men who had an interest in, and were to varying extents versed in, teachings and practices concerned with health and well being. This focus on health was maintained through the transition of the OTO into a Thelemic Order. Having noted this interest on the part of the founders of the Order as a background to our discussion, we will now move on to the theme of health as it came to be approached in the Thelemic OTO under the leadership of Aleister Crowley.

Crowley and the Elixir of Life

Crowley had become interested in occultism through the study of alchemy, which eventually led to his initiation into the Hermetic Order of the Golden Dawn in 1898. After the collapse of the Golden Dawn at the turn of the century, Crowley's continuing spiritual quest led to his reception of *The Book of the Law* in Cairo in 1904. This event marks the beginning of Thelema as the religion of which Crowley would proclaim himself the prophet. In 1907, Crowley, along with his Golden Dawn comrade George Cecil Jones, formed a Thelemic Order known simply by the initials A∴A∴. In 1910, Crowley published the rituals of the Golden Dawn in his journal *The Equinox*, which caused Golden Dawn founder Samuel Mathers to initiate legal action against him. The resulting publicity attracted the attention of Theodor Reuss, who, according to scholar Martin P. Starr, offered Crowley the VII° of the OTO when he visited him in England that year.[12] (The OTO official history of this event states that Reuss inducted Crowley into the III° on this occasion.[13])

In 1912, recognizing that Crowley understood that the Order's inner secret concerned a method of producing the hermetic medicine, Reuss insisted on initiating him to the IX° and subsequently bound him to an oath of secrecy. Reuss proceeded to grant Crowley a charter that included authority over a rite of the lower degrees of OTO that was given the name 'Mysteria Mystica Maxima', or M∴M∴M∴.. Crowley redrafted the *Manifesto* of the OTO, with the claim that the OTO teaches Hermetic Science and Yoga of all forms, and that it 'possesses the secret of the Stone of the Wise, of the Elixir of Immortality, and of the Universal Medicine'[14], and also stated,

> The Knowledge of the Preparation and Use of the Universal Medicine is restricted to members of the IX°; but it may be administered to members of the VIII° and VII° in special circumstances by favour of the National Grand Masters General, and even in particular emergency to members of lower degrees.[15]

---

[12] Crowley, *Amrita*, xii

[13] Sabazius, *History*

[14] Crowley, *The Equinox III:10*, 155

[15] Ibid., 158

Meanwhile, in the same year, Reuss published an essay in *The Oriflamme* that enunciated many basic principles of the OTO, including a hint at the inner secret teaching of the Order. 'We say in our Manifesto that we supply the duly prepared Brother with the practical means to gain even in this terrestrial life proofs of his immortality. Well, one of these means is a certain Yoga exercise'[16]. Reuss does not name this exercise, although the wording implies that it does relate to vitality and health in some manner.

By the end of 1912, Crowley and Reuss had condensed the system of Freemasonry into their own unique, workable system. The following year, Crowley composed the Gnostic Mass for use of the OTO as 'the central ceremony of its public and private celebration, corresponding to the Mass of the Roman Catholic Church'. Reuss is said to have initially been impressed with Thelema and even published a translation of the *Gnostic Mass* in German in 1918. In 1920, Reuss published his *Program of Construction and Guiding Principles of the Gnostic Neo-Christians: OTO*. These principles were to be based on ideas from Thelema and other ideas from Rosicrucianism, Gnosticism, and yoga. Crowley remained uncomfortable with the Masonic aspects of the Order, however, for a number of reasons, including his desire to spread the teachings of Thelema through the system of the OTO. The relationship

---

[16] Reuss, *'Our Order'*, 7

between Crowley and Reuss began to deteriorate in 1920 or 1921, and on November 23, 1921, Crowley stated in a letter to Reuss that it was his intention to relieve Reuss of his duties as head of the Order. Crowley succeeded to proclaim himself head of the Order, and Reuss died on October 28, 1923, apparently without having designated anyone else as successor. Crowley later insisted that Reuss had agreed to Crowley's succession in his last letter to Crowley, but this letter has never been found.[17] In any event, sanctioned by Reuss or not, Crowley was now standing at the helm of the OTO, free to implement the teachings of Thelema through its structure as he saw fit.

Despite his dismal view of the Masonic aspects of the OTO and his evident falling out with Reuss, with the path wide open for him to now completely convert the OTO into a Thelemic Order, Crowley was not about rid the Order of all of the ideas of its founders. Although toward the end of his life, when reminiscing to David Curwen, he stated that the secret teaching of the OTO at the time of his initiation 'was in a very crude and unscientific form and there was no explanation of the conditions which had to be brought about to get it to work'[18], the secret around which

---

[17] Sabazius, *History*

[18] Crowley, *Amrita*, xii. Richard Kaczynski (*Forgotten Templars,* 245-249) discusses possible origins for the source of this secret, giving evidence that it came from outside Masonry. As possible

Hartmann, Kellner, and Reuss had constructed the Order was still viewed by Crowley as one of great worth, and even more so after his own experimentation. What had Crowley found that convinced him that the original secret of the Order still deserved a prominent place in his Thelemic system?

After having been initiated into the IX° by Reuss in 1912, Crowley was armed with the ability to practise the production of the secret elixir, and in 1914 he began to keep a diary of his experiments, and the degree of success that he found in even casual workings was enough to convince him that it was worth pursuing.[19] During his American period (1914-1919), he undertook a magical retirement in New Hampshire in which the results of his experiments were so striking that after returning to Europe he devised a plan to promote his Abbey of Thelema at Cefalu as a health resort where patrons could be treated according to OTO methods, although his full plan for the Abbey was cut short by his expulsion from Italy by Mussolini

---

sources, Kaczynski cites a fictional provenance deriving from the travels of Kellner, contemporary literature on phallicism and sex worship, the possibility that Kellner learned it from one of his esoteric teachers, and the teachings of an Order known as Fraternitas Lucis Hermetica (The Hermetic Brotherhood of Light). Kaczynski considers the last possibility to be the most probable of the four.

[19] Crowley, *Amrita*, xii

in 1923.[20] Later, after returning to England, Crowley
gave a lecture entitled 'The Elixir of Life: Our Magical
Medicine' at the National Laboratory of Psychical
Research in 1932 in which he outlined some of his
theories and results of his experiments.[21] In 1933, he
wrote an 'Interim Report' in which he explained both
that the elixir was meant to be accompanied by a
programme of purification which most people found
difficult to adhere to, and also that the results of the
elixir were not meant to be permanent – repeated
dosages were needed over time. As Starr comments,
'Clearly Crowley did not think of his treatment as a
panacea; the aim was more in line with the Hindu
notion of repeated rejuvenation than with the Semitic
idea of eternal life'[22]. For some time, Crowley
continued his attempts to commercialize the elixir
therapy, establishing in London's West End in
September 1935 a clinic where patients would receive
treatments lasting for periods of three to six months.
Like many of his other ventures, however, this also
experienced financial difficulties and never became
sustainable.

---

[20] Ibid., xiv

[21] This lecture, with the accompanying essays *Elixir of Life (1)* and
Elixir of Life (2) are reprinted in *Amrita* (Crowley, ed. Martin P.
Starr).

[22] Crowley, *Amrita,* xvi

Crowley eventually gave up on the wider-ranging commercial applications of the secret formula and went back to concentrating its application solely within the membership of the OTO, attempting to foster initiates of the IX° with an understanding of the preparation of the elixir within the context of the Order's sexual magic. Crowley's approach to the magic of the Order was Western, as opposed to the Eastern Tantric approach of Reuss, a distinction highlighted by Bogdan in his 2006 essay *Challenging the Morals of Western Society: The Use of Ritualized Sex in Contemporary Occultism*.[23] It is of interest to note here that, despite any differences between Crowley's Western approach to the Order's sexual magic and his approach to the A∴A∴, which includes material of Indian origin, such as Hinduism and Yoga, Crowley had originally drawn on A∴A∴ students as recruits for his Thelemic OTO.[24] What did the two Orders have in common that might allow for such an overlap in membership? The role of Eucharistic ritual was certainly one point of commonality between the two systems, and it is to this that we will now turn our attention.

The Gnostic Mass: Eucharist as Medicine

As previously mentioned, Crowley penned the *Gnostic Mass* in 1913 as the central rite, both public and private,

---

[23] Bogdan, '*Challenging the Morals of Western Society*', 238

[24] Kaczynski, *Forgotten Templars*, 265

of the OTO.[25] Thus, although Crowley eventually gave
up on public commercial treatments using the secret
medicine, participation in the *Gnostic Mass* allows
participants who are not OTO initiates to experience
the central secret through consummation of the
Eucharist within an OTO environment. The *Gnostic
Mass* is a Eucharistic ritual in which the priest consumes
two elements, a consecrated host and a goblet of wine.
Crowley states that these elements are to be treated as
consecrated talismans,[26] and in the *Mass*, the priest
performs this consecration with a lance, converting the
elements, as it were, into spiritual substance. He then
invokes a blessing upon the elements with the words,
'Lord most secret, bless this spiritual food unto our
bodies, bestowing upon us health and wealth and
strength and joy and peace, and that fulfilment of will
and of love under will that is perpetual happiness'[27].
This statement provides an insight into the view of
health in the OTO – one in which health is achieved
through consumption of food, with the understanding
that the food is made divine in the process. The Roman
Catholic doctrine of transubstantiation immediately
springs to mind here, but rather than using elements
symbolic of the body and blood of Christ, as is the case

---

[25] Crowley, *Confessions*, 714

[26] Crowley, *Magick*, 268

[27] Ibid, 596

in the Christian tradition, Crowley indicated that the substance used is to symbolize Nature itself.

> One of the simplest and most complete of magick ceremonies is the Eucharist. It consists in taking common things, transmuting them into divine things, and consuming them... Take a substance symbolic of the whole course of Nature, make it God, and consume it.[28]

The differences with the Catholic rite do not stop here. Crowley also held that it is not even necessary that the eucharist be part of a celebration of the Gnostic Mass itself to be effective – the Creed of the *Mass* states, 'forasmuch as meat and drink are transmuted in us daily into spiritual substance, I believe in the miracle of the Mass'[29]. In other words, according to Crowley's view, it is not the Mass that makes the Eucharist, but it is the Eucharist that makes the Mass. In fact, Crowley said that the Magician should consummate a Eucharist of some sort every day, and that by so doing the Magician

> becomes filled with God, fed upon God, intoxicated with God. Little by little his body will become purified by the internal lustration of God; day by day his mortal frame, shedding its earthly elements, will become in very truth the Temple of the Holy Ghost.

---

[28] Ibid., 267

[29] Ibid, 585

Day by day matter is replaced by Spirit, the human by
the divine; ultimately the change will be complete:
God manifest in flesh will be his name.[30]

Crowley described seven types of Eucharist, numbered
according to the number of elements of which they are
composed. The Eucharist of the *Gnostic Mass*, being
composed of a host and goblet of wine, is a Eucharist of
two elements, but of the seven types, Crowley says that
the highest form of Eucharist is that of one element.

The highest Sacrament, that of One Element, is
universal in its operation… It is a universal Key of all
Magick. These secrets are of supreme importance, and
are guarded in the Sanctuary with a two-edged sword
flaming every way; for this Sacrament is the Tree of
Life itself, and whoso partaketh of the fruit thereof
shall never die.[31]

In speaking again of the single-element Eucharist,
Crowley more strongly hints at its nature with thinly
veiled sexual imagery.

---

[30] Ibid, 269

[31] Ibid. Note that Crowley follows this immediately with the
statement, 'Unless he so will'. He goes on to point out that death is
a natural occurrence, and that it would be an act of black magic to
use the Elixir of Life in a way that runs counter to the course of
natural change.

This Sacrament is secret in every respect... It is reserved for the highest initiates, and is synonymous with the Accomplished Work on the material plane. It is the Medicine of Metals, the Stone of the Wise, the Potable Gold, the Elixir of Life that is consumed therein. The Altar is the bosom of Isis, the eternal Mother; the Chalice is in effect the Cup of OUR LADY BABALON Herself; the Wand is that which Was and Is and Is To Come.[32]

The fact that the central ritual of the OTO involves consumption of a Eucharist that is consecrated with a sacred lance and within a holy grail, in combination with various not-so-subtle references to phallus and womb and seed, in addition to Crowley's description of the nature and effects of a Eucharistic sacrament, is indicative of an understanding that when a sex act is undertaken as a sacrament, not only does it contribute to physical vigour and vitality, but it may serve as the vehicle through which man approaches the divine.

Health in A∴A∴: The Holy Guardian Angel

As already mentioned, in 1907, after breaking away from the Golden Dawn but prior to his involvement with the OTO, Crowley founded a magical order known simply by its initials, A∴A∴. This new order incorporated 'Golden Dawn rituals mixed with some

---

[32] Ibid., 267

yoga and other Eastern practises'[33]. We will now explore some of these rituals in relationship to one of the primary doctrines of the A∴A∴, known as the Knowledge and Conversation of the Holy Guardian Angel.

As in the Golden Dawn, A∴A∴ grades are attributed to Sephiroth on the Qabalistic Tree of Life.[34] The grade of Adeptus Minor is attributed to the sixth Sephira, Tiphereth, and is 'characterized by the Attainment of the Knowledge and Conversation of the Holy Guardian Angel', the main theme of instruction in A∴A∴.[35] Crowley wrote a great deal about this attainment and gave instructions for it in a variety of forms, including a 91-day operation described in the Eighth Aethyr in *The Vision and the Voice*. There are a number of shorter A∴A∴ rituals, however, that are also designed to focus the mind of the aspirant on this attainment. Three of these rituals, *Liber Pyramidos*, *The Mass of the Phoenix*, and *Liber Samekh*, have Eucharistic elements, and it is these to which we will now turn our attention.

A∴A∴ Eucharistic Rituals

Liber Pyramidos

---

[33] Goodrick-Clarke, *The Western Esoteric Traditions*, 205

[34] Crowley, *Commentaries*, 33

[35] Ibid., 16

Liber Pyramidos is a ritual assigned to the Neophyte, the grade associated with the Sphere of Malkuth on the Qabalistic Tree of Life. Far below the Sphere of Tiphereth, the Neophyte nevertheless is granted a taste of Eucharistic participation with the divine. Partaking of the sacrament, he declares,

> Behold! The Perfect One hath said
> These are my body's elements
> Tried and found true, a golden spoil
> Incense and Wine and Fire and Bread
> These I consume, true sacraments
> For the Perfection of the Oil.
>
> For I am clothed about with flesh
> And I am the Eternal Spirit
> I am the Lord that riseth fresh
> From Death, whose glory I inherit
> Since I partake with Him. I am
> The Manifestor of the Unseen.
> Without me all the land of Khem
> Is as if it had not been.[36]

Incense, Wine, Fire, and Bread symbolize Air, Water, Fire, and Earth, respectively, and are consumed 'for the Perfection of the Oil', a fifth element used for consecration.[37] *Liber Pyramidos*, then, is an example of a multi-element Eucharistic ritual.

---

[36] Ibid., 71

The Mass of the Phoenix

The Mass of the Phoenix was first printed in 1913 as Chapter 44 of *The Book of Lies*, and is another example of an A∴A∴ Eucharistic ritual that invokes the Holy Guardian Angel, here referred to as the 'Child'[38]. In this ritual, the practitioner has two Cakes of Light, one of which is burned. The other is dipped in blood produced by the piercing of the skin. The invocation here is,

> Now I begin to pray: Thou Child,
> Holy Thy name and undefiled!
> Thy reign is come; Thy will is done.
> Here is the Bread; here is the Blood.
> Bring me through midnight to the Sun!

In addition to mention of the Child, the reference to the Sun is indicative of the Qabalistic solar centre of Tiphereth, and its association with the Holy Guardian Angel. The dual elements of Bread and Blood make this an example of a double-element Eucharistic ritual, comparable to that of the Gnostic Mass of the OTO. But what of the single-element sacrament of which Crowley speaks so highly? *Liber Samekh* may be seen as an example of a Thelemic ritual that includes this 'highest Sacrament'.

---

[37] Crowley, *Magick*, 60

[38] Crowley, *The Book of Lies*, 98

Liber Samekh

Liber Samekh is a ritual that Crowley wrote during his Cefalu period in the early 1920's, for the specific purpose of attainment of the Knowledge and Conversation of the Holy Guardian Angel in the Adeptus Minor Grade. A full treatment of this ritual is not possible here, but it is of interest to note that in reference to these words addressed to the Angel, 'Thou didst create the moist and the dry, and that which nourisheth all created Life', Crowley comments,

> The Adept reminds his Angel that He has created That One Substance of which Hermes hath written in the Table of Emerald, whose virtue is to unite in itself all opposite modes of Being, thereby to serve as a Talisman charged with the Spiritual Energy of Existence, an Elixir or Stone composed of the physical basis of Life. This Commemoration is placed between the two personal appeals to the Angel, as if to claim privilege to partake of this Eucharist which createth, sustaineth and redeemeth all things.[39]

Here, in a Eucharistic context, we find reference to both 'the Spiritual Energy of Existence' and 'the physical basis of Life'. Crowley states that in this ritual, the Adept recognizes the Angel as 'the True Self of his

---

[39] Crowley, *Magick*, 532

subconscious Self, the hidden Life of his physical life'[40]. What does Crowley mean by this 'hidden Life' behind the physical life, this 'True Self' of the subconscious? What is the Holy Guardian Angel as understood in Thelema? A first step toward answering these questions is hinted at in Crowley's comment with regard to Liber Samekh, 'A thorough comprehension of Psychoanalysis will contribute notably to the proper appreciation of this ritual'[41]. An examination of Crowley's position on psychoanalysis will therefore prove useful for understanding the concept of the Holy Guardian Angel in terms of psychology within the Thelemic context.

The Holy Guardian Angel and Psychology in Thelema

Sigmund Freud (1856-1939) was the founder of psychoanalysis and, in the late 1800's, was one of the first to argue that the conscious mind is really only the tip of the iceberg and that we are more fundamentally driven by animal instincts, the strongest of which is the sex instinct, or libido. Although modern magicians would come to borrow his theories, it was over the subject of the occult that he would break with his foremost student, Carl Gustav Jung (1875-1961), the founder of analytical psychology. Freud's view was that his realm was in the basement of human nature, and he did not entertain aspirations of a glorious elevation of

[40] Ibid.

[41] Ibid., 521

the human spirit.[42] Given this approach and the difference of opinion he had with Jung regarding the occult, one might suspect that Crowley's view of Freud would be a dim one, and this was indeed the case – at least initially. In *Magick*, which Crowley began writing in late 1911, he expressed his opinion of Freud's ideas in scathing terms.

> Professor Sigmund Freud and his school have, in recent years, discovered a part of this body of Truth, which has been taught for many centuries in the Sanctuaries of initiation. But failure to grasp the fullness of Truth… has led him and his followers into the error of admitting that the avowedly suicidal 'Censor' is the proper arbiter of conduct. Official psycho-analysis is therefore committed to upholding a fraud, although the foundation of the science was the observation of the disastrous effects on the individual of being false to his Unconscious Self, whose 'writing on the wall' in dream language is the record of the sum of the essential tendencies of the individual. The result has been that the psycho-analysts have misinterpreted life, and announced the absurdity that every human being is essentially an anti-social, criminal insane animal.[43]

---

[42] Suster, *Crowley's Apprentice*, 83

[43] Crowley, *Magick*, 134

This extremely negative view was written almost a decade before Crowley's composition of *Liber Samekh* at Cefalu, where he encourages the reader to gain an understanding of psychoanalysis. What had happened in the meantime that made his opinion more positive? One clue regarding the timing of this apparent change of heart is that Crowley read Jung's *Psychology of the Unconscious* soon after it was published in English in 1916. Later, in *The Law is for All*, composed between 1919 and 1922, he acknowledges the validity, in some respects, at least, of 'Dr. Sigmund Freud, and his school' and encourages the reader to consult Jung's work for further understanding.[44] Later in the same work, Crowley describes the Holy Guardian Angel in terms of the psychology of Freud and Jung, stating 'We have to thank Freud – and especially Jung – for their development of the connection of the Will of this "child" with the True or Unconscious Will, and so for clarifying our doctrine of the "Silent Self" or "Holy Guardian Angel"'[45]. In speaking further of this 'Silent Self', Crowley says, 'He is almost the "Unconscious" of Freud, unknown, unaccountable, the silent Spirit...'[46] Again, in the context of comparing the Angel to Freud's Unconscious, Crowley states that the Great Work consists principally in the solution of

---

[44] Crowley, *The Law is for All*, 147

[45] Ibid., 163

[46] Ibid., 31

psychological complexes.[47] Crowley's view of psychology thus seems to progress from a negative to a positive view over time as he expresses his ideas about the Holy Guardian Angel in psychological terms.

There are those who see a change in the opposite direction in Crowley's views in this regard over time, however. In his essay, *Varieties of Magical Experience*, Marco Pasi argues, for example, that Crowley's early attempts to psychologise the Holy Guardian Angel eventually proved obstructive to his view of his central role as the prophet of Thelema, because identifying *Aiwass*, the transmitter of *The Book of the Law*, as his personal Guardian Angel would make his reception of *The Book of the Law* valid for himself only rather than something which has universal application.[48] Pasi states that by the time he published *Magick in Theory and Practice* (1929) Crowley's understanding of the nature of the Angel had permanently changed so as to regard the Angel as a discrete being rather than as his own 'Higher Self', stating, 'Crowley rejects eventually any psychological explanation concerning the existence of praeterhuman entities'. Pasi refers to this change in Crowley's view as 'a radical innovation concerning the concept of the Holy Guardian Angel'[49].

---

[47] Ibid., 32

[48] Bogdan, *Aleister Crowley and Western Esotericism*, 75-76

[49] Ibid., 73

Crowley's own words on this seem to allow for more flexibility of interpretation, however, indicating that he may have simply chosen to view the Angel either objectively (in psychological terms, as part of the psyche) or subjectively (as though the Angel were an independent, discrete being with its own separate existence), whichever was more convenient to his purpose at the time. In *Magick*, written in the winter of 1912-1913, he says, 'We may consider all beings as parts of ourselves, but it is more convenient to regard them as independent'[50]. In 1921, Crowley wrote in *Notes for an Astral Atlas*, 'It is *more convenient* to assume the objective of existence of an "Angel" who gives us new knowledge than to allege that our invocation has awakened a supernormal power in ourselves'[51]. Erwin Hessle, a modern-day Thelemite, agrees. 'Crowley's dismissal of the term "Higher Self" in Magick Without Tears could not be interpreted as a "change in position" since he was equally dismissive of the same term over twenty years earlier in his "new comment" to The Book of the Law.'[52] Hessle points out that when Crowley talks explicitly about 'independent intelligences', he 'repeatedly insists on the point that the "reality" or "objectivity" of such things as "Angels" is

---

[50] Crowley, *Magick*, 499

[51] Ibid., 501

[52] Hessle, *The Holy Guardian Angel*, 15

'not pertinent'"[53]. Hessle concludes that on the grounds of Crowley's own words, his assertion that the Holy Guardian Angel is an 'objective individual' or an 'independent intelligence' 'need not imply an assertion that it is a wholly independent and external "being" existing entirely separately from the individual having the "vision"'[54]. This conclusion seems to agree with Crowley's view given that Crowley later again used psychological terminology in *The Equinox of the Gods*, published in 1936, stating that the Holy Guardian Angel is 'the subconscious Ego, whose Magical Image is our individuality expressed in mental and bodily form'[55].

Irrespective of the differing views regarding whether Crowley understood the Holy Guardian Angel in terms compatible with psychology, prominent modern-day Thelemites leave less doubt about whether they are comfortable with using psychological terminology to describe the nature of this spiritual attainment. James Daniel Gunther, for example, uses Jung's archetypes to explain the advent of Thelema as a psychological paradigm shift,[56] and describes the A∴A∴ Neophyte

---

[53] Ibid.

[54] Ibid., 16

[55] Crowley, *Equinox of the Gods*, 100

[56] Gunther, *Initiation*, 22

stage of initiation in terms of confronting the Shadow.[57] In speaking of the Shadow, Gunther makes reference to the 'good Angel of the Soul' and the 'evil Angel of the Soul', terms used by French occult author Eliphas Levi (1810-1875). Gunther equates these terms to the Holy Guardian Angel and the Evil Persona, respectively, and urges the aspirant not to fall victim to the attraction of the Evil Persona, 'which has much in common with what depth psychology calls the Shadow, the negative aspects of the personality'[58].

Stephen J. King also sees Thelemic initiation in parallel with the aims of modern psychology. In speaking from an OTO point of view, he states,

> The Jungian therapeutic aim of a well developed ego standpoint so the conscious and unconscious may encounter each other as equals parallels (from the thelemic standpoint) the moral teachings and training of the OTO through progressive initiation.[59]

Although this encounter between the conscious and the unconscious is described as one which occurs between equals, King maintains a sense in which the Holy

[57] Ibid., 88-89

[58] Ibid., 129

[59] King, *Active Imagining OTO,* 7. King here references Jung in J. Chodorow, ed. 'Introduction', *C.. Jung on Active Imagination* (Princeton: Princeton University Press, 1997) 12-13.

Guardian Angel is an "inner empirical deity" that brings the whole psyche, conscious and unconscious, into balance.

> The transpersonal dimension to this archetypal psyche ... was termed by Jung the Self, 'an ordering or unifying center of the total psyche (conscious and unconscious).' The Self serves as the imago Dei or inner empirical deity, a psychic authority to which the ego - which it includes yet which acts autonomously - is subordinate.[60]

In speaking of the expected effects or results of the balancing, ordering, and unifying work of the Holy Guardian Angel, Crowley stated that his objective in writing *Liber Samekh*, a ritual in which the Holy Guardian Angel is invoked, was

> to establish the relation of the subconscious self with the Angel in such a way that the Adept is aware that his Angel is the Unity which expresses the sum of the elements of that Self, ... and that this Knowledge and Conversation of his Holy Guardian Angel destroys all doubts and delusions, confers of all blessings, teaches all Truth, and contains all delights.[61]

---

[60] Ibid., 4

[61] Crowley, *Magick*, 531

How is this understood to happen in Thelema? In *Magick*, Crowley describes Tiphereth, where the Angel appears as 'the heart of the Ruach, and thus the Centre of Gravity of the Mind', and that as the Adept comes to a greater understanding of his Angel, he 'approaches the solution of the ultimate problem: Who he himself truly is'[62]. Crowley goes on to say that the Angel alone has the full power to 'organize and equilibrate the forces of the Adept...' because only Tiphereth is connected to the various parts of his mind.[63] Marcelo Motta (1931-1987), a prominent A∴A∴ figure, stated that the Angel, dwelling in Tiphereth, radiates Light on the six spheres that surround it, which 'represent the various powers of his mind'[64]. The understanding of the attainment of Knowledge and Conversation of the Holy Guardian Angel in Thelema, then, is that not only does this attainment connect one to one's own true, essential identity, but also that it serves to balance and equilibrate the mind, a process that is explained by modern Thelemites in psychological terminology.

Summary

This essay has briefly examined the theme of health in the Thelemic context. Founded by Freemasons with an interest in the Hermetic medicine, the OTO later came

---

[62] Ibid., 540

[63] Ibid.

[64] Motta, *The Commentaries of AL*, 263

to understand itself in terms of the sacramental symbolism of the Gnostic Mass, in which physical matter, in the form of food, is understood to be transmuted into spiritual substance, the alchemical Stone of the Wise which effects the eucharistic union of that which is above and that which is below.

Sacramental rituals of A∴A∴ were also discussed, with their emphasis on aiding in the attainment of the Knowledge and Conversation of the Holy Guardian Angel. This primary attainment was once viewed by Crowley, as in the present day by modern Thelemites, in psychological terms, as an 'initiation of wholeness'[65] which leads one to the understanding of his or her true identity and, in doing so, brings about a balancing of the psyche and, with it, psychological well-being.

Far from being a tangential aspect of Thelemic doctrine, examination of Eucharistic ritual in both Ordo Templi Orientis and A∴A∴ reveals the primary importance placed on health in the teachings of Thelema. In briefly examining some of these rituals in this essay, I have hoped to demonstrate that, whether viewed in terms of the Hermetic Medicine as the Stone of the Wise or as a method of attaining psychological wholeness through mystical union with the divine in the form of one's Holy Guardian Angel, the importance of well-being is a core aspect of the religious philosophy of Thelema that its founder consciously and

---

[65] King, *Active Imagining OTO*, 24

intentionally wove into the tapestry of its teachings, and which its modern proponents continue to emphasize today.

EROS DAIMON MEDIATOR AND
ELECTORAL COLLEGE

FRATER IAΩ ΣABAΩ

The revolutionary messages presented by Plato in
Symposium have to do with Eros, not understood as a
'god', but as a 'daimon mediator'[1]. According to the
founder of the Academy, Eros is a 'philosopher' and an
image of the mediation between reason and passion,
therefore between Dionysian and Apollonian elements.

This matches with Electoral College's function:
mediation between the Dionysian element contained in
the Man of Earth triad and the Apollonian element
represented by the Hermit triad. At this point we
understand that the governing body concerned
represents Eros as daimon mediator[2].

In order for an Elector to be trained in the mediating
function, a nourishing attitude is indicated:
renunciation[3]. The etymology of this word comes from

---

[1] 'There is no god but man'. *Liber Oz.*

[2] 'First falls the silly world; the world of the old grey land. Falls it
unthinkably far, with its sorrowful bearded face presiding over it;
it fades to silence and woe. We to silence and bliss, and the face is
the laughing face of Eros'. *Liber VII,* V, 37-39.

[3] *Liber CXCIV,* 9.

135

the Latin *renuntiare*, to proclaim something, from the root *nuntio*, someone who lets people know, whose noun is announcement, news and message. In the Roman Catholic Apostolic Church, the Pope's ambassador is the Nuncio. This ambassador in the Grand Lodges of OTO[4] is the Electoral College as a whole, whose president coagulates the eleven manifestations[5] of Eros[6]. In Plato's *Symposium*, this aspect of the ambassador as a mediator between man and god, is expounded through the mask of Eryximachus, a doctor and Natural philosopher. The last art called upon by Eryximachus in his speech is the *mantica*, the art of divination understood as the capacity of connecting and guaranteeing the mutual commonality between gods and men. Eryximachus explains that the art of *mantica* is aimed at knowing human beings' loves and looking after them in the proper way, so that friendship and communion between men and gods[7] can arise through honour and

---

[4] *Khem IV – 6*, Editorial by Frater Phanes, p.3.

[5] 'This electoral college consists of Eleven Persons in each country.' *Liber CXCIV,* 11.

[6] 'And there is a voice: thou knowest not how the Seven was united with the Four; much less then canst thou understand the marriage of the Eight and the Three.' *The Vision & the Voice,* The Cry of the Fifth Aethyr which is called LIT.

[7] *Symposium*, 188 B.D.

veneration of orderly Eros[8]. Therefore, Renunciation enables the Elector to refine the cognitive function as participation to the divine. The word *gnosis* is used with three meanings: knowledge; mystic communication; sexual intercourse. All three meanings can be found in *Liber DCCCXI Energized Enthusiasm. A note on Theurgy.* To know[9] corresponds then to knowledge which passes through personal, direct, singular experience of the individual, allowing him to advance in the 'mystery' through the processes of absolutely personal psychological and spiritual experience.

In order for renunciation to be nurtured, the *Daodejing* helps us:

> Thirty spokes share the wheel's hub;
> It is the centre hole that makes it useful.
> Shape clay into a vessel;
> It is the space within that makes it useful.
> Cut doors and windows for a room;
> It is the holes which make it useful.

---

[8] For Plato the orderly Eros is that force which mediates and unites the opposites, wisely blending and harmonizing them. Such Eros produces convenient effects on all living creatures, both men and animals, i.e. harmony, and so health and prosperity. It is another way to say 'Peace, Tolerance, Truth: Salutation on All Points of the Triangle; Respect To the Order. To All Whom It May Concern: Greeting and Health'. *Liber LII.*

[9] One of the Powers of the Sphinx.

Therefore profit comes from what is there;
Usefulness from what is not there[10].

But also *The Book of Lies*:

Verily, love is death, and death is life to come.
    Man returneth not again; the stream floweth not
    uphill; the old life is no more; there is a new life
    that is not his.
Yet that life is of his very essence; it is more He
    than all that he calls He.
In the silence of a dewdrop is every tendency of his
    soul, and of his mind, and of his body; it is the
    Quintessence and the Elixir of his being. Therein
    are the forces that made him and his father and his
    father's father before him.
This is the Dew of Immortality.
Let this go free, even as It will; thou art not its
    master, but the vehicle of It.[11]

A further evocative element is that the office of an
Elector begins through extroversion which is
volunteering for appointment by the Supreme & Holy
King, an attitude immediately balanced by introversion:
renunciation to every further advancement in the
Order for eleven years. The two polarities are

---

[10] Lao Tzu, *Daodejing*, chapter 11.

[11] Crowley A., *The Book of Lies*, Samuel Weiser, Inc., 1989, chapter 18.

constantly expressed in the work of the Electoral College, for on one hand it holds the most comprehensive control over the Man of Earth issues, on the other hand every Elector is 'encouraged to live in solitude, avoiding unnecessary communication even to casual neighbours, taking care of themselves in every aspect, for three months continuously, once in every two years at least'[12].

> 'Even for five hundred and eleven times nightly for one and forty days did I cry aloud unto the Lord the affirmation of His Unity'[13].

This fluctuation is designed so that one can accomplish that centroverted state whose result is neither male nor female.

Moreover, in *The Vision & the Voice*, fifth Aethyr, the seer is in front of Eros who instructs him to shoot the two arrows against him:

> Then came understanding to me, and I took forth the Arrows. The white arrow had no barb, but the black arrow was barbed like a forest of fish-hooks; it was bound round with brass, and it had been dipped in deadly poison. Then I fitted the white arrow to the string, and I shot it against the heart of Eros, and

---

[12] *Liber CXCIV*, 14.

[13] *Liber DCCCXIII*, III-1.

though I shot with all my force, it fell harmlessly from his side. But at that moment the black arrow was thrust through my own heart. I am filled with fearful agony. And the child smiles, and says: although thy shaft hath pierced me not, although the envenomed barb hath struck thee through, yet I am slain, and thou livest and triumphest, for I am thou and thou art I.

With this wonderful image, I believe that the Aethyr wanted to communicate one of the most important aspects of Eros: that Force which constantly animates all our actions and vivifies our interior world. The white arrow has no barb and it falls from the side of Eros. It is white because it's exterior action as the Sign of the Enterer, it is that Christian Agape which acts outwardly. The black arrow is as a forest of fish-hooks which means creative power addressed to the heart, the interior world, the Sign of Silence. The poison of the Hamus operates and the seer becomes That. The work of the Electoral College, thereby, requires a white arrow which operates outwardly, over the Man of Earth Triad and a black arrow which processes that Force coming from the Hermit Triad.

Plato also speaks about the twofold nature of Eros in the *Symposium* through the myth of the androgynous. In the presentation, the famous comedian poet Aristophanes points out the concept of Eros as *longing for the One*. To overcome duality one shouldn't simply look for the other half which is another individual who feels the same need; one should rather look for something much higher, 'the first Friend', as Lysis would call it[14]. The 'first Beloved' we call it. The centroverted state, therefore, neither male nor female, recalls Mercury as a messenger and the Child Horus. Our Sun is indeed a Mercurial Star, the union of the intercourse between Babalon and the Beast, V.V.V.V.V. and V.V.V., whose power loosens the swathings in order to answer the call of Nuit: 'To me! To me!'[15].

Each Elector is encouraged to give evidence of:

(I) Some branch of athletics.

(II) Some branch of learning.

In *Symposium*, Eryximachus, depicts Eros as *universal cosmic force*[16], discriminating the daimon in Heavenly Eros and Earthly Eros[17], both active in men and animals, in plants and minerals. Eryximachus says he learned this precisely from medicine[18]. The doctor,

---

[14] Plato, *Lysis*, Editore ETS, Pisa, 2005, 219 C-D.

[15] *Liber AL vel Legis*, I-65.

[16] The idea of Universal Eros has been revived by Dante and the poets of XIX century, as by the Scholastic Philosophers.

[17] Frater P. himself, in *Liber 777*, attributes Eros both to both Yesod and the path of Zain.

[18] We notice that in *Liber 52* verse 13 (number corresponding to the words AChD & AHBH i.e. Union & Love) we can read that

continues Eryximachus, is the one who can instill Eros in the bodies, making friends of those parts that are mutual enemies and instill concord in those elements that are discordant inside the body. Therefore, as we have suggested, Eryximachus understands Eros as a complex natural force that he thinks he can control through his science and art[19]. Medicine is then the weapon of the Demiurge; the architect creator of Eros. In close relation with medicine, Eryximachus refers also to athletics. In Greek culture, athletics was closely related to medicine, as both were considered arts providing bodily health. Athletics were intended to produce balance and harmony of opposites in the body, and so, health[20].

One of the few references to athletics in the works of Frater P. can be found in *Magick* in the chapter dedicated to Yama and Niyama[21]. He writes: 'The only difficult question is that of convenience, which is complicated by many considerations, such as that of

among the privileges of OTO members there is the use of the Knowledge and the Preparation of the Universal Medicine.

[19] We should appreciate the fact that Plato doesn't define Earthly Eros as something to suppress but only to offer cautiously, so that one can enjoy the pleasure of it without generating intemperance.

[20] The term health comes from the same root as salvus, which is intact, whole. Being healthy means the union of opposites. 'Also I give you power earthly and joy earthly; wealth, and health, and length of days. Adoration and love shall cling to your feet, and twine around your heart.' *Liber Tzaddi*, 31.

energy; but everybody's mind is hopelessly muddled on this subject, which some people confuse with erotology, and others with sociology. There will be no clear thinking on this matter until it is understood as being solely a branch of athletics[22]'.

In the background of this chapter, Frater P. relates the issue of continence, let's call it chastity, to concentration of energy. This is a peculiar way to speak about Eros and the union of opposites.

Concerning some branches of knowledge, in *Symposium*, Plato (through the mask of Socrates) explains that knowledge isn't people's property, something we can put our hands on, in exchange for an adequate remuneration. Knowledge can't be an object of trade because it's not a personal belonging, but a process which involves the transcendence of individuality. There are things, Plato writes, we can neither possess, nor buy, nor transmit through contact. In this way he measures the distance between Earthly Eros and Heavenly Eros. In *Liber DCCCXI*, Frater P. instructs us to grasp something about Eros, through a sharp distinction between rough and refined Eros: 'The Greeks say that there are three methods of discharging

---

[21] Yama and Niyama pertain essentially to the moral code the Aspirant realizes. This moral system, as Brother Phanes generously made us reflect upon in his lectures, is contained into Ordo Templi Orientis.

[22] Crowley, *Magick, Book 4, parts I-IV,* Weiser, 2008, p.23.

the Leyden Jar of Genius. These three methods they assign to three Gods. These three Gods are Dionysus, Apollo and Aphrodite. In English: wine, woman and song. Now, it would be a great mistake to imagine that the Greeks were recommending a visit to a brothel.' Our Brother, in this way, enables us to glimpse the magic formula hiding behind Eros, which is not the generation of wild cries but the orderly discharge of the Prometheus liberated.

Beyond all the erotic connotations of this speech, in order to become a specialist in some branches of knowledge, one should rely on personal experience, the only thing that can give 'flavour'[23]. 'Let the salt of Earth admonish the water to bear the virtue of the Great Sea. Mother, be thou adored'[24]. It's the Salt of Earth, our personal experience, that allows the Great Sea, the Understanding, to manifest its Force[25]. In the second volume of Jung's *Commentary* to *Thus spoke Zarathustra*[26] a debate arises among the participants about the nature of so-called wisdom. Jung explains

---

[23] The etymology of the word 'sapere' (knowledge) involves the word 'sapore' (flavour).

[24] Liber XV.

[25] The Force, the *Virtus* can be defined as a vital force (not necessarily a masculine property) distinctive of the contact with Eros.

[26] C.G.Jung, *Lo Zarathustra di Nietzsche*, Bollati Boringhieri, Torino 2011, second volume.

that wisdom is experiencing revelation. This is a self-manifestation on the other end of the line. In other words, it is the archetype which discloses itself, something alive, real, that is manifesting. This revelation in the Electoral College has authority, it is a *ipse dixit*, it is the last word[27]. We come back in this way to Eryximachus' speech, who calls upon the *mantica* as the capacity of linking and guaranteeing the mutual commonality between gods and men.

Another core element in *Symposium* concerning knowledge is that Eros forces both the beloved and the lover to take care of virtues. This behaviour has also a political value, because, through virtue[28] one can bring advantages to the City and the citizens, and so becoming experts in the art of governing, another quality of an Elector. The socio-political importance of Eros is called upon, in *Symposium*, through Phaedrus and Pausanias. The first calls upon the idea that if a City was formed by lovers and their beloved, it would be governed in a perfect way, because those would do everything in their power to keep themselves far from everything ugly, and they would compete in honour, inspired by Eros in this bravery. The political speaker

---

[27] Appeal from their decisions may be made to the Supreme Council. Only the Supreme and Holy King can veto.

[28] For Plato nurturing the virtues means having the capacity to join with The Beauty, i.e. the One, the Beloved.

Pausanias presents his theory that Eros' force is political, enemy of tyranny and oppression.

'For the interests of rulers – Pausanias explains – require that their subjects should be poor in spirit and that there should be no strong bond of friendship or society among them, which love, above all other motives, is likely to inspire[29]'.

Another key concerning knowledge of history and art of government is given by some of Frater Saturnus' students. In fact, he was said to define the *Daodejing* as a method aimed to develop the art of government[30] and how this attitude is the capacity of an Aspirant to become king of oneself and so being a bridge for gods (and men). All this is closely related to philosophy, another specialization of an Elector[31], as understood by the priestess Diotima in *Symposium*. Philosophy is actually Love, a quality that enables man to put himself between the saviour and the ignorant. 'This is, o Socrates – Diotima continues – the nature of the daimon', to put himself in the centre between god and man, to be an intermediate. Philosophus[32] is the one who conveys the Fire of Gods to the Man of Earth.

---

[29] *Symposium*, 201 D.

[30] The evidence is given by Frater Adjuvo in the introduction to *Liber 157*, published in the volume *'The Chinese Texts of Magic and Mysticism'*.

[31] *Liber CXCIV*, 13.

Another interesting issue is that the President of the Electoral College will summon his colleagues on the four seasons of the year. It is the Atu XIV of the Wheel: Art. In 365 days of the vulgar calendar, the Electoral College will gather 4 times. This means Squaring[33] the Circle[34]. The Art of this Governing Body, therefore, is explained in *Symposium* as *the desire of generating and giving birth* – giving a shape – *in beauty*. The Electors must have the capacity of being 'pregnant' in the body as well as in the soul in order to give shape in harmony with the divine. Acting on the Men of Earth's triad means to realize that desire of generating which will transform what is mortal into what will be *for ever and everlasting*[35].

One of the last tasks of the Elector is to sanction the passing to the Fifth Degree: *like knows like*[36]. Moreover,

---

[32] It can be helpful to examine Brother Gunther's lecture, 'The Order that has No Name among Men', being very careful about the Imperator's function in the Outer Order, following the mirroring of the Fire of Chokmah, The Beast. But also reflecting upon the Senate and his Knights Hermetic Philosophers in the OTO.

[33] Squaring is associated to number 4.

[34] Circle is associated to the 365 days.

[35] One day the Man of Earth won't need ceremonial initiations because the poison will act as leaven in his blood. The Man of Earth will be born every day to be Ecclesia.

Appeal from their decisions may however be made to the Supreme Council[37].

I developed the idea that the Supreme Grand Council of a Grand Lodge could be compared to the World of Briah which is the World of Creation. It is the first Governing body outside the Hermit Triad but close enough to understand the Word and convey its influence. This point is related to the idea of mediation of the Electoral College. In order to be mediators between the triads, the Electors must have the capacity to align the vehicle of intuition (Briah) and the one of consciousness (Yetzirah)[38] so that his decisions are a result of inspiration and not of a monkey.

All the Electors are vowed to poverty[39]. This aspect recalls the fact that Eros was born from Poros, the God of expedience and of the capacity to acquire and absorb (as well as son of Metis, goddess of perspicacity), and

---

[36] This Empedocles' aphorism comes from the fact that thinking has its origin in one's heart, because blood is the source of knowledge of things; it is a kind of microcosm where all the roots abide. Man knows the things of the world because he is built by the roots of all the things.

[37] Liber CXCIV, 14.

[38] In OTO Curriculum there are many Books that enable us to practice this, everyone according to one's temper.

[39] Liber CXCIV, 30.

Poenia, goddess of lack and poverty. Plato in
Symposium writes:

Now, as the son of Poenia and Poros, Eros is ever poor,
and far from tender or beautiful as most suppose him:
rather is he hard and parched, shoeless and homeless; on
the bare ground always he lies with no bedding, and
takes his rest on doorsteps and waysides in the open air;
true to his mother's nature, he ever dwells with want.
But he takes after his father in scheming for all that is
beautiful and good; for he is brave, strenuous and high-
strung, a famous hunter, always weaving some
stratagem; desirous and competent of wisdom,
throughout life ensuing the truth; a master of jugglery,
witchcraft, and artful speech. By birth neither immortal
nor mortal, in the selfsame day he is flourishing and
alive at the hour when he is abounding in resource; at
another he is dying, and then reviving again by force of
his father's nature[40]. And yet the resources that he gets
will ever be ebbing away; so that Eros is at no time
either resourceless or wealthy[41].

So, Eros is mediator and synthesis of lack and
possession; he is an unstable; of constant motion and
force, nevertheless he is naturally related to the Holy
One. This explains the singular power the Electoral

---

[40] The process is described in the work dedicated to Merlin by
Frater P., *Liber DCCC, The Ship.*

[41] *Symposium*, 203 C-E.

College possesses: 'Every eleven years, or in the case of a vacancy occurring, they choose two persons from the Ninth Degree, who are charged with the duty of Revolution'[42]. The unstable, constant motion and force, is then coagulated in the Revolutionary. 'It is the business of these persons constantly to criticise and oppose the acts of the Supreme and Most Holy King, whether or no they personally approve of them. Should he exhibit weakness, bodily, mental, or moral, they are empowered to appeal to the OHO to depose him; but they, alone of all the members of the Order, are not eligible to the Succession'[43]. Thus, a force in motion stands carnally next to the Most Holy King, creator of Stability, in order to promote changing and evolution. The Revolutionary cannot in any way be elected as a successor, because his nature is pure change.

Osiris, therefore, is constantly challenged by Typhon, in order to enable Orus to be born. Or to put it differently: Ra-Hoor-Khut unites with Hoor-pa-kraat in order to establish the Realm of Heru-Ra-Ha on Earth.

Note for the reader: the words 'gods' and 'men' should be always understood as the Hermit triad and the Man of Earth triad.

(Translation by Francesca Passerone, Teth Lodge)

---

[42] *Liber CXCIV*, 25.

[43] *Ibidem*, 26.

ON THE EPICLESIS

MICHAEL KOLSON

Epiclesis (from the Greek ἐπίκλησις) means invocation, and in Eucharistic practice this is related specifically to the invocation of the Holy Ghost, or sometimes the Logos, either directly or through God. It is used primarily in Christian Eucharistic celebrations of the Eastern Orthodox Churches but has also found its way back into Western Churches through a study of Eastern Liturgies.

In *Liber Aleph* Crowley gives a detailed analysis of a Eucharistic celebration called The Mass of the Holy Ghost, or *De Missa Spiritus Sancti*[1]. It is to be noted that this Mass is not the same as *Liber XV: The Gnostic Mass*, but they do have certain commonalities.

In Chapter 86, *De Formula Tota*, or On the Complete Formula, Crowley writes 'perform the Mass, not omitting the Epiklesis, and let there be a Golden Wedding Ring at the Marriage of thy Lion and thine Eagle'. This comment of the 'omitting not the Epiklesis' speaks to the importance of this part of the ceremony of the Mass of the Holy Ghost and a possible connection to the Gnostic Mass.

---

[1] See in particular Chapters 85-87.

Since, the epiclesis is important and not to be omitted it is worth looking at the same and equivalent part of the Gnostic Mass. The epiclesis in practice is, as has been said, an invocation of the Holy Ghost. The chorus of the Anthem of the Mass can be looked at as a commentary on the nature of the Holy Ghost. Starting with the line:

'For of the Father and the Son,
The Holy Spirit is the norm'.

This concept of the Holy Spirit being the 'norm' can be studied in *The Book of Lies* particularly chapters 8, 15, and 16 among others.

'Male-female, quintessential, one,
Man-being veiled in woman form.'

Here, the Holy Spirit is defined as male and female, as one quintessence. It is further elaborated and defined that man = being and woman = form. This is an important notion within Crowley's sexual metaphysics and can also be studied in *The Book of Lies* see the aforementioned chapters and Chapter 4 among others.

'Glory and worship in the highest,
Thou Dove, mankind that deifiest,'

The Dove is likened to the Holy Spirit in Jesus' Baptism, it is sometimes thought that it was at Jesus baptism, at the hands of John, that Jesus became divine; that is through the descent of the Holy Spirit Jesus was 'deified'. In the Christian Gospels it is written:

> 'And Jesus, when he was baptized, went up straightway out of the water: and lo, the heavens were opened unto him, and he saw the Spirit of God descending, and lightening upon him' (Matthew 3:16)

> 'And straightway coming up out of the water, he saw the heavens opened and the Spirit like as dove descending upon him' (Mark 1:10)

> 'And the Holy Ghost descended in a bodily shape like a dove upon him, and a voice came from heaven, which said, Thou art my beloved Son; in thee am I well pleased' (Luke 3:22)

> 'And John bare record, saying, I saw the Spirit descending from heaven like a dove, and it abode upon him' (John 1:32)[2]

We can now see how the Holy Spirit is equated to the Dove, which would of course be the same Dove that we see on the OTO's Lamen descending from the Eye of the Father into the Chalice of the Mother. The Holy

---

[2] For an interesting comparison to the descent of the Holy Spirit and magical practices see Morton Smith's excellent *Jesus the Magician* particularly pages 96-104.

Spirit is therefore of dual form, it is the seed or logos of transmission and it is also the male-female quintessence.

This is further elaborated upon in Aspects of the Mystic Marriage (Part VIII of The Gnostic Mass), which follows the Anthem. The Priest breaks off of a portion of the host with the words, translated from the Greek, 'This is my seed. The Father is the Son through the Holy Spirit'. These words of consecration again point to the same Mysteries as conveyed in the Anthem.

After the words of consecration are spoken the Priest recites AUMGN, thrice. AUMGN adds up through gematria to 100^3, its recitation three times equaling 300. In Crowley's 'An Essay Upon Number' we read '300. The letter ש, meaning "tooth" and suggesting by its shape a triple flame. Refers Yetziratcially to fire, and is symbolic of the Holy Spirit, RVCh ALHIM = 300. Hence the letter of the Spirit. Descending into the midst of IHVH, the four inferior elements, we get IHShVH Jeheshua, the Saviour, symbolized by the Pentagram' (Crowley et al. 1992, 103). It is interesting to note that the word quintessence, used in the Anthem, comes from the Latin for 'fifth essence'. Here relating to one aspect of the Pentagrammaton and the name of Jesus.

The particulate is then depressed into the Cup by the Priest and Priestess with the word HRILIU. This word

---

[3] See *Magick in Theory and Practice*, Chapter VII, part V.

is from *The Vision and the Voice*, Second Aethyr where it is translated as 'the shrill scream of orgasm' (Crowley et al. 1998, 242) In *The Heart of the Master* it is said to be the Voice of the Dove (Crowley 1992, 39), further tying this word to the symbol of the Holy Ghost.

The cup is covered, the Lance is retrieved and then the Priest joins hands and strikes his breast. The Holy Ghost having been invoked by song and gesture is now invoked explicitly by the triple recitation of 'O Lion and O Serpent that destroy the destroyer be mighty among us'. This is the logical location of the epiclesis within the Mass as the Holy Ghost has now become manifest through the comingling of the particulate into the cup. Compare the Mozarabic Mass were the epiclesis uses the words *'Adesto, adesto Jesu, bone Pontifex, in medio nostril: sicut fuisti in medio nostril: sicut fuisti in medio discpulorum tuorum'* or 'Be present, be present in our midst, O Jesus, great High Priest: as thou wert in the midst of thy disciples.' Jung quotes this passage as an example of the epiclesis and further explains 'This naming likewise has the force of a summons. It is an intensification of the *Benedictus qui venit*, and it may be, and sometimes was, regarded as the actual manifestation of the Lord, and hence as the culminating point of the Mass.' (Jung 1975, 213)

Sabazius writes of this moment in the Mass:

...the Priest strikes his breast, once, just before invoking the Lion and Serpent prior to communion. This time, the people of the congregation do not repeat the gesture.

In this instance, the striking of the breast does not symbolize fidelity and fellowship; neither does it symbolize grief or penitence or self-denial, as it does in the Roman Catholic Mass, it symbolizes the opening of the heart to receive (or emit) the influence of a particular force being invoked: the force of Baphomet, the Lion and Serpent 'that destroy the destroyer', the dialectic union of opposites that conquers death.

This is further shown by the Cakes of Light themselves. In Crowley's commentary to *The Book of the Law* published in *The Law is for All* we read:

> These two kinds of 'blood' are not to be confused. The student should be able to discover the sense of this passage by recollecting the Qabalistic statement that "the blood is the life," consulting *Book 4, Part III*, and applying the knowledge which reposes in the sanctuary of the Gnosis of the Ninth Degree of O.T.O. The "child" is "Babalon and the Beast conjoined, the secret saviour," the being symbolized by the egg and the serpent hieroglyph of the Phoenician adepts. The second kind is also a form of Baphomet, but differs from the "child" in that it is the

lion-serpent in its original form [emphasis added] (Crowley 1988, 284).

We here see that the Lion Serpent is equated to Babalon and the Beast conjoined and to Baphomet, it is also the 'child'. Of which one could see as the resultant of the union of the Priest and Priestess. Returning to *Liber Aleph* Crowley writes 'The Substance is the Father, the Instrument is the Son, and the Metaphysical Ecstasy is the Holy Ghost, whose Name is HRILIU' (Crowley 1991 Chapter 87) indicating quite clearly that the commixture in the cup is representative of the Holy Spirit. In the Syrian interpretation of the Eucharist the words of consecration represent the death of Christ while the commixture shows his resurrection. St. Chysostom refers to the commixture as 'The fullness of the Holy Spirit.' (Davies 1966, 56). It is of course, therefore, fitting that the people communicate in an 'attitude of Resurrection'.

Secret Light

Reflections on the Rosy Cross

TAU NEKTARIOS

The Heart of the Rose

> O Rose thou art sick.
> The invisible worm,
> That flies in the night
> In the howling storm:
>
> Has found out thy bed
> Of crimson joy:
> And his dark secret love
> Does thy life destroy.

The Sick Rose by Saint William Blake

'in the heart of the Rose there is the secret light that men call midnight'

Liber 418 15th Aethyr

Abomination of Desolation

'The only way to be really born is by annihilation – to be born into Chaos, where Pan is the Saviour.'

Liber 415 *The Paris Working* Opus III

Enter the Temple, the Holy of Holies, gold rich with red.

Hear a scapegoat utter his last lie.

Smell, perfume pervading, Pan, hair matted and pungent.

Hooves sinking into the moist earth.

With secret sense, spiral horns reach and touch infinity, encompassing All.

> Another prophet shall arise, and bring fresh fever from the skies; another woman shall awake the lust & worship of the Snake; another soul of God and beast shall mingle in the globèd priest; another sacrifice shall stain the tomb; another king shall reign; and blessing no longer be poured To the Hawk-headed mystical Lord!
>
> Liber AL III:34

The Abomination of Desolation is raised over the Temple, crowning a pyramid of Annihilation; '*For he is ever a sun, and she a moon*' (Liber AL I:16). Conjoined in passion with the Beast, in her right hand the Mother of Abominations, BABALON, holds aloft '*the Holy Grail aflame with love and death*' (Liber LXVVII, Atu XI). Led to the Gate of the Sun, humanity is vivified by the sacrament of the Aeon.

At the heart of the Sun, as of the Rose, a secret light, the Night of Pan, primal and unconscious subsistence of the magical and transformative power of the eucharist, 'bestowing upon us health and wealth and strength and joy and peace, and that fulfilment of will and of love under will that is perpetual happiness' (Liber XV).

As brothers fight ye

Hammer held high; Cain strikes with full force. Abel's eyes open in bare surprise at the ferocious intimacy of the attack. Abel falls, blood staining his apron, head bleeding into the dry earth. The earth Cain tilled for meagre harvest cries out.

> God asked Cain, 'Where is your brother Abel?' 'I do not know,' replied [Cain]. 'Am I my brother's keeper?'

> God said, 'What have you done? The voice of your brother's blood is screaming to Me from the ground.

> Now you are cursed from the ground that opened its mouth to take your brother's blood from your hand.

> When you work the ground, it will no longer give you of its strength. You will be restless and isolated in the world.

Genesis 4:9-12

Cain's fratricide marks the true and final expulsion from Eden. His blood seal – curse and protection, conquering death, staining the tomb - drives him ever to the Orient. *'Death is forbidden, o man, unto thee'* (Liber AL II:73). The cursed earth, an outer inversion of the *'sangréal'* sanctifying earth and humanity, necessarily establishes the very conditions for initiation.

> The shedding of blood is necessary, for God did not hear the children of Eve until blood was shed. And that is external religion; but Cain spake not with God, nor had the mark of initiation upon his brow, so that he was shunned by all men, until he had shed blood. And this blood was the blood of his brother. This is a mystery of the sixth key of the Taro, which ought not to be called The Lovers, but The Brothers.

Liber 418 2nd Aethyr

The laughing face of Eros

At Mamre during the hottest part of the day, Abraham sits at the entrance of his tent as three strangers, angels, approach the camp. Serving them with meat, yoghurt and milk, the strangers affirm the now elderly wife Sarah will bear a son.

> Sarah was listening behind the entrance of the tent, and he was on the other side. Abraham and Sarah were

already old, well on in years, and Sarah no longer had female period. She laughed to herself, saying, 'Now that I am worn out, shall I have my heart's desire? My husband is old!'

God said to Abraham, 'Why did Sarah laugh and say, 'Can I really have a child when I am so old? Is anything too difficult for God? At the designated time, I will return, and Sarah will have a son.'

Sarah was afraid and she denied it. 'I did not laugh,' she said.

Abraham said, 'You did laugh.'

Genesis 18:10-15

At the time appointed Sarah gives birth to a son. Seemingly commemorating Sarah's laughter at Mamre, Abraham names the boy Issac '*he will laugh*'. Some years pass and God tests Abraham,

> Take your son, the only one you have – Issac – and go away to the Moriah area. Bring him as an all-burned offering on one of the mountains that I will designate to you.

Genesis 22:2

An angel halts the rough blade held by the patriarch's age-withered hand as it lowers to the altar-bound boy. Isaac cheats death. A ram caught by its horns in a nearby thicket completes and sublimates the sacrifice.

Another father brings his son to sacrifice, yet the Christ, like Issac, has the last laugh.

> Yes, they saw me; they punished me. It was another, their father, who drank the gall and the vinegar; it was not I. They struck me with the reed; it was another, Simon, who bore the cross on his shoulder. It was another upon Whom they placed the crown of thorns. But I was rejoicing in the height over all the wealth of the archons and the offspring of their error, of their empty glory. And I was laughing at their ignorance.
>
> Second Treatise of the Great Seth

In the secret light, the formula of substitution and sacrifice is raised to passionate identification - the Brothers as Lovers. The trickster-like switch of Issac and the redeemer Christ is sublimated as Eros, passionate and self-slain.

> Although thy shaft hath pierced me not, although the envenomed barb hath struck thee through, yet I am slain, and thou livest and triumphest, for I am thou and thou art I.
>
> Liber 418 5th Aethyr

The laughing face of Eros is now the Ambassador of Pan, the Saviour,

> First falls the silly world; the world of the old grey land.

> Falls it unthinkably far, with its sorrowful bearded face presiding over it; it fades to silence and woe.

> We to silence and bliss, and the face is the laughing face of Eros.

> Smiling we greet him with the secret signs.

> He leads us into the Inverted Palace.

> Liber 7 V: 37 – 41

and

> 'the sun of midnight is ever the son'

> Liber AL III:74

Regenerate the world

> 'I swoop down upon the black earth; and it gladdens into green at my coming.'

> Liber 90

In these Mysteries we reach a liminal edge of consciousness, a substratum of being known through symbol and ceremony.

Here is the effective operation of the sacrament and its sacrificial preparation. The burnt flesh offerings of the Temple, Christ at Golgotha, the passion of Cain and Abel, the ram in the thicket, the sacrifice of Life and Joy ('true warrants of the Covenant of Resurrection') - each a sacrifice to stain the tomb for 'the Cross is both Death and Generation, and it is on the Cross that the Rose blooms.' (Liber ABA *The Formula of the Holy Graal*).

Here then is healing, at the heart of the Rose, the sun of midnight; the secret light, gladdening into green, the Light invoked in the Priestly charge to the Lord of the Aeon, '*Let Thy Light crystallize itself in our blood, fulfilling us of Resurrection.*' (Liber XV)

> 'This shall regenerate the world, the little world my sister, my heart & my tongue, unto whom I send this kiss.'
>
> Liber AL I:53

EUCHARIST: FROM SELF TO GOD

There is a long history of the use of sacrifice and sacrament in the pursuit of contact with God.

The use of the Eucharist[1] is a vital practice in the context of Thelema but may be neglected due to general misunderstanding and in reaction to its use historically. The practice of consuming the Eucharist is seemingly simple in itself, but its results or rewards are *golden*.

We can see the historical precedents to the Thelemic Eucharist in the Christian theology and even further back to the Jewish Temple practices. These historical associations can create negative emotional responses when the topic of the Eucharist is discussed. Those that have come to Thelema from a background where they have been betrayed or otherwise dismayed by the Christian Church often have issues reconciling the use of our many shared words. This can be an additional problem if they come into an ecclesiastical expression of Thelema, in particular the Gnostic Catholic Church, which shares much of the same language.

---

[1] 'The Greek noun εὐχαριστία (eucharistia), meaning "thanksgiving", appears fifteen times in the New Testament' <https://en.wikipedia.org/wiki/Eucharist#Other_terms>

Throughout the Bible, we find many early practices and traditions that we would recognise as Eucharistic. There is some risk of vague hand waving at this point, as the legitimacy of any Biblical content can be argued and contested. For our purposes, it needs to be taken as assumed that the Bible is a mix of historical facts, mythology, and a great deal of revisionist editing.

In early Jewish history, there was a ritual on The Day of Atonement, which occurred once a year. The High Priest of the Temple entered the Holy of Holies alone and made an offering of his own blood. This was a start to a tradition of an exchange of *life* enabling contact with the Divine. With time, animals replaced the blood of the Priest himself and as the theologian Margaret Barker summarized[2] 'this was recognized as a substitute for the self-offering of the high priest himself.' She also used an effective quote from Romans which bears repeating in full:

> I appeal to you therefore, brothers and sisters, by the mercies of God, to present your bodies as a living sacrifice, holy and acceptable to God, which is your spiritual worship. [3]

---

[2] Margaret Barker, *The Revelation of Jesus Christ: Which God Gave to Him to Show to His Servants What Must Soon Take Place (Revelation 1,1)* (London: Clark, 2004), 5.

[3] Romans 12:1 (NRSV)

These earlier Temple traditions influenced the writers of Christ's time and laid a foundation of *sacrifice* as part of spiritual worship. In that earlier period, on the Day of Atonement two goats were sacrificed. One was to contain or banish Azazel[4], the leader of the fallen angels. The other was sacrificed in the Holy of Holies as a form of redemption or atonement for the peoples. The high priest is said to be changed on emerging from the Temple, 'His face is radiant because he has been in the divine presence which has transformed him into the LORD'[5]. This transformation is key here, the high priest has been filled with the Divine and radiates this outwards to those that then witness him. This filling oneself with God becomes a salient point in Crowley's writing about the Eucharist.

But as this *blood* was a substitute for the *life* of the high priest, it was considered only a partial offering, and had to be repeated. Barker[6] strongly suggests that it was later through Christ offering his own blood that the redemption became *eternal*.

This was the first evolution towards what became the Eucharist. Taking the substituted *life* and replacing it with the actual *life*. This substitution may be caught up in metaphor and myth, but it does represent a

---

[4] Barker, *The Revelation of Jesus Christ*, 45.

[5] Barker, 85.

[6] Barker, 45.

transformation of ideas. Margaret Barker speculates on some of the more practical forms of this earlier tradition which we see evolve into the Eucharist of Christianity:

> The role of the bread in the temple is another mystery. Twelve loaves "the Bread of the Presence" (literally "the Face") were set on a golden table in the great hall of the temple, together with incense and flagons of drink offerings (Exod. 25.29-30). The bread became holy while it was in the temple before being taken in it was placed on a marble table but when it was brought out it was placed on a table of gold because it had become holy (*m. Shekalim 6.4*). The loaves were eaten by the high priest every Sabbath, perhaps the origin of the weekly celebration of the Eucharist.[7]

Following this line of inquiry in her other books, she further refines the idea, drawing clearer connections between the old and new traditions:

> The two temple rituals originally exclusive to the high priests were carrying blood into the holy of holies on the Day of Atonement and eating the most holy Shewbread on the Sabbath. These were combined to become the Christian Eucharist.[8]

---

[7] Barker, *The Revelation of Jesus Christ*, 387.

[8] Margaret Barker, *Temple Theology: An Introduction* (London: SPCK, 2004), 10.

This earlier history demonstrates an emerging attempt to connect with the Divine, but one that is highly external in practice. The *self* was substituted with animals, and the act itself was only carried out by the high priest. The people themselves were not connected to this divine transformation, there being a distinct separation between the High Priest, the priests, the people, and further still, the women of society. Experiencing God was reserved for certain select families and the occasional prophet.

The early Christian expression of the Eucharist derives from the *Last Supper*, which occurred during a *Passover* meal (combining the new Theology of Christ with the old traditions from the Second Temple, and even further back to the First Temple). The event is described or otherwise referenced in the canonical Gospels[9], Mark having the clearest illustration of this:

> ...Jesus took a loaf of bread, and after blessing it he broke it, gave it to the disciples, and said, "Take, eat; this is my body." Then he took a cup, and after giving thanks he gave it to them, saying, "Drink from it, all of you; for this is my blood of the covenant...[10]

---

[9] Matthew 26:17–30, Mark 14:12–26, Luke 22:7–39 and John 13:1–17:26

[10] Matthew 26:26–28

This provides the scaffolding for the Eucharist as it later emerged. It took the bread, the wine and an explicit reference to blessings (or giving thanks). The more specific term for this is *epiklesis*[11], a term that becomes more significant as we continue to explore the Eucharist in the Thelemic context.

Rewinding briefly to the dawn of Man, we can imagine an evolution to this point. At the first emergence of a spiritual man, *he* made sacrifices[12] to the *Divine* with blood from his hunts. This continued for quite some time, and by repetition, this understanding became integrated into human consciousness. Later, this sacrifice moved inward, so that the Priest would offer their own blood and body to appease the *Divine*, which in turn evolved to make use of symbolic offerings of the same *self*. At the birth of Christianity, this offering became an *actual* self-sacrifice at the crucifixion.

The Eucharist within the Roman doctrine is, a gateway between the Communicant and the *Divine*, although it does act by 'bestowing the gift of the Spirit, the

---

[11] '...from Ancient Greek: ἐπίκλησις "invocation" or "calling down from on high" ' <https://en.wikipedia.org/wiki/Epiclesis>

[12] There are probably some very good anthropological and paleontological studies on this topic. I can not recommend any currently. So this whole statement is based on a personal interpretation.

Eucharist functions as a sacrament of Unity.'[13] The goal is the Unification with the Divine Will, although this is still outside of the communicant. It is not controlled or initiated by them.

We have gone from the Eucharist (or connection to the Divine) being entirely the domain of the high priest, to a point where the priest can, through the Mass, act as an intermediary between God and the people. Providing them a connection to the Divine through the application of the Eucharist.

This maintained the idea of it as being a sacrifice, in particular, a remembrance of the crucifixion and all that entails, 'but a sacrifice only inasmuch as it is a memorial of the one sacrifice that was accomplished by and for all on the cross".[14]

The simplest way to begin looking at the Eucharist in Thelema is to read the clear description Crowley provided us with

> One of the simplest and most complete of Magick ceremonies is the Eucharist.

---

[13] Enrico Mazza, *The Eucharistic Prayers of the Roman Rite* (Collegeville: The Liturgical Press, 2009), 203.

[14] Enrico Mazza, *The Eucharistic Prayers of the Roman Rite* (Collegeville: The Liturgical Press, 2009), 178.

It consists in taking common things, transmuting them into things divine, and consuming them.

So far, it is a type of every magick ceremony, for the reabsorption of the force is a kind of consumption; but it has a more restricted application, as follows.

Take a substance symbolic of the whole course of nature, make it God, and consume it.[15]

This seemingly simple practice is given a very thorough description and very detailed application in Chapter XX of *Magick in Theory and Practice*. As with many passages in *Liber ABA* there is layered meaning to what has been written, and a careful review of the passages would be likely to bear fruit for anyone so invested.

This particular section of the book is divided into twenty-two chapters, which coincides with the number of trump cards in the Tarot deck or the paths on the Tree of Life. The corresponding Major Arcana card, to the Eucharist chapter, is *The Aeon*; the corresponding path is *Shin* (ש).

A quick review of the matching chapter in *The Book of Thoth* does not reveal any explicit correspondences with the Eucharist (or seemingly related matters). But the

---

[15] Aleister Crowley et al., *Magick: Liber ABA, Book Four, Parts I-IV*, 2nd rev. ed (York Beach, Me: S. Weiser, 1997), 267.

first sentence[16] 'In this card it has been necessary to depart completely from the tradition of the cards, in order to carry on that tradition.' gives an insight of its own. The new Aeon has a new view of things, so then perhaps with the Aeon of Horus, the Eucharist has also a new meaning and range of action. There is no longer the celebration of the glory of self-sacrifice. There is now an understanding that the Divine can exist in all of us, 'There is no god but man.'[17]. And 'Every man and every woman is a star.'[18]

Using the reference tables in *Liber ABA*[19] we can see on the path of Shin the *two elements* attributed here are both *fire* and *spirit*. This can be easily paralleled with the well-known quote by Crowley 'Invoke often! Inflame thyself with prayer!'.

Within Chapter XX, Crowley encourages the Magician to partake of the Eucharist daily, no less than three times over the course of three or four pages. He doubles down stating 'It is of more importance than any other magical ceremony, because it is a complete

---

[16] Crowley, Aleister, *The Book of Thoth* (Samuel Weiser, Inc, 1971), 115.

[17] Liber LXXVII 'Liber OZ'

[18] Liber AL vel Legis, Chapter 1, verse 3

[19] Aleister Crowley et al., *Magick: Liber ABA, Book Four, Parts I-IV*, 2nd rev. ed (York Beach, Me: S. Weiser, 1997), 546.

circle'[20], which is a telling indication of how he felt about the topic.

In Crowley's letters to his magical son, in the chapter *De Cultu*[21] he also indicated the importance of the Eucharist (referred to as Mass in the text) and its daily performance

> Neglect not the daily Miracle of the Mass, either by the Rite of the Gnostic Catholic Church, or that of the Phoenix. Neglect not the Performance of the Mass of the Holy Ghost, as Nature herself prompteth thee.[22]

His examples here cover both OTO ritual and A∴A∴ ritual, and The Mass of the Holy Ghost. This particular Mass is described further in *Liber Aleph* across several chapters.

The basis of any of the Eucharistic acts is to consume the Sacraments. As it is written in *Liber ABA* these can be of a composite nature. Although in the Christian church the wafer is used in more modern times, Crowley notes that this can be substituted with the

---

[20] Crowley et al., *Magick*, 269.

[21] Trans. 'On Discipline'

[22] Aleister Crowley, *Liber Aleph Vel CXI: The Book of Wisdom or Folly, in the Form an Epistle of 666, the Great Wild Beast to His Son 777, Being the Equinox, Volume III Number VI*, Rev. ed (York Beach, Me: S. Weiser, 1991), 16.

more complex *Cakes of Light*. We have them described in *Liber AL vel Legis*, Chapter III, verses 23 – 29.

> For perfume mix meal & honey & thick leavings of red wine: then oil of Abramelin and olive oil, and afterward soften & smooth down with rich fresh blood.

> The best blood is of the moon, monthly: then the fresh blood of a child, or dropping from the host of heaven: then of enemies; then of the priest or of the worshippers: last of some beast, no matter what.

> This burn: of this make cakes & eat unto me. This hath also another use; let it be laid before me, and kept thick with perfumes of your orison: it shall become full of beetles as it were and creeping things sacred unto me.

> These slay, naming your enemies; & they shall fall before you.

> Also these shall breed lust & power of lust in you at the eating thereof.

> Also ye shall be strong in war.

> Moreover, be they long kept, it is better; for they swell with my force. All before me.

The first three of the verses talk about the *recipe* for the Sacrament, and the remaining verses give some ciphered indication of their use.

Although the Sacrament of the Cake of Light is a singular item in itself, it is composed of parts that have their own attributes. The meal is earthy. The honey, lunar. The leavings of red wine (which is primarily composed of tartaric acid) is a raising agent and may be related to Bacchus. Olive oil calls to mind Athena and wisdom. The Oil of Abramelin is in itself composite, which brings a deeper layer to this otherwise *simple* wafer.

The next ingredient which seems to have caused the most discussion and debate is the blood. Some of the choices offered are reasonably obvious, and in the New Comment[23], Crowley writes a long passage about this topic. His discussion does include references to the Sanctuary of the Gnosis and to alchemical processes; neither of which are suitable to be explored in the context of this survey. However, this particular component does make reference back to the blood that is a notable part of the history of the Eucharist. The animal sacrifices of the early Temple period and then the symbolic *blood of Christ* that is part of their celebration.

---

[23] Crowley, Aleister, *The Law Is for All* (Llewellyn Publications, 1975), 284.

A fascinating word in this set of verses is the word *orison* which quite simply means 'a prayer[24]'. This can be related to the word *epiklesis*, as the division between prayer or an invocation at this point may be moot.

Lust as a word is used twice, and as Crowley suggests in the New Comment, this is not related to the idea of Lust in a Puritan sense but is the raising of energy or *fire*. Much like the spirit and fire that dwell on the path of Shin.

The use of a rising agent, as directed by the voice of Aiwaz in the Book of the Law, adds a new component to the history of the Eucharist. Traditionally bread during the time of *Passover* was unleavened and even today, the wafer used in the Christian-inspired Masses are thin and unleavened. The underlying importance of this change can be read in the section 'Mystery of the Leaven' in Daniel Gunther's book, *Initiation in the Aeon of the Child: The Inward Journey*.[25] Historically the process of fermentation (and rising of the bread) was associated with corruption or decay. He further details the act of fermentation which *stirs up*, and in this case, does the same in the soul of the consumer of the Cake of Light.

---

[24] Walter W. Skeat, *An Etymological Dictionary of the English Language* (Mineola, N.Y: Dover Publications, 2005), 415.

[25] J. Daniel Gunther, *Initiation in the Aeon of the Child: The Inward Journey* (Lake Worth, FL : Newburyport, MA: Ibis Press ; Distributed to the trade by Red Wheel/Weiser, 2009), 133.

Drawing on the alchemical literature, Gunther aligns the leavening agent with the *Salt of Tartaruss*[26], which is where we most likely get the basis for the name of *tartaric acid*.

The most publicly known expression of the Mass and the Eucharist is *Liber XV*, 'The Gnostic Mass', of the Ecclesia Gnostica Catholica. A beautiful rite that at first sight appears to be a combination of a mystery play, a dramatic ritual, hints of the OTO degree system, and quite prominently, the Eucharistic rite. The Eucharist appears to take place primarily in section VI 'Of the Consecration of the Elements' and section VIII 'Of the Mystic Marriage and Consummation of the Elements'. Although it could be readily argued that section VII 'The Office of the Anthem' is an important part of this particular sequence as part of the *epiklesis*. It is part of the invocation that is required in the preparation of the Sacraments.

The Sacramental elements, which make up the Eucharist, in the Gnostic Mass is the Cake of Light (or *wafer*) and a Chalice of Wine. Crowley's description[27] of the *Eucharist of two elements* covers the details of this quite well. The wafer represents the pantacle (and of corn) whilst the chalice represents water. These can also

---

[26] Reading his references in footnote 13 on these pages is highly recommended.

[27] Crowley et al., *Magick*, 267.

represent the Sun and Bacchus in turn. These are also a symbolic representation of flesh and blood much like the earlier Sacramental rites in the pre-Christian Temple.

Based on a page count using the 'Blue Equinox'[28] the sections that are related directly to the Eucharist are about one-third of the rite itself. A diagram by Barker[29] which correlates the Tabernacle with the seven days of Creation has the first third of the Temple, which contains the Holy of Holies, standing behind the veil. In the Gnostic Mass, the preparation of the Eucharist takes place on the altar, which is situated behind the veil in the area which corresponds to the Holy of Holies. The place where the Eucharist is prepared and consecrated is also the place where God is manifested.

Although reminiscent of the Roman Rite, where there is the Clergy and there is the Communicants (or People), the Gnostic Mass changes this dynamic. The *lay folk* come to the Veil that would normally hide the Holy of Holies. This has been laid open for them, rather than being shielded. The whole procedure of consecrating the Sacrament and preparing it has been made available to them. Another change that has been

---

[28] Aleister Crowley and Ordo Templi Orientis, *The Equinox: The Official Organ of the A∴A∴* (San Francisco, Calif.; [Enfield: Weiser ; [Airlift, distributor, 2007), chap. Liber XV.

[29] Margaret Barker, *Temple Theology: An Introduction* (London: SPCK, 2004), 18.

introduced here is the addition of the feminine element in the consecration of the Sacrament. This creates a balance that had been previously removed.

First documented in *The Book of Lies,* Chapter 44, Crowley provides us with another form of Mass. This one is designed explicitly for use by one person. He describes it as 'exoteric'[30], being an outward practice of the Mass.

The Mass of the Phoenix is a short ritual containing some seemingly simple invocations and the use of Sacraments. The instructions involve two Cakes of Light, fire, and the Magician's own blood. This is consumed and he rises as if a Phoenix. At first sight, this Mass appears to be the Eucharist of Two elements (much like the Gnostic Mass), but the extended commentary on this chapter, which is found in Chapter 62 'Twig?', *The Book of Lies*, describes all the elements involved. Being the Bell, the Fire, the Knife, and the Cakes of Light. These represent the senses of sound, sight, touch, taste, and smell. The description of this combination of elements in *Liber ABA* varies, using a rose and wine for the last two portions. The magician brings the Universe onto themselves, using their blood and Cake of Light combined to illustrate the transformation from lower to higher. Using their

---

[30] Crowley et al., *Magick*, 268.

prayer they are consumed in holy fire and reborn, as the Phoenix[31].

There are examples of other uses of the Eucharist in published and unpublished rituals from Crowley. There is no inherent benefit to describing them all here, but there is one particularly good example that is based on an official A∴A∴ ritual.

It is related to the formula of the Neophyte. As a colour insert in *Equinox IV:1* there is a holograph of Crowley's illuminated version of *Liber DCLXXI vel Pyramidos* (or 'Liber Pyramidos'). It echoes material he would have encountered during his earlier association with the Golden Dawn:

> Behold! the Perfect One hath said
> These are my body's Elements
> Incense and Wine and Fire and Bread
> Tried and found pure, a golden Spoil.
>
> These I consume, true Sacraments,
> For the Perfection of the Oil
> – For I am clothed about with Flesh
> And I am the Eternal Spirit.

---

[31] Aleister Crowley, *The Book of Lies, Which Is Also Falsely Called, Breaks: The Wanderings or Falsifications of the One Thought of Frater Perdurabo (Aleister Crowley), Which Thought Is Itself Untrue.* (San Francisco, Calif.: Weiser Books, 1981), 134.

I am the Lord that riseth fresh
From Death, whose Glory I inherit
Since I partake with Him. I am
The Manifestor of the Unseen.

Without me all the Land of Khem
Is as if it had not been.[32]

The elements of the Sacrament are made Godly and consumed (through the senses) and fill the Magician. The prayer or invocation explicitly talks about *consumption* and the in-filling of the bodily shell ('clothed about with flesh') containing the divine ('And I am the Eternal Spirit'). Much like in *The Mass of the Phoenix*, the Magician is risen after the consumption of the Eucharist. Although in this instance the imagery is more closely associated with The Risen God (Osiris), whereas the Phoenix is formulated around a different mythological concept.

The consumption of the Eucharist is not intended to provide instant results. It is a slow process that transforms the Magician so that they are prepared for their next steps. It comes to mind that this *day-by-day*

---

[32] Aleister Crowley, *Commentaries on the Holy Books and Other Papers: The Equinox, Volume Four, Number One* (York Beach, Me: S. Weiser, 1996), 71.

Author note: Any errors in the text are the result of my own transcription.

nature of the Eucharist seems to be a barrier to some people properly engaging with it. The gradual transformation seems anathema to modern lifestyles. But as with all *true* good things, patience and persistence is required.

The Angel admonishes us regarding this point of patience quite clearly:

> Wolf's bane is not so sharp as steel; yet it pierceth the body more subtly.

> Even as evil kisses corrupt the blood, so do my words devour the spirit of man.

> I breathe, and there is infinite dis-ease in the spirit.

> As an acid eats into steel, as a cancer that utterly corrupts the body; so am I unto the spirit of man.[33]

Another of our Holy Books, using The Aeon as a signpost, provides us with further inspiration and understanding; that with patience, the goal will be reached and the monument built:

> Then also the Pyramid was builded so that the initiation might be complete. [34]

---

[33] Liber Cordis Cincti Serpente, Chapter 1, verses 13 – 17

Back in *Liber ABA*, Crowley finishes his essay on the Eucharist by making it abundantly clear that the Eucharist is part of the Magician's preparation[35] for the initiation that is the Attainment of the Knowledge and Conversation of the Holy Guardian Angel.

Through this process of infusing one's self with the Divine, the Temple that is our bodies is purified and gilded, that we may hear the *voice* and be suitably prepared for that experience.

> The magician becomes filled with God, fed upon God, intoxicated with God. Little by little his body will become purified by the internal lustration of God; day by day his mortal frame, shedding its earthly elements, will become in very truth the Temple of the Holy Ghost. Day by day matter is replaced by Spirit, the human by the divine; ultimately the change will be complete; God manifest in flesh will be his name[36]

Working onward, looking upon high. Purify yourself patiently and constantly. With time and dedication, God will indwell. It will be hard and daunting. Built on a past that we have transformed into something greater. Go from the self to God.

---

[34] Liber Arcanorum των Atu του Tahuti Quas Vidit Asar in Amenti sub figura CCXXXI, verse 20

[35] Crowley et al., *Magick*, 269.

[36] Crowley et al., *Magick*, 269.

Finally, again the words of the Angel:

> Let not the failure and the pain turn aside the worshippers. The foundations of the pyramid were hewn in the living rock ere sunset; did the king weep at dawn that the crown of the pyramid was yet unquarried in the distant land?[37]

---

[37] Liber Cordis Cincti Serpente, Chapter 5, verse 51

THE PROOF IS IN THE PUDDING

MARKO MILENOVIC

Do what thou will shall be the whole of the Law.

The crown jewel of the work of the Outer College of the A∴A∴ is the Knowledge and Conversation of the Holy Guardian Angel. The Outer College curriculum trains you to be ready for it but doesn't tell you who or what the Angel is. There is only a promise that He is there, at the end of the Path, and if you work hard you will reach Him.

Neither this little essay nor any other will help you understand what the Holy Guardian Angel is. No amount of books written on this subject can bring you any closer to Him or help you understand who He is and how to get to Him. There is but one way to do that – eat the pudding. That is why at the end of this essay you will not know who He is nor the precise ritual and/or meditation needed to get to Him. What this text will give you is an overview of the process that will inevitably lead you to Him. Not that I don't want to do it or that I am forbidden to do it – I can't. It is impossible for one person to explain to another who the Angel is and what it feels like to have experienced Him. Only those who have the experience will recognise others who have had it too. And they will do so in Silence. One does not yell it from rooftops.

But I expected...

It is truly hard not to expect things when one starts to do anything. When you start exercising you expect a healthier and stronger body. When you start a diet you expect to lose weight. And that is normal. The problem arises when something very vague such as the Holy Guardian Angel is the ultimate aim of one's endeavour. It is hard not to have expectations but it's also very dangerous to have them. Before moving on it would be good to address some misconceptions right away.

First of all, you don't *have* Him. He is not a pet to be had. He is not an item on the astral shelf that you will pick up one day only for you to have. I understand that it is the deficiency of languages and that it's the same as saying 'I have a friend'. However, this little language deficiency can lead to the second problem – entitlement.

Same as with friends, one is not entitled to the Angel. He is not assigned to you when you are born, silently waiting for you to sober up and see Him. Just as friends are not assigned to you when you are born. Friendship is earned. Parents spend countless hours teaching their children social skills so that once they start exploring the world on their own, they are able to make friends. The whole work of the Outer College of the A∴A∴ is precisely about that – preparing you to be able to observe and communicate with the Angel.

Next thing we need to address is Aleister Crowley. Every one of us has had their own Path that led them to Crowley and Thelema. It was a general spiritual exploration for some. For others, rebelling against the established religions of their forefathers. What awaits all of us is facing Crowley for what he was and learning not to mix the planes. This skill is very hard to acquire but is the most useful one to have in your tool belt. Not just when it comes to Crowley but when it comes to you too.

The first step is facing Crowley the 'demon' and outgrowing him. Crowley was a spiritual genius but he was also human. With all his faults. Crowley was also a trickster. He had different methods for different students and those methods may sometimes seem plain sadistic. Unless you learn to make a difference between the man and his work you will be haunted by the demon Crowley which will hinder your Great Work quite a bit, if not leading you to leave it completely. My suggestion is to read various biographies, especially those dealing with specific portions of his life in details such as the India or the USA periods[1] and then try to see beyond the image.

Crowley developed as a person throughout his life. My approach is to observe the development of his ideas through time and to be very careful what value I give to his statements when he was young. If mid twenties

---

[1] The works of Tobias Churton are a good choice

are behind you, try to remember what you did, said and thought back then. One of the things that Crowley did, which resulted in long term damage, was claiming the following: *'The spirits of the Goetia are portions of the human brain'*[2]. Many practitioners of Goetia will never forgive him for this. Yet, you should remember that he was 29 when he wrote the introduction to his edition of Goetia. My suggestion is to go to Crowley in his late years and see what he has to say on the same subject:

> Now, on the other hand, there is an entirely different type of angel; and here we must be especially careful to remember that we include gods and devils, for there are such beings who are not by any means dependent on one particular element for their existence. They are microcosms in exactly the same sense as men and women are. They are individuals who have picked up the elements of their composition as possibility and convenience dictates, exactly as we do ourselves... I believe that the Holy Guardian Angel is a Being of this order. He is something more than a man, possibly a being who has already passed through the stage of humanity, and his peculiarly intimate relationship with his client is that of friendship, of community, of brotherhood, or Fatherhood. He is not, let me say with emphasis, a mere abstraction from yourself; and that is why I have insisted rather heavily that the term

---

[2] Crowley, *The Book of the Goetia of Solomon the King*, p.3

'Higher Self' implies a damnable heresy and a dangerous delusion[3].

The Oaths

Those who decide to walk the lonely Path of the A∴A∴ will sign different Oaths during their career. Those Oaths are publicly available in the document called *Liber Colegii Sancti svb figura CLXXXV*. All of them are two page documents containing the Oath and the Task list for each grade. Each Oath contains a single sentence that sums up the essence of what Student needs to achieve. The Task list contains practices that will lead to that end. I always suggest to my Students to go through their Oath & Task very thoroughly as they contain pearls of wisdom that will help them understand the work at hand and how they should conduct themselves. That work is often described as a pyramid where Probationers have a rather broad foundational work which is slowly trimmed down with each grade only to leave a single task at the top.

Let us look at each essential sentence of the Outer College Oaths:

---

[3] Crowley, *Magick Without Tears,* p.166

Probationer	obtain a scientific knowledge of the nature and powers of my own being
Neophyte	obtain control of the nature and powers of my own being
Zelator	obtain control of the foundations of my own being
Practicus	obtain control of the vacillations of my own being
Philosophus	obtain control of the attractions and repulsions of my own being
Dominus Liminis	obtain control of the aspirations of my own being
Adeptus Minor	attain to the knowledge and conversation of the Holy Guardian Angel

If you pay attention to each of the sentences you will notice the process of trimming down one's being. This is a slow and painful process. There is nothing fun in spiritual exploration no matter which path you decide to take.

So, our work starts at Probationer grade. At this point the Student is told to study publications in Class B[4] *and apply himself to such practices of Scientific Illuminism as seemeth him good*[5]. This is a testing period. One that should not be treated as something light. During this period you are tested by the Order and by yourself to see if you are actually capable of doing the work. A lot of Students naively think that this grade is a joke and that they'll just run through it. A lot of them get stuck here for years or decades. For you see, the judge for your advancement may officially be your Instructor but it is also you. It is easy to pretend in front of others that you are the greatest magician in the world but you can't lie to yourself when you know that you aren't capable of doing your practices in a disciplined manner for more than two days.

So, once Students face the 'nature and powers of their own being' also known as 'facing the fact that they are weak and lazy' there comes the next step. They are allowed into the Outer College where more structured work is given. The Student can no longer choose what they do. The aim is now very precise thus making the practices very specific.

---

[4] *Cf.* Crowley, *Liber ABA, Appendix I, Literature Recommended to Aspirants*

[5] Crowley, *Liber Colegii Sancti svb figura CLXXXV,* p. 4

If you take a look at the five Oaths between Probationer and Adeptus Minor you will notice that they all have the word 'control' in them. The aim of this control is to become the master of your body and mind. But why? What does this have to do with the Holy Guardian Angel? Let us take a look at the practices that each grade is given to do in order to understand this.

We start with material in Class B which is pretty wide. Probationers are allowed to use their own judgement when deciding which practices to do as long as they serve the purpose of the Oath. Once they become Neophytes their work can be pretty much be summed up as: spiritual hygiene and concentration. Both of these, if performed regularly and properly will result in improvement of Student's focus. Neophytes are told to *'practise Liber O in all its branches'*. That in turn requires to train our minds and to develop our focus.

Those who pass a rigorous test may move on to the Zelator grade. This grade tells us that *'He shall pass Examinations in Liber E, Posture and Breathing'*. Liber E lists practices are derived from Crowley's time in India and Ceylon. He was greatly influenced by time spent there and practices learned within the frameworks of Hinduism and Buddhism. Crowley was able to extract the essence of Raja Yoga and convert it to practices given in Liber E and elsewhere. So, what is a Zelator expected to do? Develop control of the foundations of his being, of course. The foundation of our being is our body. That is where posture and breathing techniques from yoga come into place. It is really hard to expect to be able to control your mind if you can't control your body. Achieving this is a long and painful process. And I don't mean psychologically painful. Try sitting in a single position, motionless for over 30 minutes. What a Zelator aims for is to reach that point where body is no longer an obstacle and when clearing one's thoughts with breathing exercises becomes natural.

Once this body & mind self-control is achieved the work doesn't stop. I've noticed over the years that a lot of Students tend to observe the grades as self-contained things. You pass the exam of the Neophyte and that's it, you no longer need what you've learned. I blame the education in most countries for this where certain knowledge is acquired only to pass an exam and then quickly forgotten. This approach is bound to fail. What one learns on the first grade is something they will need for the remainder of their lives. It is active knowledge that we improve and advance with each step we make on the Path.

So, our Zelator has learned to control his body and breathing. Zelator becomes a Practicus and now faces vacillations or the inability to decide between different opinions or actions; indecision. The Practicus grade is where our intellect is exposed completely. The practices given on this grade are such that even the most intellectual Student will become sick of their own intellectualisation of things. Very interesting insights are reached here. And intellect is trimmed off in a sense that we start to understand our own thought process thus being able to control it even more. Liber XIII tells us that the Practicus grade gets 'Instruction in Philosophical Meditation (Jñāna yoga)' which is 'Union by Knowledge'.

Once the Practicus passes the exhausting exam only one step is left before the Angel and that is the grade of Philosophus. Liber XIII tells us that the Philosophus grade gets 'Instruction and Examination in Methods of Meditation by Devotion (Bhakti-Yoga)' which is fiery devotion to the Divine. By this point one should be deeply inflamed with Aspiration.

Once this grade is passed the Student reaches Dominus Liminis which is not technically a grade but a threshold between the Outer and Inner Orders. That doesn't mean being idle, as the Oath reminds us. Dominus Liminis is tested in control of thought through Liber III, cap III. By this moment Student should have became master of both mystical (yoga) and magical (ceremonial) paths.

But to what end? To a careful reader it will be clear that all this training has a purpose. It is obvious that by the time one becomes Adeptus Minor they should have emptied their minds and filled their hearts. They have only one task now - the Knowledge and Conversation of the Holy Guardian Angel. To perceive Him, to be able to hear Him and converse with Him one needs to be able to achieve exalted states of mind. One has to be able to be one-pointed. It is the top of the pyramid that we are aiming for.

So, who is the Angel? He is what is left when you empty your mind and fill up your heart. This is the closest thing I can say about Him and still sound sane. It is impossible to convey into words something achieved when all words have ceased. Thus the only answer of those who know Him is and always will be Silence.

Knowledge and Conversation of the Holy Guardian Angel

One expectation that I haven't covered in my introduction was the expectation of the experience of the Angel. First of all notice that the whole process is called Knowledge and Conversation. It is not a single event where everything happens. The Knowledge is a long process that happens in the Outer College. It is something built bit by bit and we come to know His presence gradually, as we work to prepare ourselves for Him[6]. The whole experience will not be a flash of light where one comes to realise the truth about the Universe and ones own being. This whole process is nicely described as building of a relationship between two lovers. It starts with a kiss. Subtle. So subtle that we don't even notice it. That is when the Angel shows Himself to us early on but we are too loud and too

---

[6] See J. Daniel Gunther, Angel & Abyss, p. 342 - 351

chaotic to even notice it. In most cases it takes the completion of the Outer College for Students to realise when this first encounter happened.

It then builds until the grand finale. And even that grand finale is not a single moment. Our relationship with the Angel is something that is built, achieved and then consumed – it is a process that takes time. It is a process best achieved in Silence.

> My Fairy Prince is a dark boy, very comely; I think every one must love him, and yet every one is afraid. He looks through one just as if one had no clothes on in the Garden of God, and he had made one, and one could do nothing except in the mirror of his mind. He never laughs or frowns or smiles; because, whatever he sees, he sees what is beyond as well, and so nothing ever happens. His mouth is redder than any roses you ever saw. I wake up quite when we kiss each other, and there is no dream any more. But when it is not trembling on mine, I see kisses on his lips, as if he were kissing some one that one could not see.[7]

The process described here is long, hard and very private. Is it worth your time? I think it is. Should you believe in what I wrote here? Absolutely not. Go and test it. Don't waste time debating. Eat the pudding so

---

[7] Crowley, *The Wake World*, p. 3

that you know if it's any good. Once you do, you won't have to explain anything to anyone.

'Sit still. Stop thinking. Shut up. Get out!'

Love is the law, love under will.

FRATER O.I.P.

Already he had shown me that I, in my office as Baphomet,
was the rock on which the New Temple should be built[1]

I am Baphomet, that is the Eightfold Word that shall be
equilibrated with the Three.[2]
Liber A'ash, 18

Binario Verbum Vitae Mortem et Vitam Aequilibrans[3]

When Aleister Crowley became Grand Master General
X° in the OTO he took on the name of the mysterious
idol that the Knights Templar were accused of
worshipping during the trials of 1307 – Baphomet.
This essay is an attempt to explore the potential
doctrinal and historical reasons why Crowley took on
this name in an OTO and EGC context; as well as its
broader relation to Thelemic doctrine, and the
relationship between the two Orders (OTO and
A∴A∴).

---

[1] Crowley, *The Confessions of Aleister Crowley*, 833.

[2] The numbers 8 and 3 may have significance to initiates of the I°
of the OTO.

[3] Levi, *The Book of Splendours*, 118.

Since I began writing this essay many years ago[4], more people have explored this theme and some of these ideas in detail, but I hope this small offering still contains something of interest, and contributes to the ongoing discussion. I dedicate it with gratitude to Frater Shiva X°, who has continually encouraged me along my long and stumbling path in eternity.

One of the first historical references to Baphomet is from 1195 in a poem titled 'Senhors, per los nostres peccatz', a crusaders song written by Gavaudan (1195-1215) who was a soldier and troubadour:

---

[4] I can find evidence of starting to work on the core of these concepts in 2010 but may have begun prior to this.

Profeta sera.n Gavaudas	Gavaudan shall be a prophet
qu.el dig er faitz, e mortz als cas!	for his words shall become a fact. Death to those dogs!
e Dieus er honratz e servitz	God shall be honoured and worshipped
on Bafometz era grazitz.	where Mahomet is now served.[5]

As can be seen in the translation Baphomet (Bafometz) is likely a corruption of Mahomet or Mohamed, the founder and prophet of Islam (and EGC saint), who was known to meditate for weeks at a time in a cave on Jabal an-Nour (The Mountain of Light), and it was here that he was visited by the Angel Gabriel and received his first revelation.

ٱلْحَجَرُ ٱلْأَسْوَد

Through the midnight thou art dropt, O my child, my conqueror, my sword-girt captain, O Hoor! and they shall find thee as a black gnarl'd glittering stone, and they shall worship thee.

Liber LXV, V: 6

---

[5] Kastner, *Gavaudan's Crusade Song*, 142–150.

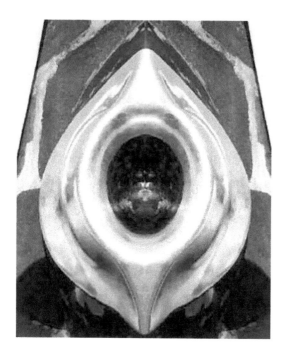

In Islamic tradition the stone placed at the Kaaba by the
Prophet dates back to the time of Adam and Eve and
fell from "Jannah"[6] to show Adam and Eve where to
build an altar (the first temple on Earth), becoming a
link between heaven and earth. Its black colour is said
to represent the extinction of the ego needed to
progress towards God. The stone has been worn
smooth by the generations of Muslim pilgrims, who
have touched it for the expiation of their Sins.
However, the Kabba and the black stone predates Islam,
and was once a pilgrimage site for the Nabateans.

---

[6] جنّة - Literally a garden (Paradise)

Similar temples and acts of worship can be seen at other Nabatean sites such as Petra in Jordan.

Semitic cultures in the Middle East were known to use unusual stones to indicate religious sites or sites of worship.

Blocks representing Nabataean God "Dushara" in Petra (Photo by the author)

In another tradition it is said that the stone is an Angel who had previously been placed by God in the Garden of Eden to protect Adam. This angel was punished for being absent when the forbidden fruit was eaten and was turned into the black stone.

The Islamic prophet Muhammad solves a dispute by lifting the black stone (الحجر الأسود) into position at al-Kaaba

In the above image the Prophet can be seen lifting the black stone into its position in the Kaaba based on Ibn Ishaq's *Sirah Rasul Allah*[7] (The Life of Muhammad). It shows the elders of the clans holding the corners of a cloth in which the stone was placed at Mohammed's request. Here we may see disordered elements (the clan

---

[7] Ishaq, *The Life of Muhammad*, 84-87.

elders who could not decide who should place the stone back in the rebuilt Kaaba) joined by a unifying influence (spirit) represented both by the black stone and the Prophet. Herein is also the element of chance (or perhaps some would argue fate), as the elders decided to wait for the first person to walk through the gate, and ask that person to make the decision for them. Here was can see Muhammad's role, and Islam's in uniting warring clans and unifying a fragmented society in common purpose.

The name Baphomet also appears in Raymond Llull's (1232 – 1315) *Libre de la doctrina pueril* ('The Book on the Instruction of Children') and turns up again in the fabricated essay written by Joseph von Hammer-Purgstall (1774 – 1856) titled '*Mysterium Baphometis revelatum*' (The Secret of Baphomet is Revealed), which was published to discredit Freemasonry and link the Fraternity to the Knights Templar.

Under torture in 1307 some Knights Templar did confess to the worship of this idol, while it was denied by others, and the descriptions of this 'Baphomet' varied greatly: such as a severed head; a cat or a head with three faces. Although false charges were brought against other enemies of King Phillip, Baphomet seems to have been unique to the Templars. Some modern scholars propose that the name Baphomet is indeed an Old French corruption of Muhammad, and that the charges against the Templars stem from the integration of some Islamic elements into their beliefs due to their time spent in the Holy Land. Some authors also posit that prior to Islam the Kaaba was the site of fertility rights, and that the word Kaaba is derived from the old Semitic KBA, which referred to the female genitals.[8]

It should be noted that others argue against this view on the origins of the name and do not think the Christian Templars would take on Islamic elements. For example Hugh Schonfield believed that Baphomet when written in Hebrew (בפומת) could be converted by Atbash to Sophia (שופיא), Wisdom.[9] We will return to Wisdom later in this essay. Another alternative that has been given is **Ba**sileus philoso**phorum met**aloricum; "the sovereign of metallurgical philosophers."[10]

Frater Shiva has lectured about the Templar archetype, its relationship to freemasonry, and its transmission to initiates of the OTO. Regardless of the real historical facts, this archetype is embedded in the psyche of the Western world. Both the image of the Templars and Baphomet still play out in our culture. It should be noted that the connection between warriors and a religious or spiritual dimension is certainly not isolated to the Western world. This is perhaps explained by a warrior's proximity to death, and the need for

---

[8] Zalewski, *The Crucible of Religion*, 269.

[9] Schonfield, *Essene Odyssey*, 164.

[10] Klossowski, *The Baphomet*, 164–165

philosophical and religious structures to assist them to cope with the psychological stress this creates.

The image of Baphomet most commonly recognized today bears little resemblance to the descriptions given at the Templar trials, but is the image of Baphomet, or 'The Sabbatic Goat'[11], that was produced by Eliphas Levi in his *Dogme et Rituel de la Haute Magie*.

---

[11] Levi also calls the figure, "The Baphomet of Mendes", Mendes being the Greek for the Egyptian city Djedet or 'Per-Banebdjedet -The Domain of the Ram Lord of Djedet'. The chief deities worshiped in Djedet were the ram deity *Banebdjedet* (Ba of Osiris), and his consort Hatmehit, who is a fish goddess. With their child Har-pa-khered ("Horus the Child"), they formed the triad of Mendes.

Levi wrote elsewhere about Baphomet. In part three of *The Book of Splendours* he dedicates a section to Baphomet, interestingly called "The Flaming Star". Here he seems to clearly connect Baphomet to the Sphinx (with some additions):

> Sometimes he is shown with a beard, the horns of a male goat, the face of a man, the breasts of a woman, the mane and claws of a lion, the wings of an eagle and the hooves of a bull.[12]

Levi further writes, "He is a hold-over from the Cherubs of the ark and the Holy of holies".

The two cherubim, according to Philo represented the two greatest of the heavenly powers. The first was the creative power, which was called God, and the second was the kingly power, which was the Lord. "The divine presence was discerned between them." Philo also stated that the name meant, "recognition and full knowledge."[13] Christian tradition later built on this and taught that the "cherubim are those who know God, who are filled with Wisdom and then pour this into others."

> The Lord God drove out the man; and at the east of the garden of Eden he placed the cherubim, and a

---

[12] Levi, *The Book of Splendours*, 118.

[13] Barker, *An Extraordinary Gathering of Angels*, 121.

flaming sword which turned every way, to guard the
way to the tree of life.
Genesis 3

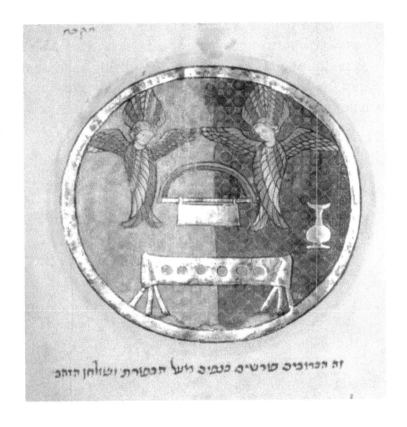

*Two cherubim stand on either side of the Ark of the Covenant,
their colourful wings spread over it. The golden Table of the show
bread and the golden Manna Vessel stand beneath them. British
Library, London. Date : c.1280*

Also, Levi writes of Baphomet that, "he is the guardian of the key to the temple."[14]

Levi also seems to point at the archetypal nature of Baphomet when he writes, "These hybrid creations of impossible animals gave to understand that the image was not an idol or reproduction of a living thing, but rather a character or representation of something having its experience in thought." [15]

Levi further points to the mysteries connected to Baphomet when he states in *The Key of the Mysteries*:

> ...the Templars, for example, who are much less to be blamed for having worshipped Baphomet, than for allowing its image to be perceived by the profane. Baphomet, pantheistic figure of the universal agent, is nothing else than the bearded devil of the alchemists. One knows that the members of the highest grades in the old hermetic masonry attributed to a bearded demon the accomplishment of the Great Work.[16]

Aleister Crowley felt a great connection between himself and Eliphas Levi (considering himself his reincarnation), so it is not surprising that he saw a relationship between himself and this, to some, still

---

[14] Levi, *The Book of Splendours*, 119.

[15] Ibid., 118

[16] Levi, *The Key of the Mysteries*, 148.

confrontational image. But what did he see as the significance of this name in relation to the OTO? In the *Confessions of Aleister Crowley* he discusses the name Baphomet, stating that "for six years and more I had tried to discover the proper way to spell this name. I knew that it must have eight letters, and also that the numerical and literal correspondences must be such as to express the meaning of the name in such a way as to confirm what scholarship had found out about it, and also to clear up those problems which archaeologists had so far failed to solve".

By Gematria Crowley came to the spelling BAFOMIThR (or he was given the spelling by the Wizard Amalantrah), which equals 729[17]. This has the same value as the Aramaic Kephas (Πέτρος) or rock, which is the name Jesus is said to have given to the apostle Peter as the foundation of his Church.

> You are Peter, and on this rock I will build my Church, and the gates of hell will not prevail against it. (Matt. 16:18)

Crowley further writes that, "The R has been suppressed as a blind – it blinded me all right!- and because the sun has been concealed (in the Aeon of

---

[17] 9 cubed (9^3) = 729

Osiris, I suppose)..Note: One of the Wizard's favorite veils was the Winged Beetle – the Concealed Sun![18]"

Now, why did Crowley believe that the name *must* have eight letters? Any one even casually familiar with the Hermetic Qabalah would know that the number 8 refers to the Sephiroth Hod and Mercury ($\math\ {\wideimpl}$) or Thoth. From the Golden Dawn Z.1 paper, which Crowley would have been intimately familiar with, Mercury is attributed to three Sephiroth on the Tree of Life: Kether, Hod and Yesod. It is in Yesod that Thoth is seen as a "sexual or generative moon god."[19] Here we immediately see a possible connection with the "Eightfold Word" and the mysteries of the OTO[20] We also see a clear connection to Mercury in Levi's depiction, with the Caduceus rising up from

---

[18] Crowley, *The Magical Record of the Beast 666*, 68.

[19] 'Note that there are Three basic forms of Thoth,...first, Thoth the Speaker of the Work (and Word) of the Universe. He thus stands at Kether, the Tree of Life being his Speech. The second is Thoth we see in Hod, as messenger from beyond the Abyss, (there is a conscious play on words here). The third is the sexual or generative Moon God, who stands in Yesod, (the Sphere of the Moon, in the sign of the Enterer, leaning forward over the Thirty-Second Path, called, in the Tarot, "The Universe"'.

[20] In this iteration of this essay I have not touched on Crowley's writing in relation to the "eight genii of the desert," "the eight Elements of Fu-hsi." in the Soul of the Desert, but I would direct the reader to the writings of Frater Shiva X°.

Baphomet, who is seated upon a 'cubic stone'[21] (which itself seems to be supported by a sphere). Now Baphomet here is essentially androgynous (as is Mercury) or bisexual, in that it is a combination of both male and female elements – active and passive.

Levi writes:

> The caduceus, which replaces the generative organ, represents eternal life; the scale-covered belly typifies water; the circle above it is the atmosphere; the feathers still higher up signify the volatile; lastly, humanity is depicted by the two breasts and the androgyne arms of this sphinx of the occult sciences.[22]

Here we can refer back to the previous quote from Levi where he appears to be making a connection between the figure of Baphomet and that of the Sphinx.

The Caduceus itself could be seen as phallic (clearly indicated above by Levi), but the figure also displays prominent breasts. This androgynous nature of Baphomet is perhaps also seen in the older versions of the 'Devil' card in the Tarot, where a male and a female figure are seen chained to Baphomet (or more

---

[21] An Ashlar is a "square black of building stone. In Masonry, the perfect Ashlar signifies the rough stone brought to perfection and readied to become the cornerstone of the Temple." (Gunther, *Initiation in the Aeon of the Child*, 196.)

[22] Levi, *Dogma and Ritual of High Magic*, 309.

specifically to the stone[23]). The Devil card is attributed
to the number XV: יה – "The Monogram of the
Eternal, the Father one with the Mother, the Virgin
Seed one with all-containing space."[24]

[23] In relation to the symbolism of the Stone in depth psychology
Carl Jung writes of a, '*aliquem alium internum,* 'a certain other one,
within', quoting Ruthland, or an 'inner friend of the soul', which I
would associate with the H.G.A. in the doctrine of the A∴A∴
'The alchemists projected the inner event into an outer figure, so
for them the inner friend appears in the form of the "Stone"…'
(Jung, *The Archetypes of the Collective Unconscious,* 131 – 133)

[24] Crowley, *Magick: Book 4,* 277

We can perhaps see further hints at the mysteries of Baphomet in Levi's *Dogma and Ritual*, and the connection to Mercury in his, somewhat odd, depiction of the Pentagram and Tetragrammaton – the Pentagram clearly depicted on the forehead of Baphomet (remembering Levi's section relating to Baphomet in *The Book of Splendours* is called "The Flaming Star").

As with Baphomet the Caduceus is placed as a phallus, with an even more obvious indication of its Mercurial nature; but also seemingly combined with the astrological symbol for Venus (♀) again highlighting the combination of Male and Female as seen in Baphomet (although androgynous Mercury is primarily male). This lower symbol (the circle surmounted by a cross) could also be seen as a symbol of the *prima materia*, the material basis of the Great Work conjoined with the Messenger of the Gods, from above the Abyss.

...and is thus the influence of the supernals descending through the Veil of Water (which is blood) upon the energy of man, and so inspires it.[25]

It could also be both these symbols, with the formula of "love under will" vital to the process of the marriage of Earth and Heaven.

It is interesting to note the darkened right-hand side of the Pentagram, as also seen in the image of Baphomet, perhaps as an indication of the 'upright and the averse'- the 'bright and the dark'.

> I who comprehend in myself all the vast[26] and the minute[27], all the bright[28] and the dark[29], have mitigated the brilliance of mine unutterable splendour, sending forth V.V.V.V.V. as a ray of my light, as a messenger unto that small dark orb.

---

[25] Crowley, *The Book of Thoth*, 85.

[26] Nuit

[27] Hadit

[28] Therion

[29] Babalon

Liber X, 2

The symbols for the Sun and the Moon are also present
(Male and Female)[30] as are the words אדמ ADM and
חוה EVE, the first Man and Woman in the Book of
Genesis. If we write Adam and Eve (Hava) in Hebrew (
אדמ וחוה) we get 70[31]- ע – The Devil – Atu XV –
with its clear depiction of Baphomet.[32]

---

[30] "Note that Sol and Luna are direct images of the masculine and
feminine principles, and much more complete Macrocosms than
any other planets. This is explained by their symbols in the Yi
King, ☷ and ☵. Note also that Yesod appears openly, this being
the Queen Scale, in the violet robes of the spiritual-erotic
vibrations referred to above." (Crowley, 777 *and other Qabalistic
Writings of Aleister Crowley,* 81.)

[31] It is also interesting that one of the texts used by the early
Christians and Greek speaking Jews (and later derided and
associated with 'The Golden Calf') was a Greek translation of the
Old Testament sometimes simply called LXX (70). The legend
surrounding the texts is that they were translated by 70 (or 72)
Jewish scholars during Ptolemy Philadelphus reign in Egypt.

[32] 'The Old Testament is full of attacks upon kings who celebrated
in "high places"; this although Zion itself was a mountain!'
(Crowley, *The Book of Thoth,* 106-107.)

Zion, as pointed out by J. Daniel Gunther, refers to Binah, where
sit the Masters of the Temple.

"The word ABRAHADABRA is from Abrasax, Father Sun, which
adds to 365. For the North-South antithesis see Fabre-d'Olivet's
Hermeneutic Interpretation of the Origen of the Social State of

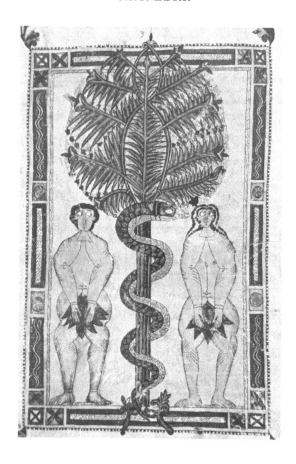

Man. Note that sax also as a Rock, or stone, whence the symbol of
the Cubical Stone, the Mountain of Abiegnus, and so forth"
(Crowley, *The Law is for All*, 24.)

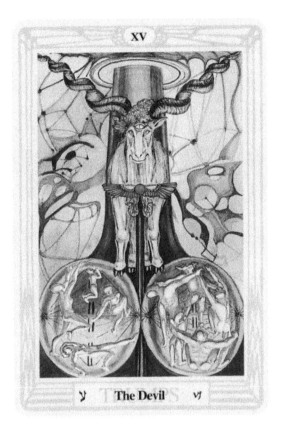

This blending of male and female in the figure of Baphomet seems central to Crowley's understanding and identification. In *The Book of Thoth* Crowley writes of Baphomet that

> Its pictorial correspondence is easily seen in the figures of Zeus Arrhenotheus and Babalon. [33]

---

[33] Crowley, *The Book of Thoth*, 67.

Earlier, in his discussion of Zeus Arrhenothelus[34] Crowley states that,

> It is only in Zeus Arrhenothelus that one gets the true Hermaphrodidic nature of the symbol in unified form. This is a very important fact, especially for present purpose, because images of this god appear again and again in alchemy. It is hardly possible to describe this lucidly; the idea pertains to a faculty of the mind which is **"above the Abyss"**.[35] (my emphasis)

In his personal diary Crowley shares further insights into the nature and relationship of Baphomet:

> When I was Levi I drew myself as Ayin or Baphomet, 'The Devil', with Beast's Head. This is the Beast throned, crowned, exalted; the leaper, the erect, the butter-in. Her womb is my city, Babel. This Ayin is therefore my Phallic Will, My Holy Guardian Angel, Aiwaz, who was afterwards called Satan. Distinguish their Ayin-Baphomet crowned from the Teth-Therion ridden. I am Ayin-King in Her city, Pe, Baphomet of Babalon; and she is also Babalon, Whore astride Therion in Teth. Her name seems the same both ways; perhaps always 7 whether I am 6 or 8.[36]

---

[34] The hermaphroditic form of the creator.

[35] Crowley, *The Book of Thoth*, 64.

[36] Crowley, *The Magical Record of the Beast 666*, 198.

It is clear here that Crowley is identifying himself directly with Baphomet (connecting it with what he saw as his past incarnation). It is also worth noting the connection of Babalon with Pe (פ). This is 'her city', in which Crowley sees himself as Ayin-King (remembering what Philo states about "the kingly power"). In the *Book of Thoth*, Crowley writes of Atu XVI (The Tower or War), "This suggests another (and totally different) interpretation of the card...The destruction of the garrison may therefore be taken to mean their emancipation from the prisons of organized life, which was confining them. It was their unwisdom to cling to it."

"Unwisdom" – I will return to the concept of 'Wisdom' later in this essay in relation to the Temple in Jerusalem and The Woman Clothed with the Sun.

Whore of Babylon by William Blake (1809)

From this, if we conjoin Babalon (7) with Baphomet (8), we again are taken back to 15, which resolves back to 6 (1+5), the Sun-Therion, and the Mystic Number of the Masters of the Temple - "the idea pertains to a faculty of the mind which is "above the Abyss".

Here we see Crowley associating Baphomet with his Office of The Beast and its relationship with Babalon and the dual nature of the Beast, as 6 or 8 – as the Sun or as Mercury – Therion or Baphomet. Also, very interestingly, we see here Crowley making a connection between Baphomet and his Holy Guardian Angel – defined as Aiwaz. In an earlier diary entry Crowley records:

> Later – I invoked Aiwaz, was shown a phantasm of Baphomet, and suddenly determined to recognise this for Him! I was instantly rewarded by the Word and Oath of an Ipissimus.[37]

When I read this entry the image of Atu V enters my mind, as I personally see this card as a depiction of Aiwaz – Crowley's Holy guardian Angel (V being ו the "Prince").

> He seemed to be a tall, dark man in his thirties, well-knit, active and strong, with the face of a savage king, and eyes veiled lest their gaze should destroy what

---

[37] Ibid., 140.

they saw. The dress was not Arab; it suggested Assyria or Persia, but very vaguely[38]

Further, Gunther makes clearer the connection between the Hierophant and the Masters of the Temple, making reference to the downward pointing V, formed by the Hierophant's left hand forming the Greek Λ, showing a connection to Atu VIII.

Gunther writes, "rather than the Roman V, he is forming the Greek Λ, which equates to the Hebrew ל, attributed to Atu VIII, Adjustment, and Libra (♎) in the Zodiac. M.A.A.T."[39]

---

[38] Crowley, *The Holy Books of Thelema*, Viii.

[39] Gunther, *The Angel and the Abyss*, 280.

These two letters form the vessica in which M.A.A.T. stands as a guardian of the gate through which the aspirant must pass in order to enter the supernal triad (as one who has passed that gate and stands in balance); where the heart is weighed against the feather of truth.

> Also the lady Maat with her feather and her sword abode to judge the righteous.
>
> For Fate was already established.

Liber CCXXI: 11

Both The Hierophant and Adjustment are ruled by ♀, the goddess of Love, whose symbol encompasses the whole Tree of Life. This symbol is also featured in The Hieroglyphic Triad (Book III of *The Inward Journey*), 'The Bar of Heaven' in which the Sephiroth and their Trigrams are displayed on the symbol of Venus – "Who is he that hath the **key** to the gate of the evening star" (my emphasis) – the evening star of course being ♀ (although sometimes ☿). This quote is taken from the 7th Aethyr (DEO) whose astrological attributions also pertain to BABALON[40]. Also, as before quoted from Levi regarding Baphomet: "He is the guardian of the **key** to the temple". (my emphasis).

Keys feature repeatedly throughout this essay in connection to Baphomet, Peter and Mithras.

---

[40] 7 is also a number of BABALON

Further to this, in *The Heart of the Master*, in his Instruction to Atu V Crowley writes:

> "Offer thyself Virgin to the Knowledge and Conversation of thine Holy Guardian Angel!
> All else is a snare."[41]

Additionally, in *The Book of Thoth*:

> But the main reference is to the particular Arcanum which is the principle business, the essential of all magical work; the uniting of the microcosm with the macrocosm.[42]

* * *

In the Book of the Dead the deceased recited the 42 negative confessions. Not things that the deceased is, but things the deceased is not. The aspirant is not filled with Truth, but is found to be devoid of falsehood. The path of true initiation is one of reduction.

---

[41] Crowley, *The Heart of the Master*, p. 61.

[42] Crowley, *The Book of Thoth*, 78.

There were also 42 "Assessors of Maat" who participated in the weighing of the heart in Maat's name. If the feather and the heart were in balance, the deceased then was found to be Maa Kheru – true of voice, vindicated or justified.

In a Thelemic sense the aspirant is found to have "no life therein" (Liber CLVI, 6); has divested themselves of "all thy goods" (Liber CLVI, 7).

In Sepher Sephiroth the first entry under 42 states, "the Number of the letters of a great name of GOD terrible and strong, and the Assessors of the Dead"[43].

Most of us who study the Qabalah are familiar with the Shem HaMephorash (שם המפורש) and that it is a 72 letter name. However, tradition has it that this is not

---

[43] Crowley, 777 and other Qabalistic Writings of Aleister Crowley, 178

the only number of letters associated with Shem HaMephorash. It also has 12, 22 and 42 letter variations.

Some argue that it is this 42 letter name of God that is used by the High Priest on the Day of Atonement during the recitation of his confessional.

> The Midrash also states that Genesis opens with a bet and closes with a mem because it alludes to the name of God enunciated by the High Priest on the Day of Atonement[44]

This connects to the 42 negative confessions of the deceased in the Book of the Dead, when the High Priest confesses his sins and those of Israel onto the goat. But this is the opposite of the Egyptian tradition, where it is a positive confession, where the High Priest acknowledged his and Israel's "sin". However, it is also seen that the negative confession in the Egyptian tradition proves the deceased is deserving of eternal life in the fields of Aaru (reeds). Whereas in the Jewish tradition a sacrifice is required in relation to the confession; it requires death.

It is interesting that this number, which is associated with the dead is also a number that strongly ties to the power of creation. 42 also reduces to 6, the sun, God in the Macrocosm and the Phallus in the Microcosm.

---

[44] Alter, *Why the Torah Begins with the Letter Beit*, 111.

The Great Name of Creation has 42 letters and leans to the left, and is the source of creation. The Great Name of Redemption has 72 letters and leans to the right, and rescues us from oppression and returns us to God.[45]

42 is also the numeration of Moses's mother Jochebed (יוכבד), who was a midwife and is said to be the mother of 600,000 souls.

---

[45] Spiegel, "42 Letter Name of God". University of Utah. Accessed 11 April, 2020.
https://www.cs.utah.edu/~spiegel/kabbalah/jkm010.htm

Also the phrase 'my heart' – לבי has a value of 42. This parallels the tzimtzum[46] creation story where G-d withdraws into himself leaving a space like His heart where creation begins. Kabbalists teach this Name is from the first 42 letters of the Bible with each portion, each line of 6 letters bearing the "magical potency" of the entirety.

> The 42 Letter Name is also the force behind the mitzvah[47] for a man to marry and procreate. The antithesis of procreation is death.[48]

> The Forty-two Letter Name associates with the seven days of creation. The 'workings of creation' – Ma'aseh Bereshis has the initials Mem Bet in Hebrew. The gematria value of Mem Bet – מב is 42.[49]

42 is also the gematria of אמא (the Supernal Mother, unfertilised).[50]

---

[46] Contraction

[47] "commandment", מִצְוָה

[48] Spiegel, "42 Letter Name of God". University of Utah. Accessed 11 April, 2020.
https://www.cs.utah.edu/~spiegel/kabbalah/jkm010.htm

[49] Ibid

[50] Whereas (52) אימא is the Supernal Mother containing the seed.

Another interesting association with the number 42[51] is it is the combined numeration of the Tarot cards Death (XIII), Art (XIV) and The Devil (XV), bringing the archetype associated with the goat (Baphomet / PAN) and Death as a machine for transformation (Life through Death), and its connection to the Word ON.[52] Here we have represented pictorially the three paths that lead to Tiphareth, the sun. The realisation of Godhead in the consciousness.

---

[51] In Japanese culture 42 is popularly considered an unlucky number for men (Yakudoshi – 厄年); but Risuke Ootake states that this is a misconception and that the number is a, "harmonious fusion of yin and yang. Produced by multiplying the number six, associated with yin, by the number seven, associated with yang, the age of forty-two is thus considered a midway point in a person's life at which they leave the first half of their journey (yin) and enter the second (yang); presumably they have attained some semblance of good judgement by this age. This belief in the omnipotent influence of yin and yang is based on the notion that, for better or worse, all phenomena are governed by the laws of heaven." (Ootake, *Katori Shintou-ryu: Warrior Tradition*, 239.)

[52] There is also an interesting gematria, which was shared with me by a Sister of the Order where one hundred and twenty in Hebrew is, one hundred (46) מאה, and twenty is (620) עשרים. This gives a total of 666.

When discussing Baphomet in *The Book of Thoth* Crowley states that:

> Von Hammer-Purgstall was certainly right in supposing Baphomet to be a form of the Bull-god, or rather, the Bull-slaying god, Mithras; for Baphomet should be spelt with an "r" at the end; thus it is clearly a corruption meaning "Father Mithras".[53]

Atu V is attributed to the Hebrew letter ו (V) and to the astrological sign of Taurus, the Bull, linking it immediately to both V.V.V.V.V. and Baphomet (and perhaps to Aiwaz who, as we saw earlier, Crowley identified with Baphomet). Both The Hierophant and Baphomet are depicted giving the 'Sign of V' (the Hierophant with his left hand and Baphomet with both

---

[53] Crowley, *The Book of Thoth*, 67.

hands[54]). I also cannot help but see Baphomet reflected in Atu V in the symbol of the inverted Pentagram with the 'upright' Pentagram on the 'forehead' containing a "dancing male child"[55] - the product of the union of opposites.

Also if we read in Liber VII, IV: 41-43,

> On ancient skin was written in letters of gold: Verbum fir Verbum.

> Also Vitriol and the **hierophant's** name V.V.V.V.V.

> All this wheeled in star-fire, rare and far and utterly lonely – even as Thou and I, O desolate[56] soul my God! (my emphasis)

It is also interesting that one of the traditional titles of Atu V was 'The Pope' of which St. Peter is considered the first by the Roman Catholic Church. I also cannot help to think that the Wand held by the hierophant has the appearance of an old-fashioned key.

---

[54] Although we could interpret the upraised Wand whose colours are based on deep indigo – Saturn / Binah.

[55] Crowley, *The Book of Thoth*, p. 78.

[56] Remembering the goat for Azazel's connection to desolate places.

The key being the mysteries and mastery of the three, "interlocking magical formulae"[57] represented by the three Aeons and their deities – Mother, Father and Son. The magick of the New Aeon incorporates those of the past, bringing them into a wholeness.

It is also worth noting in the traditional images of "the Pope" below the key is displayed on the right, whereas the Hierophant hold it on the left. This is on the side of the Pillar of Severity – no longer the Pillar of Mercy headed by the Father.

---

[57] Crowley, *The Book of Thoth*, 79.

Christ surrounded by the Cherubim (in Christian tradition the four cherubs have been associated with the Four Evangelists in various combinations.1 The "four living creatures" from Rev 4:7) and Atu V (The Hierophant)

There is also the presence of the 'A and Ω'[58] in Levi's depiction of the Pentagram; above and below the Caduceus. The term 'A and Ω' is first seen in the Book of Revelation (verses 1:8, 21:6, and 22:13) where it is a title of Jesus (τὸ Α καὶ τὸ Ω) - "I am the Alpha and Omega, the first and the last."[59]

Crowley very directly associated Christ and Mercury during the Paris Working[60], and we see on the Pledge

---

[58] A + Ω = 1 + 800 = 801 = 9 (Yesod)

[59] We also see the Alpha and the Omega in J.F.C. Fullers rendering of Baphomet, along with the dove and the serpent assigned to the downward and upward pointing hands. Baphomet also sits above the pyramid of initiation (downward pointing) and within the zodiac (compared to Fullers other painting called "The Portal of the Outer order"). This image is reproduced at the end of this essay.

[60] "In the beginning was the Word, the Logos, who is Mercury; and is therefore to be identified with Christ. Both are messengers;

forms we sign in the OTO the Caduceus with the Seal
of Baphomet[61]. The Caduceus is also the Wand of the
Chief Adept in the A∴A∴.

> The symbol represents the wand of the Chief Adept,
> showing that the authority is derived from the
> superiors; were it not so, this card would be
> thoroughly disastrous.[62]

---

their birth-mysteries are similar; the pranks of their childhood are
similar. In the Vision of the Universal Mercury, Hermes is seen
descending upon the sea, which refers to Mary. The Crucifixion
represents the Caduceus; the two thieves, the two serpents; the cliff
in the Vision of the Universal Mercury is Golgotha; Maria is
simply Maia with the solar R in her womb. The controversy about
Christ between the Synoptics and John was really a contention
between the priests of Bacchus, Sol, and Osiris, also, perhaps, of
Adonis and Attis, on the one hand, and those of Hermes on the
other, at that period when initiates all over the world found it
necessary, owing to the growth of the Roman Empire and the
opening up of means of communication, to replace conflicting
Polytheisms by a synthetic Faith. (This is absolutely new to me,
this conception of Christ as Mercury.)"

(Crowley, Neuburg and Desti, *The Vision & the Voice With
Commentary and Other Papers: The Collected Diaries of Aleister
Crowley,* 359.)

[61] This seal is a Gryllus, which belonged to an early period of
Roman art and considered to be Gnostic in origin. This ring
depicts a Rooster, Ram and a Man. The man is Silenus, companion
and tutor to the wine god Dionysus.

[62] Crowley, *The Book of Thoth,* 191.

I would refer you to Frater Shiva's Belgrade lecture from 2016 for a more detailed exploration of this symbolism and the interrelationship between the two Orders.

This is the wand of the Praemonstrator of the A∴A∴ (the Teaching Adept), and it "signifies the initiation of Life in the Natural and the Spiritual world."[63]

When describing Atu XV, Crowley writes:

> The roots of the Tree are made transparent, in order to show the innumerable leapings of the sap; before it stands the Himalayan goat, with an eye in the centre of his forehead, representing the god Pan upon the highest and most secret mountains of the earth. His creative energy is veiled in the symbol of the Wand of

---

[63] Frater Shiva, *Aspiring to the Holy Order*.

the Chief Adept, crowned with the winged globe and the twin serpents of Horus and Osiris.[64]

In relation to the connection between Christ and Mercury it is interesting to note Crowley's comment that, "this is absolutely new to me, this conception as Christ as Mercury." Crowley should have been familiar with this connection through the Golden Dawn's 'The Vision of the Universal Mercury' – "Christus de Christi, Mercury de Mercurio" – "I am Hermes Mercurius, the Son of God".[65]

In addition to this, there are teachings in the writing of Helena Blavatsky that also make the connection between Mercury and Christ, in relation to the gnostic figure of Chnoubis (a Lion Serpent showing a direct link to Baphomet):

> The solar Chnouphis, or Agathodaemon is the Christos of the Gnostics, as every scholar knows. He is intimately connected with the seven sons of Sophia (Wisdom), the seven sons of Aditi (universal Wisdom), her eighth being Marttanda, the Sun, which seven are the seven planetary regents or genii. Therefore Chnouphis was the spiritual Sun of Enlightenment, of Wisdom, hence the patron of all the Egyptian Initiates,

---

[64] Crowley, *The Book of Thoth*, 105.

[65] Regardie, *The Complete Golden Dawn System of Magic*, 61 -63.

as Bel-Merodach (or Bel-Belitanus) became later with
the Chaldeans.

Repeating Iamblichus, Champollion shows him to be
"the deity called [[Eichton]] (or the fire of the celestial
gods – the great Thot-Hermes), to whom Hermes
Trismegistus attributes the invention of magic.[66]

Crowley also identifies the Lion Serpent with the
H.G.A. in his commentary to Liber Samekh:

> Repetition fortifies him to realise the nature of his
> Attainment; and his Angel, the link once made,
> frequents him, and trains him subtly to be sensitive to
> His holy presence and persuasion. But it may occur,
> especially after repeated success, that the Adept is not
> flung back into his mortality by the explosion of Star-
> spate, but identifies with one particular "Lion Serpent,"

---

[66] Blavatsky, *The Secret Doctrine*, 210 – 211.

continuing conscious thereof until it finds its proper place in space, when its secret self flowers forth a Truth, which the Adept may then take back to earth with him.

Samekh also gives a further hint to the connection between Christ and the Lion Serpent

PhI-ThETA-SOE

Thou shining Force of Breath! Thou Lion-Serpent-Sun! Thou Saviour, save!

An amazingly beautiful description, from what I consider one of Crowley's most important commentaries. Here we can also see a connection between the Lion Serpent, who is also Baphomet, and the H.G.A. and Christ. One can also infer a connection to the sexual mysteries, and kundalini as key to this process and the process of initiation. It is all kundalini.[67]

During the Paris Working, Crowley records in relation to the Caduceus:

---

[67] "Now let him not only fill his whole being to the uttermost with the force of the Names; but let him formulate his Will, understood thoroughly as the dynamic aspect of his Creative Self, in an appearance symbolically apt, I say not in the form of a Ray of Light, of a Fiery Sword, or of aught save that bodily Vehicle of the Holy Ghost which is sacred to BAPHOMET, 23 by its virtue that concealeth the Lion and the Serpent that His Image may appear adorably upon the Earth for ever." Liber Samekh

The Caduceus contains a complete symbol of the Gnosis. The winged sun or phallus represents the joy of life on all planes from the lowest to the highest. The serpents (besides being Active and Passive, Horus and Osiris, and all their other well-known attributions) are those qualities of Eagle and Lion[68] respectively, of which we know, but do not speak. It is the symbol which unites the Microcosm and the Macrocosm, the symbol of the Magical operation that accomplishes this. The Caduceus is Life itself, and is of universal application. It is the universal solvent.[69] - *Solve Et Coagula.*

Along a similar vein, Erich Neumann writes of the god Pan:

Pan, in his capacity as the custodian of the secrets of Nature, brings with him the key to the depths. This time, the tempter is not refused but accepted, for it

---

[68] "Let the Lion and Eagle duly prepare themselves as Prince and Princess of Alchemy – as they may be inspired. Let the Union of the Red Lion and the White Eagle be neither in cold nor in heat ... Now then comes the time when the elixir is placed in the alembic retort to be subjected to the gentle warmth.... If the Great Work be transubstantiation then the Red Lion may feed upon the flesh and blood of the God, and also let the Red Lion duly feed the White Eagle – yea, may the Mother Eagle give sustain-molt and guard the inner life." (Valentine, "The Triumphal Chariot of Antimony", 34-47)

[69] Crowley, *The Confessions of Aleister Crowley*, 721.

seems that, nowadays, it is only the man who, as he "strives with might and main", does not shun the danger of downfall and of chaos, that "can be redeemed."[70]

In a way the symbol of Pan / Baphomet serves as a powerful symbol of the "new ethic" explored by Neumann – "The alliance between Faust and Mephisto is the alliance of modern man with the shadow and evil, which makes it possible for him in the first place to undertake his journey through the fullness of life, right down to the Mothers and up again to the Eternal Feminine."[71]

Neumann identifies the shadow as "the "guardian of the threshold", across which the path leads into the nether realm of transformation and renewal. And so, what first appears to the ego as a devil becomes a psychopomp, a guide of the soul, who leads the way into the underworld of the unconscious." [72] Here we can also loop back to Crowley's (and Levi's) association with Mercury and Baphomet, and Mercury as a psychopomp.

William Breeze in his essay 'De Harmonia Mundi' writes in relation to Baphomet, "He has a caduceus for

---

[70] Neumann, *Depth Psychology and a New Ethic*, 116.

[71] Ibid., 116.

[72] Ibid., 143.

a phallus, hinting at the importance of vibration and vibration control in sexual magick, from the slow frequencies of the "ophidian vibrations" to the "shrill scream of orgasm". Employed externally, rather than internally in trances or vision, the forces indicated by these symbols relate to the siddhis of Yoga, and in magick and sorcery, the powers of fascination and glamor".[73]

Crowley also makes a connection between BAPHOMET and the siddhis, stating that,

> The eight Siddhis should refer to the Eight Letters of Baphomet.

B   Gnana
A   Expansion to Nuit
P   Power to destroy
H   Pranayama: Levitation
O   Power to create
M   Transformations
I   Contraction to Hadit
T   Gnana[74]

As you can see the above was prior to Crowley being instructed in the correct spelling of the name. It is also

---

[73] Breeze, "De Harmonia Mundi", *Arcana V : music, magic and mysticism*, 17.

[74] Crowley, *The Magical Record of the Beast 666*, 54.

interesting if we take the 'A' and 'I' from the above – expansion and contraction, we have Aleph and Yod, which equals 11, ABRAHADABRA, the Great Work accomplished. Overall, it shows a balance in the Word, a word that begins and ends with Gnana, knowedge, but "It is knowledge inseparable from the total experience of reality, especially a total or divine reality (Brahman)."[75]

As stated, earlier Crowley identified Baphomet as 'Father Mithras' – Mithras being the subject of a pre-Christian worship with many similarities to the

---

[75] *Britannica.com* ."jnana (Indian religion) - Britannica Online Encyclopedia".

Christian Myth. Interestingly, Mithras is often depicted as being born from a rock. Mithraism had a series of 7 initiations, believed related to the 7 planets, and it seems that much of the ritual of Mithraism involved feasting.

76

Associated with Mithraism is a lion headed image sometimes called Arimanius or Aion, but there is continued debate over the name of this deity. In the

---

[76] "And I believe in the Serpent and the Lion, Mystery of Mystery, in His name BAPHOMET." (Crowley, *Magick: Book 4, Liber Aba*, 585.)

image above we can see the presence of the Caduceus, which also appears in the common image of Mithras, the 'Banquet', where a torchbearer points a caduceus towards the base of an altar, from which flames spring up. In the above image you can also see Aion holding two keys, as if to form a gate.

In reference to this we can return to St. Peter (Πέτρος), as in some iconography and artworks associated with him, like Arimanius, he is depicted holding two keys. [77]

> And I will give unto thee the keys of the Kingdom: and whatsoever thou shalt bind on Earth shall be bound in heaven: and whatsoever thou what loose on earth shall be loosed in heaven. (Matthew 16:19)

---

[77] Another possible etymology for the name Baphomet is Maphtah Bet Yahweh; 'Key to the House of God' (Von Hammer).

Traditionally one of these Keys given to St. Peter is
Gold and the other silver. The gold Key represents
forgiveness, which comes from God; the other
repentance, which comes from man (or the individual)
– *as above, so below*. An analogy could also be drawn
between this and what Crowley calls the 'reciprocating
formula' in Magick in Theory and Practice.

> It will be noted, however, that in this invocation of
> Thoth which we have summarized, there is another
> formula   contained,   the   Reverberating   or
> Reciprocating formula, which may be called the
> formula of Horus and Harpocrates. The magician
> addresses the God with an active projection of his will,
> and then becomes passive while the God addresses the
> Universe. In the fourth part he remains silent,
> listening, to the prayer which arises therefrom.[78]

---

[78] Crowley, *Magick in Theory and Practice*, 19.

Another interesting aspect of St. Peter is the story that
he was also crucified, but at his request was crucified
upside-down.

As J. Daniel Gunther discusses in his lectures on A∴A∴
doctrine, the image of the crucified Peter, although
never identified as such, likely has a relationship with
the Tarot Card called the 'Hanged Man'. If we open
up the *Book of Thoth* we find that in relation to 'The
Hanged Man' Crowley writes,

> It is then to Water that the Adepts have always looked
> for the continuation (in some sense or other) and to
> the prolongation and perhaps renovation of
> life'…'The legend of the Gospels, dealing with the

Greater Mysteries of the Lance and the Cup (those of the god Iacchus = Iao) as superior to the Lesser Mysteries (those of the God Ion = Noah, and the N-gods in general) in which the Sword slays the god that his head may be offered on a plate, or disk, says: And a soldier with a spear pierced his side; and thereforth there came out blood and water, waiting beneath the Cross or Tree for that purpose, in a Cup or Chalice; this is the Holy Grail or Sangréal (Sangraal) of Monsalvat, the Mountain of Salvation.[79]

Crowley also writes:

Nor is it an accident that St. Peter was a fisherman. The Gospels, too, are full of Miracles involving fish, and the fish is sacred to Mercury, because of its cold-bloodedness, its swiftness and its brilliance.[80]

It is tempting to also link St. Peter with Mercury / Thoth, as in religious folklore St. Peter guards the gates of heaven and keeps a book with the names of all those that are to be admitted. Mercury guides the dead in the underworld ("Persephone, through Tartaros dark and wide, gave thee for ever flowing souls to guide." (Orphic Hymn 57 to Chthonian Hermes) and Thoth is involved in the judgment of the dead. Thoth is also the

---

[79] Crowley, *The Book of Thoth*, 98-99.

[80] Ibid., 101.

scribe and messenger of the gods as St. Peter could also be seen as through his continuation of 'Christ's' teachings through the Gospels.

* * *

In the system of the A∴A∴ there is a link made between BABALON and Baphomet in the sign of Mulier[81] (a woman; female), which is one of the N.O.X. signs, and I am interested in what I see as a connection between V.V.V.V.V., BABALON and then here to Baphomet.

> And for this is BABALON under the power of the Magician, that she hath submitted herself unto the Work; and guardeth the Abyss. And in her is perfect purity of that which is above; yet she is sent as the Redeemer to them that are below. For there is no other way into the Supernal Mystery but through her, and the Beast on which she rideth...[82]

> The master flamed forth as a star and set a guard of Water in every Abyss.[83]

---

[81] Mulier. Isis in Welcome. Sign of Babalon. Attitude of Baphomet.

[82] Crowley, Neuburg and Desti, *The Vision & the Voice With Commentary and Other Papers: The Collected Diaries of Aleister Crowley,* 3rd Aethyr, p. 213

[83] Liber Trigrammaton sub Figura XXVII

Blessed, blessed, blessed; yea, blessed; thrice and four times blessed is he that hath attained to look upon thy face. For I will hurl thee forth from my presence as a whirling thunderbolt[84] to guard the Ways, and whom thou smites shall be smitten indeed. An whom thou lovest shall be loved indeed[85]

---

[84] 'In the Aeon of the Child, the Thunderbolt is one of the symbols of Messiah.' Gunther, *Initiation in the Aeon of the Child*, p. 119

[85] Crowley, Neuburg and Desti, *The Vision & the Voice With Commentary and Other Papers: The Collected Diaries of Aleister Crowley,* 1st Aethyr, p. 250

86

Lamed is the King's Daughter, satisfied by Him, holding His "Sword and Balances" in her lap. These weapons are the Judge, armed with power to execute His Will, and Two Witnesses "in whom shall every

---

[86] In reference to his image of 'The Sabbatic Goat' Eliphas Levi writes, 'This Pantheistic figure should be seated on a cube, and its footstall should be a single ball, on a ball and a triangular stool'.

(Levi, *Transcendental Magic*, XV.)

Initiates of the Oasis degrees in the Man of Earth of the OTO. should also look to the basic shapes used in the construction of their Temples.

Truth be established" in accordance with whose testimony he gives judgment.[87]

If we looked at the letters of the Messiah's name (V.V.V.V.V., "the Light of the World Himself."[88]) we get 30 (.ו.ו.ו.ו.ו). 30 is ל and is attributed to ♎[89] and Atu VIII in The Book of Thoth called 'Adjustment'. In this card again we see the 'A and Ω'; the beginning and the end[90]. "The Trump represents The Woman Satisfied"[91]. "It is the final adjustment in the formula of Tetragrammaton, when the daughter, redeemed by her marriage with the Son, is thereby set up on the throne of the mother"[92]

---

[87] Crowley, *Magick: Book 4, Liber Aba*, 155.

[88] "Then spake Jesus again unto them, saying, I am the light of the world: he that followeth me shall not walk in darkness, but shall have the light of life." (John 8:12)

[89] "Libra, *Lamed*, is the Scarlet Woman (shamelessly boasting) alone". Crowley, *The Magical Record of the Beast 666*, 198.

[90] "But as Thou art the Last, Thou art also the Next, and as the Next do I reveal Thee to the multitude". Liber LXV, Ch III, Vs. 61

[91] Crowley, *The Book of Thoth*, 87.

[92] Ibid., 86.

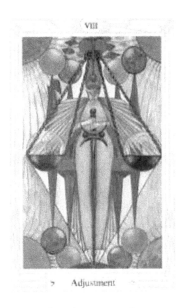

Adjustment

Crowley hints at this "satisfaction" more clearly in one of his diary entries where is described the card "Justice" as "The satisfied womb."[93]

The shape of the central figure also seems to suggest a downward pointing phallus, with the spheres as testes, in opposite arrangement to The Devil. The creative energy in Atu VIII and Atu XV also seem complementary. One more constrained and geometrical, the other less structured and wild, but still focused or directed. "It is the Tree of Life as seen against a background of the exquisitely tenuous, complex, and fantastic forms of madness, the divine

---

[93] Crowley, *The Magical Record of the Beast 666*, 196.

madness of spring…"[94]. "The sign of Capricornus is rough, harsh, dark, even blind; impulse to create takes no account of reason, custom, or foresight."[95] This is in contrast to Atu VIII where, "at the corner of the card, are indicated balanced spheres of light and darkness, and constantly equilibrated rays from these spheres form a curtain, the interplay of all those forces which she sums up and adjudicates."[96]

The Devil is primal energy of what seems a more "personal"[97] type, the Goddess of Justice works on an "impersonal plane."[98] Perhaps the Devil shows the Adept leaping from incarnation to incarnation, as they are sworn to do, whereas Justice sits beyond temporal experience. She is "the Annihilation of Illusion".[99]

Libra is ruled by Venus and in it Saturn is exalted (Binah / BABALON). I see here a possible relationship to V.V.V.V.V. through the eight pointed Star of the Messiah; Atu VIII and the eightfold name of Baphomet. There is also a distinctly sexual aspect to this card (if

---

[94] Crowley, *The Book of Thoth*, 105.

[95] Ibid., 106.

[96] Ibid., 87.

[97] "The sign is ruled by Saturn, who makes for selfhood and perpetuity." (Ibid., 105.)

[98] Ibid., 87.

[99] Ibid., 256.

more subtle than in Atu XV; and the direction of the flow of energy seems reversed). I see these two Atu as different ends of the initiatory spectrum (here writing in a strictly A∴A∴ context). We read in chapter 3 of Liber 333.

> The Man delights in uniting with the Woman; the Woman in parting from the Child.

> The Brothers of A∴A∴ are Women: the Aspirants to A∴A∴ are Men. [100]

The sign of ♎ in the system of the A∴A∴ is associated with the signs of Sa and Neter, showing a marriage, or unity of Man and God.

---

[100] Crowley, *The Book of Lies*, 12.

"These two formulae, Solve et Coagula, are now explained, and the universe is exhibited as the interplay between these two."

In Christianity the 8-pointed star is that of redemption or regeneration and is associated with baptism (baptismal fonts often have an octagonal base). Also in Christianity baptism and circumcision are considered equivalent, and, because of the Jewish tradition, Jesus was said to have been circumcised and named when he was 8 days old.

> ...they formerly did not obey, when God's patience waited in the days of Noah while the ark was being prepared, in which a few, that is, **eight persons**, were brought safely through water. Baptism, which corresponds to this, now saves you, not as a removal of dirt from the body but as an appeal to God for a good conscience, through the resurrection of Jesus Christ, who has gone into heaven and is at the right hand of God". (1 Peter 3:18-22, ESV).[101] (my emphasis)

> And I confess one Baptism of Wisdom, whereby we accomplish the Miracle of Incarnation.[102]

In this respect it is also interesting that during the Amalantra working Crowley asked "the wizard for an

---

[101] Right hand of God – Binah

[102] Crowley, *Magick: Book 4, Liber Aba*, 585.

It is also interesting that by 'ATHBaSH Temura' Baphomet = Sophia (wisdom) and one possible etymology of Baphomet that has been suggested is the Greek 'Baphe Metis'; Baptism of Wisdom, although this is dubious.

equivalent geometrical figure [of Baphomet]". The wizard says: "The segment of an octagonal column".[103] Here combining a phallic symbol and the number 8.

Also if we look at the name Jesus written in Greek we have 'Ἰησους', with tnge, reflected in the Hebrew:

אני יהוה לא שניתי[104]

I am the Lord, I change not. (Malachi 3.6)

Again, if we take the Anointed One, the Messiah, spelling it in full in Hebrew without using any final values we get

מימ שינ יוד חית

888[105]

It is interesting to note that all the letters in this word in full contain י :

The letter Yod is the first letter of the name Tetragrammaton, and this symbolises the Father, who is Wisdom; he is the highest form of Mercury, and the Logos, the Creator of all worlds.[106]

---

[103]Churton, *Aleister Crowley The Biography*, 217.

[104] 888

[105] In the Confessions Crowley calls 888 "the number of Redemption". (Crowley, *The Confessions of Aleister Crowley*, 834.)

Concealed within Mercury is a light which pervades all parts of the Universe equally; one of his titles is Psycopompos, the guide of the soul through the lower regions.[107]

In Hebrew, ADNI, 65. The Gnostic Initiates transliterated it to imply their own secret formulae; we follow so excellent an example. ON is an Arcanum of Arcana; its significance is taught, gradually, in the OTO. Also AD is the paternal formula, Hadit; ON is its compliment, NUIT; the final yod signifies "mine" etymologically, and essentially the Mercurial (transmitted) hermaphroditic virginal seed – "The Hermit of the Tarot. The use of the Name is therefore to invoke one's own inmost secrecy, considered as the result of the conjunction of Nuit and Hadit. If the second A is included, its import is to affirm the Operation of the Holy Ghost, and the formulation of the Babe in the Egg, which precedes the appearance of the Hermit.[108]

In connection to this, if we take the Hebrew for A∴A∴, spelt in full, and the Hebrew for OTO, spelt in full, we have 222 and 666. If we then add these values together (222 + 666) we have:

---

[106] Crowley, *The Book of Thoth*, 88.

[107] Ibid., 89.

[108] Crowley, *Magick: Book 4, Liber Aba*, 509.

888

Is this number (and the image of Baphomet) representative of the Mystic Marriage between the A∴A∴ and the OTO? A bridge between the temporal and the eternal. Another Hebrew word that equals 888 is חפף – to cover; shelter; shield – "*under the shadow of the wings*" (LIBER DCLXXI vel PYRAMIDOS).

* * *

In 1906, on the 17th of April (my birthday and the Day before the great San Francisco Earthquake) Crowley wrote,

> Ere Sol in Aries makes bright spring weather
> Eight Star and Six shall have kissed together[109]

He wrote this after kissing his old Golden Dawn college Elaine Simpson (Sr. Fidelis). At this time Crowley was coming to terms with the Augoeides, and he had identified Fidelis at as 'El Istar'. Ishtar is a goddess associated with the ancient city of Babylon and is seen as a Goddess of fertility and sexuality. She is also a deity of war and death. Called the 'Great Whore' she was a patron of prostitutes and sacred prostitution served as part of her worship. Ishtar is also symbolized

---

[109] Churton, *Aleister Crowley*, The Biography, 120

by the eight-pointed star; the morning star and the evening star[110].

Aleister Crowley was the Prophet of the New Aeon, as was *Muhammad* (Mahomet / Baphomet) and other before him, as appointed by the Messiah; the A and Ω; V.V.V.V.V., who is depicted by a Star of eight rays.[111]

I knew that it must have eight letters.

---

[110] ♀

[111] "I now see the eightfold star of Mercury suddenly blazing out; it is composed of four fleurs-de-lys with rays like antlers, bulrushes in shape between them. The central core has the cypher of the grand master, but not the one you know. Upon the cross are the Dove, the Hawk, the Serpent and the Lion. Also, one symbol yet more secret." (Crowley, *The Vision & the Voice With Commentary and Other Papers: The Collected Diaries of Aleister Crowley, 1909-1914 E.V.,* 373.)

If we look to the Book of Lies chapter 7:

THE DINOSAURS

> None are They whose number is Six: else were they
> six indeed.
> Seven are these Six that live not in the City of the
> Pyramids, under the Night of Pan.
> There was Lao-tzu.
> There was Siddartha.
> There was Krishna.
> There was Tahuti.
> There was Mosheh.
> There was Dionysus.
> There was Mahmud.
> But the Seventh men called PERDURABO; for
> enduring unto The End, at The End was Naught
> to endure.
> Amen..[112]

Here we see the list of what Crowley describes as "a list of those special messengers of the Infinite who initiate periods."[113] He calls them 7, counting Lao-tzu as 0, but there are actually 8 'Dinosaurs', who's number is Six, the 'Mystic Number of the Masters of the Temple'. [114]

---

[112] Crowley, *The Book of Lies*, 24

[113] Ibid., 25

[114] 1+2+3 = 6

Could the letters 'V' that make up the Star of the Messiah also be the footsteps of the 'Anointed One' over the Aeons?

Besides this, in the context of the OTO and E.G.C., Aleister Crowley, as Baphomet, also serves as the founder of our Church of Light, life, Love and Liberty.[115] Like St. Peter before him (according to the Catholic Church) Baphomet is the rock (Πέτρος) or cornerstone on which our Church, 'the new Temple' is to be built.

> So far, the Wizard had shown great qualities! He had cleared up the etymological problem and shown why the Templars should have given the name Baphomet to their so-called idol. Baphomet was Father Mithras, the cubical stone which was the corner of the Temple. [116]

Another thing to note is that in Exodus and Leviticus it is indicated that the High Priest wore eight "holy

---

[115] Interestingly the proclamation given by the Deacon during the Ceremony of the Introit in the Liber XV announces, '*I proclaim the Law of Light, Life, Love, and Liberty in the name of IAO*'. IAO = 17 = the Thunderbolt, one of the symbols of the Messiah in the New Aeon. Also 1+ 7 = 8. We can also see that Atu XVII is 'The Star', attributed to the letter ה, the letter that connects that which is below the Abyss with that which is above.

[116] Crowley, *The Confessions of Aleister Crowley*, 833.

garments" (bigdei kodesh) whereas other priests wore only four.

> You shall make holy garments (bigdei kodesh) for your brother Aaron, for honour and glory (l'kavode u'l'tiffaret). (Shemot 28:2)

In Hebrew "holy garments" is בִּגְדֵי הַקֹּדֶשׁ which by gematria is 428. The same number as that of Chasmalim (חשמלים), The Brilliant Ones; Angels of Chesed, and of Tiphareth in Briah.

> For honor and glory" may be interpreted in this manner: In order that he [Aaron] will be revered and elevated in such magnificent and splendid garments. As the text states: "With a robe of righteousness He has enwrapped me; **like a bridegroom**, who, priest-like, dons garments of glory. (Yeshayahu 61:10) (my emphasis)

Another interesting hint the Crowley gives regarding the nature of Baphomet is in *The General Principles of Astrology,* where he states that, "We must then regard this Devil as the Emperor in disguise, beneath a veil..."[117] Crowley refers back to the older forms of the card and that the torch and the cup depicted are the same as the sceptre and Orb as held by The Emperor. It is not hard to see the connection in the Thoth Deck

---

[117] Crowley and Adams, *The General Principles of Astrology*, 41.

reimagining of the image with the two rams staring over the Emperors shoulders. He also draws a parallel between the pentagram (or pentacle) and the "Pope" card, which is another earthy sign – Taurus. Both of these are sovereigns in their own rights (One temporal, the other spiritual). In older versions of The Emperor, he is shown throned on a cube, as is Baphomet in the rendering by Eliphas Levi.

Although the Emperor card shows depictions of rams, and the Devil is a goat, both are described as Himalayan in The *Book of Thoth* (a mountain range, a symbol of "high places"). The horns on the depiction of the Devil spiral up, whereas the horns of the rams spiral down.

The First Temple, the Scapegoat and the Woman Clothed with the Sun

> For the life of the flesh is in the blood, and I have given it to you upon the altar to make atonement for your souls; for it is the blood that makes atonement for the soul.
> Leviticus 17, 11

The concept of a goat as a carrier of the blame of others would be familiar to us all. But in the Old Testament this is not represented by a single goat but by two; one goat 'for Azazel', the other 'for the Lord'.

In the Hebraic tradition and in the Old Testament are references to the source of the scapegoat. The history of the scapegoat has its ancient roots in the temple in Jerusalem, and in this rite I see a connection with the Templar idol – one goat for the altar, for the Lord, and the other accursed – for Azazel (the upright and the averse; the bright and the dark). But to my mind these two goats meet at the same place beyond the veil. One takes the upright path, the other the averse. Just as the Priest in the Gnostic Mass (Liber XV) comes from and returns to the Tomb (returns to the earth), after he has gone beyond the veil and offers the sacrifice of life and joy.

In the Book of Enoch Azazel is a fallen angel, and in the Bible is associated with the scapegoat rite and represents desolate places. Although it should be noted

that biblical and rabbinical scholar Arnold Ehrlich
stated that "Azazel – No one knows who he is or what
he is. What previous scholarship said about him has no
substance and cannot be relied upon."[118] To me this
uncertainly and mystery adds more to the power of
Azazel, and his association with the Day of Atonement.
Azazel is a question seeking an exclamation.

Aron Pinker states that:

> Scholars believed that if the meaning of Azazel could
> be deciphered all would fall in place. However, to this
> day the meaning of Azazel eludes categorical
> definition. The approaches that have been adopted for
> interpreting the term Azazel essentially fell into four
> types: name of a supernatural entity, name or
> description of a place, abstract noun, description of the
> dispatched goat, and, miscellaneous opinions.[119]

Azazel is also said to be a hard rocky cliff (from which
the sacrificial goat was pushed off), or can be
interpreted as 'to be sent away' or 'to carry away'.

It is also written that the goat was designated for evil,
and that by incorporating this evil in the ceremony it is
elevated again to God.

---

[118] Ehrlich, *Mikra Ki-Pheshuto*, 227.

[119] Aron Pinker, A Goat to Go to Azazel,
http://www.jhsonline.org/Articles/article_69.pdf, accessed 02 Jan
2020

Others have written that the inclusion of Azazel is meant as atonement for sexual crimes, and others that Azazel is a representation of the forces of Nature.

The Azazel goat is associated with desolate places where it is driven away, seems to have a reflection in Revelation when the Woman Clothed with the Sun escapes into the wilderness, after the child is taken to heaven ("caught up unto God, and to his throne"), leading to the "War in Heaven."

> And to the Woman were given two wings of a great eagle that she might fly into the wilderness...
> Revelation 12:14

Tobias Churton writes that, "there is clearly a link between the tradition of the Yezidis concerning the angel Ezazil and the angel who appeared in late antiquity as Azazel. Azazel is singled out for special censure in the famous Book of Enoch (IX.6) as one that revealed to men "the eternal secrets which were in heaven which men were striving to learn..."[120]

James M. Pryse in his *The Apocalypse Unsealed* gives an interesting and relevant, in our context, interpretation of the Woman (who is identifies with the Virgin Mother).

---

[120] Churton, "Aleister Crowley and the Yezidis", *Aleister Crowley and Western Esotericism,* 188-189.

> The Virgin Mother being sushumna, the two wings of the Eagle are ida and pingala. The winged Woman represents the objective, or substantial, working of the kundalini…[121]

Pryse also alludes to the dual nature of the Woman (as with Baphomet) when he writes, "As the Word-Mother, the White Virgin of the Skies, whether called Diana, Aphrodite, or Mary, she is the pure ether, the Logos-Light, or primordial force-substance; and as the Fallen Woman, the Queen of the Abyss, she is the parturient energy of nature, the basis of physical life…"[122] The Woman represents both Heaven and Earth; the upright and the averse.

In Leviticus it is written of the form and purpose of the sacrifice of the "scapegoats":

> He shall then slaughter the people's goat of sin offering, bring its blood behind the curtain, and do with its blood as he has done with the blood of the bull: he shall sprinkle it over the cover and in front of the cover.
>
> Thus he shall purge the Shrine of the uncleanness and transgression of the Israelites, whatever their sins; and

---

[121] Pryse, *The Apocalypse Unsealed: Being and Interpretation of the Initiation of Ioannes*, 160.

[122] Ibid., 155.

he shall do the same for the Tent of Meeting, which
abides with them in the midst of their uncleanness.
Leviticus 16: 15 - 16

The breasted, goat headed, hermaphroditic image of
Baphomet created by Levi could be interpreted to be an
archetypal link to the female aspect of El Shaddai.
"Now Shaddai has been translated in various ways,
most often by Almighty, but the usual meaning of this
Hebrew word is breasts, suggesting that El Shaddai had
a female aspect."[123] "A female aspect", both male and
female, and here Wisdom is seen to be female.

> The other part of Malachi's prophecy is often
> overlooked, or mistranslated. When Elijah returns:
> 'The Sun of Righteousness shall rise with healing in
> **her wings**'[124]. The sign in heaven in Revelation 12 is
> the Queen of Heaven in the holy of holies with the
> ark. She is clothed with the sun and crowned with the
> stars[125], and she gives birth to the Messiah. Later she
> flies with the wings of a great eagle to escape from the

---

[123] Barker, *Where Shall Wisdom be Found?*,
http://orthodoxeurope.org/page/11/1/7.aspx.

[124] It is also interesting to note in the Pancavimsa Brahmana,
"Those who know have wings".

[125] "My head is jewelled with twelve stars; My body is as milk of
the stars; it is bright with the blue of the abyss of stars invisible."
Liber LXV Ch. I vs 28

serpent. This vision is set exactly in the centre of the
Book of Revelation.[126] (my emphasis)

As can be read above the Queen of Heaven is the same
as the Woman clothed with the sun; mother of the
Messiah. She is also the goddess worshipped in
Jerusalem in the 7th century B.C.E. according to Barker.

Here we can make a connection to the dual nature of
Baphomet, and Baphomet's winged aspect and
connection to the cube (on which Baphomet is throned
in the representation published by Levi).

> Wisdom describes herself in the holy of holies in
> Proverbs 8. In the temple, this had been constructed as
> a **perfect cube** and lined with gold to represent the
> light and fire of the divine presence (2 Chron.3.8);
> here in Proverbs 8 it is the state beyond the visible and
> temporal creation. Wisdom was herself begotten and
> brought forth in this state (Proverbs 8.24-25), and she
> was beside the Creator as he established the **heavens**
> and marked out the foundations of the **earth**. She
> witnessed the creation. She was also the Amon [127], a
> rare Hebrew word which probably means craftsman;

---

[126] Barker, *Where Shall Wisdom be Found?*,
http://orthodoxeurope.org/page/11/1/7.aspx.

[127] "Amon is Wisdom who assisted at the creation and later
appeared in the gnostic texts as the Demiurge, the agent of the
creation." (Barker, *The Great Angel: A Study of Israel's Second God*,
202.)

in the Greek it became harmozousa, the woman who
joins together, or the woman who maintains the
harmony (Prov.8.30) (my emphasis)

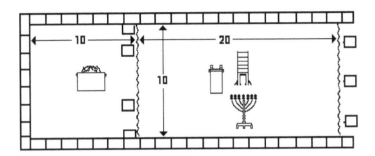

Tabernacle with the holy and holy of holies (inner sanctuary)

Wisdom is that which binds together, and brings into
harmony; a marriage of heaven and earth.

My adepts stand upright; their head above the heavens,
their feet below the hells.

Liber XC, 40

Wisdom says: be strong! Then canst thou bear more
joy. Be not animal; refine thy rapture!

Liber AL, II: 70[128]

---

[128] Noting that this is verse 70, ayin, the Devil

It is this harmony that the Isralites were trying to maintain through the Day of Atonement.

> In English, Yom Kippur is the "Day of Atonement" — a name that (perhaps surprisingly) does not mean expiating guilt, but comes from the Middle English onement (that is, harmony). In Hebrew, it is from a root that means to cover. The English and Hebrew are thus not entirely equivalent. The idea of at-one-ment invests the day with three aspects: being at one with Jewish identity; being at one with God; and being at one with other people. Each element is both a confirmation and a challenge.[129]

Margaret Barker defines Wisdom as "one of the names of the female aspect of God. She illuminates the human mind and helps us to better understand creation."[130]

From the above reference we see wisdom associated with a "perfect cube", her dwelling place; the holy of holies – this being the throne of Baphomet. There is a connection here between the word "Amon" and its association with craftsmen and freemasonry, the

---

[129] Raymond Apple, "Being at one: The challenge of Yom Kippur," *ABC News*, October 8 2019, 1:41pm Updated Tue 8 Oct 2019, 1:47pm, https://www.abc.net.au/religion/the-challenge-of-yom-kippur/11582690.

[130] Barker, *An Extraordinary Gathering of Angels*, 422.

"joining together" that builds the temple. Harmozousa is "the bringer into harmony".

It is also of note that the word Ka'aba, the name of the holiest shrine in Islam, means cube (كَعْبَة).

> The poem in Proverbs 8 also describes her as the one who joins together, or the one who holds in harmony. Since one role of the angels was to make connections between different aspects of human perception – to "inspire"- Wisdom had a special place at the head of the angels, holding them all together. They were her children, and by their work enabled Wisdom to permeate the creation.[131]

> Wisdom describes herself in the holy of holies in Proverbs 8. In the temple, this had been constructed as a perfect cube and lined with gold[132] to represent the light and fire of the divine presence (2 Chron. 3.8); here in Proverbs 8 it is the state beyond the visible and temporal creation.[133]

> There are the tablets found at the site of ancient Ugarit (on the coast of Syria) which describe their great goddess Athirat, the same name as Asheratah. She was their Great Lady, the Virgin Mother of the <u>seventy</u>

---

[131] Ibid., 186.

[132] ☉ - Tiphareth

[133] Barker, *Temple Theology: An Introduction*, 81.

<u>sons</u> [134]of the high god El (a god who was often depicted as a bull); she was a sun deity, she was the Lamp of the gods, the Bright One, and her symbol was a spindle. She had several names: Athirat, Rahmay and Shapsh. She was the nursing mother of the earthly king, who was known as the Morning Star and the Evening Star (cf. Rev. 22.16), and it seems that she was represented by the <u>winged sun disk</u> over the head of the king, showing that she was his heavenly mother.[135]

Now what does that signify? Notice that the first goat is for the altar, and the other is accursed; and that it is the accursed one that wears the wreath. That is because they shall see him on that Day clad to the ankles in his red woollen robe, and will say, 'Is not this he whom we once crucified, and mocked and pierced and spat upon? Yes, this is the man who told us that he was the Son of God. But how will he resemble the goat? The point of there being two similar goats, both of them being fair and alike, is that when they see him coming on the Day, they are going to be struck with terror at the manifest parallel between him and the goat. In this ordinance, then, you are to see typified the future suffering of Jesus. (Ep. Barnabas 7).[136]

---

[134] 70, Ayin, Baphomet

[135] Barker, *Temple Theology: An Introduction* , 79–80.

[136] Barker, *The Gate of Heaven*, 44 – 45.

Here we see that Christians draw a clear parallel with the Day of Atonement, the goat and Christ. But was this association just with the goat representing Azazel, driven out into the desolate place or was it both of the goats. Was Christ simultaneously driven away via the path of desolation, but also served as the sacrifice within the Temple – Christ moved again beyond the veil as High Priest in the holy of holies.

Levi comments that, "The old sanctuaries contain no further Mysteries, and the significance of the objects of the Hebrew cultus is comprehensible for the first time. Who does not perceive in the golden table, crowned and supported by the Cherubim which covered the ark of the Covenant, the same symbols as those of the twenty-first Tarot Key? The Ark was a hieroglyphical synthesis of the whole kabbalistic dogma.' [137]

The twenty-first Key being, "The microcosm, the sum of all in all. Hieroglyph, KETHER, or the Kabbalistic Crown, between four mysterious animals. In the middle of the Crown is Truth holding a rod in each hand."[138] I would refer you to the below quote from verse 7 of Liber CCCLXX regarding Truth.

---

[137] Levi, *Transcendental Magic*, 394.

[138] Ibid., 393

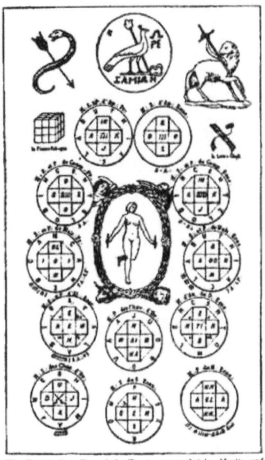

The Twenty first Key of the Tarot, surrounded by Mystic and Masonic Seals

Returning briefly to the cube that is the throne of Baphomet, and the shape of the Holy of Holies in the Temple in Jerusalem; in Revelation this is also interpreted as the shape of "the holy Jerusalem", but this

Jerusalem of Revelation has no Temple, "for the Lord God Almighty and the Lamb are the temple of it." (Revelation 21:22).

Pryse explains that, 'to solve this element of the puzzle it is only necessary to unfold the cube, thereby disclosing a cross, which represents the human form – a man with outstretched arms.'[139]

Liber A'ASH vel Capriconi Pneumatici sub figura CCCLXX

> For two things are done and a third thing is begun. Isis and Osiris are given over to incest and adultery. Horus leaps up thrice armed from the womb of his mother. Harpocrates his twin is hidden within him. Set is his holy covenant, that he shall display in the great day of M.A.A.T., that is being interpreted the Master of the Temple of A∴A∴, whose name is Truth.

> Liber CCCLXX, 7

Liber A'Ash is "*The book of Creation or the Goat of the Spirit*", and in "a Syllabus of the Official Instructions of the A∴A∴ it was stated that the text "*contains the true secret of all practical magick*".

---

[139] Pryse, *The Apocalypse Unsealed: Being and Interpretation of the Initiation of Ioannes*, 30 – 33.

A'ash in Hebrew being Ayin and Shin meaning creation (עש). Ayin = 70 and Shin 300 giving 370, the number of the Holy Book. 370 is also the value of עקר, a foundation or basis.

The Book, "analyses the nature of the creative magical force in man, explains how to awaken it, how to use it and indicates the general as well as the particular objects to be gained thereby."[140] The book also has a specific relationship to the Dominus Liminis of A∴A∴ who is expected to study and practice the formula of the Rose Cross, as preparation for the mysteries of the Knowledge and Conversation of the Holy Guardian Angel.

Charles Stansfeld Jones in the introduction to his commentary on Liber A'ash stated that, "if the Phallus is the Creator in the Microcosm, why should it not be used, under will, to create any necessary thing or state whatever"? [141]

So we have a clear indication here that the mysteries of Liber 370 relate to the dual mysteries of the A∴A∴ and the OTO.

We can also refer back to Margaret Barker's comments about Wisdom; "She illuminates the human mind and helps us to better understand creation."

---

[140] Crowley, *The Holy Books of Thelema*, xxxiii.

[141] Aleister Crowley et al., *Commentaries on the Holy Books and Other Papers*, 351

Kwan Yin / Kannon

> This also is compassion: an end to the sickness of earth.
> A rooting-out of the weeds: a watering of the flowers

Liber XC, 26

> This wine is such that its virtue radiateth through the cup, and I reel under the intoxication of it. And every thought is destroyed by it. It abideth alone, and its name is Compassion.[142]

Liber 418, the 12 Aethyr

Kwan Yin is "Popularly known in the West in the present feminine form as the "Goddess of Mercy" or the "Buddhist Madonna," and hailed by Henry Adams as the sexless "merciful guardian of the human race"[143] It is said that every house has a Kuan-Yin.

Kwan Yin is the Chinese translation of the bodhisattva known as Avalokiteśvara, who embodies the compassion of all Buddhas. The name is translated as "lord who gazes down (at the world)". The world is said to be implied.

---

[142] Crowley, Neuburg and Desti, *The Vision & the Voice With Commentary and Other Papers: The Collected Diaries of Aleister Crowley, 1909-1914 E.V,* 149.

[143] Tay and Yin, "The Cult of Half Asia", 147.

While Amita[144] (Japanese, Amida) vows to take the sentient beings after death into a world where the retribution of karma is no more effective, Kuan-yin caters to the human desire to rise above our own karma even while in this life."[145] In this way, to draw a comparison to Thelema, she represents the "labour and heroism of incarnation" and is a redeemer.

C.N. Tay further writes that, "In popular religion Kuan-Yin is an object for worship and devotion; but the illumined may find in him an ideal and tangible aid for concentration and mental tranquilisation, through which they may identify themselves with the universal mind."[146]

In line with this universality of the deity:

If needed as a Buddha or a Hinayana teacher, he appears as such; if as Brahma, or Indra, or Isvara, or a deva, a king, an elder, a citizen an official, a brahman, a monk, nun, or male of female disciple, then he appears as such. If needed in the form of a wife of an elder, citizen, official or brahman, he appears as such; or if as youth or maiden, he appears as such. If needed as a god, or a demon, he so appears.[147]

---

[144] The principle Buddha in Pure Land Buddhism.

[145] C. Tay and Yin, "The Cult of Half Asia", 147 – 148

[146] Ibid., 148

Yet, "Although Kuan-Yin appears in many forms, reality is one. Although Kuan-yin traverses the world, he remains unmoved."[148]

The above resonates with a description of Mercury by Thomas Vaughn, where the dragon states of itself:

> I am the poysonous dragon[149], present everywhere and to bee had for nothing. My water and my fire dissolve, and compound; out of my body thou shalt draw the Green and the Red lion; but if thou dost not exactly know mee thou wilt with my fire destroy thy five senses. A most pernicious quick poyson comes out of my nostrils, which hath been the destruction of many. ... I am the Egg of Nature known only to the wise . ... I am called ... Mercury. ... I am the old dragon that is present everywhere on the face of the earth; I am father and mother; youthful and ancient; weak and yet most strong; life and death; visible and invisible; hard and soft; descending to the earth and ascending to the heavens; most high and most low; light and

---

[147] Ibid., 154

[148] Ibid., 156

[149] In Japan one of the incarnations of Kannon is Seiryu (青龍) or the Blue Dragon, with a special connection to Kiyomizu Dera in Kyoto and is said to protect the city in the East. In both Chinese and Japanese representations of Kwan-yin / Kannon she is sometimes shown standing atop a dragon.

heavy. ... I am dark and bright; I spring from the earth
and I come out of heaven.[150]

The Magical Writings of Thomas Vaughan, (1621-1666)

*Buddhist Goddess Kannon on a
Dragon by Katsushika Hokusai
(1814)*

So why would I be taking about a popular Buddhist
"goddess" in a paper about Baphomet. There is a clue
that was pointed out to me by Frater Shiva.

---

[150] Raff, *Jung and the Alchemical Imagination*, 96.

In Liber 58 *An Essay Upon Number*, there is a paragraph that states that:

> In Daath is said to be the Head of the great Serpent Nechesh or Leviathan, called Evil to conceal its Holiness (משיח = 358 = נחש, the Messiah or Redeemer, and מלכות = 496 = לויתך, the Bride.) It is identical with the Kundalini of the Hindu Philosophy, the Kwan-se-on of the Mongolian Peoples, and means the magical Force in Man, which is the sexual Force applied to the Brain, Heart, and other Organs, and redeemeth him.

Now, Kwan-se-on is Crowley's rendering of Kwan-Yin. The quote above uses the term "mercy", but Kwan-Yin is commonly associated in English with compassion: "maternal love and infinite compassion."[151]

I wonder if Crowley's Kwan-se-on is actually a rendering of "Kanzeon" (観世音), which is another name for Kannon / Kuan-yin in Japanese, made up of the kanji for "outlook", "World" and "sound". There are similar renderings of this in other languages, such as the Korean "Gwan-se-eum" (관세음). I assume Crowley is using "Mongolian" in a very general sense, as in Mongolian Kwan-yin is Nidü-ber üjegči.

---

[151] Tay and Yin, "The Cult of Half Asia", 151.

Thousand-armed Kannon (木造千 手観音坐像, mokuzō senjū kannon zazō) at Sanjūsangen-dō, Kyoto, Japan

If we then look to Liber 71 *The Voice Of Silence,* verse 94 of part 3, reads:

The more thou dost become at one with it, thy being melted in its BEING, the more thy Soul unites with

that which IS, the more thou wilt become
COMPASSION ABSOLUTE.[152]

To this Crowley comments:

This verse throws a little further light upon its
predecessor. COMPASSION is really a certain
Chinese figure whose names are numerous. One of
them is BAPHOMET.[153]

One must assume, based on the previous references,
that the "Chinese figure" is Kwan Yin.

The following verse is:

Such is the arya Path, Path of the Buddhas of
perfection.[154]

To which Crowley simply comments:

This closes this subject"[155], as if to deliberately draw
attention to it, subtly.

---

[152] Crowley et al., *Commentaries on the Holy Books and Other Papers*, 333.

[153] Crowley et al., *Commentaries on the Holy Books and Other Papers*, 334

[154] Ibid., 334.

[155] Ibid., 334

In the preceding verse COMPASSION is also integral:

> There Kleśa is destroyed for ever, Tanhâ's roots torn out. But stay, Disciple ... Yet, one word. Canst thou destroy divine compassion? Compassion is no attribute. It is the LAW of laws—eternal Harmony[156], Alaya's SELF; a shoreless universal essence, the light of everlasting Right, and fitness of all things, the law of love eternal.

Crowley comments:

> It would be improper here to disclose what is presumably the true meaning of this verse. One can only commend it to the earnest consideration of members of the Sanctuary of the Gnosis, the IX° of the OTO[157]

In his commentary Crowley identifies kleśa with, "Love of worldly enjoyment", and tanhâ as "the creative force."[158] Crowley is also explicitly linking the mysteries of Compassion to those of the IX°.

In one of her "inner group" teachings Blavatsky is recorded to have said, "The Pratyeka Buddhas do not

---

[156] Harmozousa

[157] Crowley et al., *Commentaries on the Holy Books and Other Papers*, 333

[158] Ibid., 333

go beyond the 3rd Cosmic Plane. They have conquered all their material desires, but have not yet freed themselves from their mental and spiritual desires."[159]

Pratyeka Buddhas are sometimes called "solitary" and refers to someone who has attained Buddahood without a teacher. They also do not accept students and do not work in order for others to attain. They accept their attainment for themselves.

Further Blavatsky states, "It is the **Buddha of Compassion** only that can transcend this third macrocosmic plane"[160]. (my emphasis).

This "third macrocosmic plane" (or solar plane) is called Jiva: The Universal Life, and was one of Blavatsky's sevenfold description of the manifested universe.

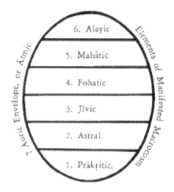

---

[159] Blavatsky, *The Inner Group Teachings of H.P. Blavatsky*, 35.

[160] Ibid., 35.

It is a Sanskrit word that means "soul, life, vital breath". In Hinduism and Jainism, a jiva is a living being; the immortal essence of a living organism. The word is derived from the Sanskrit verb-root jīv, which means to "to breathe or to live".

In the Bhagavad Gita we have:

न जायते म्रियते वा कदाचिन्
नायं भूत्वा भविता वा न भूयः
अजो नित्यः शाश्वतोऽयं पुराणो
न हन्यते हन्यमाने शरीरे

The Self is never born nor dies, nor having been, ceases at any time to be: unborn, eternal, unalterable and primeval, it is not slain when the body is slain.
 Bhagavad Gita, 2.20

Blavatsky further writes about the principle of Jiva:

More than any other, the life principle in man is one with which we are most familiar, and yet are so hopelessly ignorant as to its nature. Matter and force are ever found allied. Matter without force, and force without matter, are inconceivable. In the mineral kingdom **the universal life energy is one and unindividualized**; it begins imperceptibly to differentiate in the vegetable kingdom, and from the lower animals to the higher animals, and man, the differentiation increases at every step in complex progression.[161] (my emphasis)

The amount of Kinetic energy to be expended during life by one particular set of physiological cells is allotted by Karma—another aspect of the Universal Principle—consequently when this is expended the conscious activity of man or animal is no longer manifested on the plane of those cells, and the chemical forces which they represent are disengaged and left free to act in the physical plane of their manifestation. Jiva—in its universal aspect—has, like Prakriti, its seven forms, or what we have agreed to call "principles." Its action begins on the plane of the Universal Mind (Mahat) and ends in the grossest of the Tanmatric five planes—the last one, which is ours. Thus though we may, repeating after Sankhya philosophy, speak of the seven prakritis[162] (or "productive productions") or after the phraseology of the Occultists of the seven jivas—yet, both Prakriti and Jiva are indivisible abstractions, to be divided only out of condescension for the weakness of our human intellect. Therefore, also, whether we divide it into

---

[161] Blavatsky, "The Life Principle", https://www.blavatsky.net/index.php/life-principle accessed 12/04/2020

[162] प्रकृति (Nature) – In one sense a primal creative or natural force.

four, five or seven principles matters in reality very little.[163]

Now in general "compassion" is considered a vice in Thelemic doctrine, but what appears above is a very different type of compassion, this is not the compassion that is the "vice of kings" (AL II, 21).

If we look to the other great source of our doctrine where the above quote comes from, *The Vision and the Voice*, we find that compassion appears 7 times by my count.

> This wine is such that its virtue radiateth through the cup, and I reel under the intoxication of it. And every thought is destroyed by it. It abideth alone, and its name is Compassion.[164]

This quote is from the Aethyr called LOE (♋ ♎ ♍), to which Crowley notes, "these are all aspects of BABALON".[165] This Aethyr also contains certain

---

[163] Blavatsky, "The Life Principle", https://www.blavatsky.net/index.php/life-principle accessed 12/04/2020

[164] Crowley, Neuburg and Desti, *The Vision & the Voice With Commentary and Other Papers: The Collected Diaries of Aleister Crowley, 1909-1914 E.V.*, 149.

[165] Crowley et al, *Commentaries on the Holy Books and Other Papers*, 148.

mysteries of the OTO, as pointed out by Frater Shiva in some of his lectures.

If we convert the three astrological attributions to their associated tarot cards we get a very neat sequence, The Chariot, Adjustment and The Hermit. These are Atu VII, VIII and IX. If we add up these numbers we get 24 (the hours of the day with its origins in ancient Egypt) and it is also the number of:

אהובי

He whom I love; and

אוהבי

He who loves me

There is a certain sense of concealment in all three of these cards. In none can you fully see the face of the central figure. One is concealed, by a helmet, the other partly concealed by a mask, and the last (The Hermit) is facing away.

The Aethyr gives an indication of the nature of Compassion (compared with compassion).

> Thus do they shut themselves off from the company of the saints. Thus do they keep themselves from

compassion and from understanding. Accursed are they, for they shut up their blood in their heart.[166]

Above the teaching of the Aethyr is that a quality of a Black Brother is that they "keep themselves **from** compassion", and they keep themselves "**from** understanding" (my emphasis)[167]. Their wine is one of delusion and their understanding is false.

> Thus they make war upon the Holy One, sending forth their delusion upon men, and upon everything that liveth. So that their false compassion is called compassion, and their false understanding is called understanding, for this is their most potent spell.[168]

Here we have a clear indication that there are two types of 'compassion' that we are looking at, there is the false "compassion" and the true "Compassion" or "COMPASSION".

True Compassion is of the nature of Baphomet and BABALON:

---

[166] Crowley, Neuburg and Desti, *The Vision & the Voice With Commentary and Other Papers: The Collected Diaries of Aleister Crowley, 1909-1914 E.V,* 151.

[167] Binah – The Understanding

[168] Crowley et al., *Commentaries on the Holy Books and Other Papers*, 151-152

Blessed are the saints, that their blood is mingled in the cup, and cannot be separate anymore.[169]

If we take the Hebrew attributions of the Tarot cards we have:

חלי[170]

This is a word meaning sickness and has a value of 48. The word can also mean an ornament or Jewell (a pierced thing) and is from the verb חלל (halal), to pierce. 48 is the combined value of the above:

אהובי
He whom I love; and

אוהבי
He who loves me

Interplay and exchange (piercing and interlocking).

I was stricken as a bird by the bolt of the thunderer; I was pierced as the thief by the Lord of the Garden.

---

[169] Ibid., 151

[170] In this we can also see a reference back to the Supernal Mother, with The Chariot on one side of Adjustment carrying the Grail or Cup, while on the other The Hermit, who is Yod, the seed (the combination of these sees the mother transformed from אמא to אימא.

Liber LXV, IV: 40

In these three Tarot cards we also have a beautiful image of the Master of the Temple of A∴A∴.

We have the bearer of the Holy grail, "It is of pure amethyst, of the colour of Jupiter, but its shape suggests the full moon and the great Sea of Binah." On the other side we have the Hermit, "whose cloak is the colour of Binah." Finally, between these two, the seed and the grail, is, "the equilibrium of all things…the daughter, redeemed by her marriage with the Son, is thereby set up on the throne of the mother." She is the Alpha and the Omega, she is 8, she is Christ (the redeemer and the redeemed) - She stands in equilibrium:

> Equilibrium stands apart from any individual prejudices…She represents Manifestation, which may always be cancelled out by equilibration of opposites[171]

Here we see the True Compassion, or COMPASSION ABSOLUTE, is a state in which one has transcended duality; it is a virtue of one who has become one with the Universal Life:

> Thou shalt mingle thy life with the universal life. Thou shalt keep not back one drop.[172]

---

[171] Aleister Crowley, *The Book of Thoth*, 88.

But one can also ask, what does this mean, to become one with the Universal Life. The writings on tantra and Buddhism give some hints:

> Manipulation of the forces of good and evil provide the power. Wisdom and compassion are the means. The adamantine jewel enfolded by the lotus is the symbol. The Liberation of ourselves and all sentient beings is the goal. Perfect at-onement with pure undifferentiated Mind, a synonym for the stainless Void, is the fruit...The victory entails a shattering revolution of consciousness, progressive diminution of cherished egos and, ultimately, the burning up of the last vestiges of self.[173]

> Compassion is very detailed and precise, so it is necessary to have discriminating awareness of wisdom, which does not mean discriminating in terms of acceptance and rejection, but simply seeing things as they are.[174]

> When through prajna, the point is reached where shunyata[175] and karuna[176] are indivisible, there emerges bodhicitta (the Bodhi-mind). Bodhicitta is that which

---

[172] Liber CLVI, 3.

[173] Blofeld, *The Tantric Mysteries of Tibet*, 32.

[174] Fremantle and Trungpa, *The Tibetan Book of the Dead: The Great Liberation Through Hearing in the Bardo*, 21

all they has been a limit has fallen away and all the positive qualities of mind have become active. 'This active aspect of bodhicitta is what is meant by karuna. On this level, karuna is compassion in the true sense of that word – con-passio, "to feel with." This means to feel with what is real. It goes with the recognition of what is real and valuable in itself, not by some assigned or projected value which is basically subjective in character.[177]

We must observe that benevolence in the face of bliss, compassion in the face of sorrow, satisfaction in the face of meritorious conduct, indifference in the face of demerit, of other persons, are not sentiments which are recommended for their intrinsic moral value, but as means whereby the yogin attains the spiritual peace with is required for his task, all this in agreement with the a-moral characteristic of Yoga. It is also for this reason that the tendency will be towards indifference –

---

[175] Translated as "emptiness" or "void", but Guenther and Trungpa argue that this is a highly positive term, not negative, and a state of "openness"; an ability to perceive the "field", not just the forms within the field.

[176] Karuna is translated as "compassion" or "self-compassion", but again Guenther and Trungpa state that the word derives from the root *kr*, which denotes action.

[177] Guenther and Trungpa, *The Dawn of Tantra*, 32 -33.

the sentiment recommended in certain cases – becoming generalised so that it extends to all cases.[178]

In some ways Crowley addresses this in his commentary to Liber Samekh in relation to the nature of the H.G.A.,

> The main purpose of the ritual is to establish the relation of the subconscious self with the Angel in such a way that the Adept is aware that his Angel is the <u>Unity</u> which expresses the sum of the elements of that Self, that his normal consciousness contains alien elements introduced by accidents of environment...[179]

The Angel represents a Unity of the elements of the Adept. These elements do not cease to exist, but there is a perception or understanding of them as a field of experience. The consciousness of the Adept does not cling to these elements as do the Black Brothers, who have shut themselves up. They are there to function as tools for the Adept to express or enact his Will.

In a diary entry from 27 May 1919 Crowley writes:

> I note as to 'pain', that as 'I' am equally any other space-mark, 'I' exist and suffer so long as anything

---

[178] Tola and Dragoneti, *The Yogasutras of Patanjali: On Concentration of Mind*, 125.

[179] Crowley, *Magick: Book 4, Liber Aba*, Samuel Weiser, 531.

does. So, if Existence is Sorrow, Compassion is the token of adeptship; but then what right has a Buddha to 'pass away'? Of course, he has no choice in the matter, but then – oh, I can't think tonight!

Although as Thelemites we embrace that 'Existence is pure joy', but in the above we see Crowley meditating on the nature of Compassion, and its link to adeptship.

In my opinion the Compassion we are exploring here is equivalent to one of the tripartite elements in the attainment of the Master of the Temple – "He must completely identify Himself with the Infinite and Impersonal Love of all things." [180]This is the Compassion of those who have successfully crossed the Abyss, and reside in the City of the Pyramids; they have become the Alpha and the Omega, the beginning and the end. They are both in Heaven and in Earth. They are BABALON and the BEAST conjoined (BABALON and BAPHOMET). They are those who have gone beyond the veil; and returned to the tomb of the earth. They are the Compassionate ones who take in the whole Tree of Life. They have mingled their life with the universal life.

Greeting of Earth and Heaven![181]

---

[180] Gunther, *The Angel and the Abyss*, 193.

[181] Crowley, *Magick: Book 4, Liber Aba*, Samuel Weiser, 585.

To conclude (for now) this exploration of Baphomet, I can do no better than to quote from Tobias Churton, where, in his excellent book *Occult Paris*, he states of Baphomet, '…the faithful Catholic adept who knows what the church has long forgotten or misunderstood or supressed, Baphomet is the Key. For in this image, as he conceives it, is the symbol of mastery: the resolution of opposites in a higher unity…'[182]

Solve – Coagula

AMEN

---

[182] Churton, *Occult Paris*, 94.

So therefore the beginning is delight, and the End is delight, and delight is in the midst, even as the Indus is water in the cavern of the glacier, and water among the greater hills and the lesser hills and through the ramparts of the hills and through the plains, and water at the mouth thereof when it leaps forth into the mighty sea, yea, into the mighty sea.

Liber CCCLXX, 39

SELECTED BIBLIOGRAPHIES BY ARTICLE

Typology of Will in the Writings of Aleister Crowley, Meister Eckhart and Carl Gustav Jung

Krzysztof Azarewicz

Campbell, J., *The Hero with a Thousand Faces*, Princeton and Oxford: Princeton University Press 2004.

Crowley, A., *The Book of Lies*, York Beach, ME: Weiser 1981.

Crowley, A., *The Heart of the Master*, Tempe, AZ: New Falcon Publications 1992.

Crowley, A., *The Holy Books of Thelema*, York Beach, ME: Weiser 1983.

Crowley, A., *Liber 777 and Other Qabalistic Writings of Aleister Crowley*, ed. Israel Regardie, York Beach, ME: Weiser 1977.

Crowley, A., *Liber Aleph vel CXI. The Book of Wisdom or Folly*, ed. Hymenaeus Beta, York Beach, ME: Weiser 1991.

Crowley, A., *Magick Without Tears*, St. Paul, MN: Llewellyn Publications 1973.

Crowley, A., *The Equinox* I(2), London: Simpkin, Marshall, Hamilton, Kent & Co. LTD 1909.

Crowley, *The Equinox* III(10), York Beach, ME: Weiser 1997.

Crowley, A. *The Equinox* IV(1), York Beach, ME: Weiser 1996.

Crowley, A., *The Revival of Magick and Other Essays*, Tempe, AZ: New Falcon Publications 1998.

Eckhart, *The Complete Mystical Works*, trans. and ed. Maurice O'c. Walshe, New York, NY: The Crossroad Publishing Company 2009.

Feuerstein, G., *The Encyclopedia of Yoga and Tantra*, Boston and London: Shambhala 2011.

Jung, C.G., *Man and His Symbols*, New York, London: Anchor Press 1988 .

Marlan, S., *The Black Sun. The Alchemy and Art of Darkness*, Texas A&M University Press 2015

Saraswati, *Kundalini Tantra*, Munger, Bihar: Yoga Publications Trust 2000.

Archival source:

London, Warburg Institute, Gerald Yorke Collection: NS 117 Typescript copies of letters annotated by Gerald Yorke.

When meditation goes bad

Cynthia Crosse

Dr Miguel Farias and Catherine Wikholm (2015). The Buddha Pill: Can meditation change you? London: Watkins Publishing.

J. Daniel Gunther (2009). Initiation in the Aeon of the Child. Florida: Ibis Press.

_____(2014). The Angel & The Abyss. Florida: Ibis Press.

Daniel M. Ingram (2008). Mastering the Core Teachings of the Buddha. London: Aeon Books.

Jack Kornfield (1993). A Path with Heart. USA: Bantam Books.

Robin Lee (Dec 10, 2015). The Dark Side Of Being Full Of Light. Robin Lee, http://www.rebellesociety.com/2015/12/10/robinlee-darksideoflight/

Health in Thelema: The Stone of the Wise & The Holy Guardian Angel

Shawn Gray

Bogdan, Henrik. 'Challenging the Morals of Western Society: The Use of Ritualized Sex in Contemporary Occultism.' The Pomegranate: The International Journal of Pagan Studies 8:2 (2006), 211–246.

Bogdan, Henrik, and Martin P. Starr, eds. Aleister Crowley and Western Esotericism. Oxford: Oxford University Press, 2012.

Crowley, Aleister. Magick: Liber ABA. Boston, MA: Weiser, 2004.

Crowley, Aleister. The Book of Lies. San Francisco, CA: Red Wheel / Weiser, 1981.

Crowley, Aleister. The Confessions of Aleister Crowley: An Autohagiography. Edited by John Symonds and Kenneth Grant. New York: Hill and Wang, 1969.

Crowley, Aleister. The Equinox of the Gods. Scottsdale: New Falcon, 1991.

Crowley, Aleister. The Law Is for All. Edited by Louis Wilkinson and Hymenaeus Beta. Tempe, AR: New Falcon, 1996.

Crowley, Aleister. Amrita: Essays in Magical Rejuvenation. Edited by Martin P. Starr. Kings Beach, California: Thelema Publications, 1990.

Crowley, Aleister et al. Commentaries on the Holy Books. Vol. IV. The Equinox 1. York Beach, ME: Weiser, 1996.

Crowley, Aleister et al. *The Equinox Volume III No. 10.* Vol. III. 10. York Beach, ME: Red Wheel / Weiser, 1990.

Goodrick-Clarke, Nicholas. *The Westerrn Esoteric Traditions: A Historical Introduction.* Oxford: Oxford University Press, 2008.

Gunther, J. Daniel. *Initiation in the Aeon of the Child.* Lake Worth, FL: Ibis, 2009.

Hessle, Erwin, *The Holy Guardian Angel.* 2010. <http://www.erwinhessle.com/writings/pdfs/The_Holy_Guardian_Angel.pdf> [accessed 14 July 2013].

Kaczynski, R. *Forgotten Templars: The Untold Origins of Ordo Templi Orientis.* R. Kaczynski, 2012.

King, Stephen J., *Active Imagining O.T.O.*, Paper presented at Sydney, Australia, 2013.

Motta, Marcelo, *The Commentaries of AL: Being The Equinox, Vol. V, No. 1.* 1st Row Books, 2013. <http://www.lulu.com/shop/aleister-crowley/the-commentaries-of-al-being-the-equinox-vol-v-no-1/ebook/product-20977164.html> [accessed 19 June 2013].

Reuss, Theodor, 'Mystic Anatomy', The Magickal Link, Spring-Summer 1994, 8-9.

_____Our Order', The Magickal Link, Spring-Summer 1994, 5-8.

Sabazius, and AMT, *History*, US Grand Lodge Ordo Templi Orientis <http://oto-usa.org/oto/history/> [accessed 29 August 2013].

Suster, Gerald. *Crowley's Apprentice: The Life and Ideas of Israel Regardie*. York Beach, ME: Samuel Weiser, 1990.

On the Epiclesis
Michael Kolson

Bradshaw, Paul F. *Eucharistic Origins*. New York: Oxford University Press. 2004.

Crowley, Aleister. *The Book of Lies*. Devon: Haydn Press. 1962.

_____*The Confessions of Aleister Crowley*. New York: Hill and Wang. 1969.

_____*The Heart of the Master*. Scottsdale: New Falcon Press. 1992.

_____*The Law is for All*. Las Vegas: Falcon Press. 1988.

_____*Liber Aleph vel CXI: The Book of Wisdom or Folly*. York Beach: Samuel Weiser. 1991.

_____*Magick: Liber ABA. Book IV. Parts I-IV*. Second Revised Edition. York Beach: Samuel Weiser. 1994.

Crowley, Aleister et al. *The Equinox*. Vol.1, no. 4. York Beach: Samuel Weiser. 1992.

_____*The Vision and the Voice with Commentary and Other Papers*. York Beach: Samuel Weiser. 1998.

Davies, J.G. *A Select Liturgical Dictionary*. Richmond: John Knox Press. 1966.

Jung, C.G. *Psychology and Religion: West and East*. Princeton: Princeton University Press. 1975.

Scriven, David and Lynn Scriven. *Red Flame: A Thelemic Research Journal*. No. 2. Ordo Templi Orientis. 1995.

Smith, Morton. *Jesus the Magician*. New York: Barnes and Noble. 1993.

Baphomet

Fr. O.I.P.

Alter Michael J. Why the Torah Begins with the Letter Beit. United States: Jason Aronson, Incorporated, 1998.

Apple, Raymond, "Being at one: The challenge of Yom Kippur," ABC News, October 8 2019, 1:41pm Updated Tue 8 Oct 2019, 1:47pm, https://www.abc.net.au/religion/the-challenge-of-yom-kippur/11582690

Barker, Margaret, Temple Theology: An Introduction. London: Society for Promoting Christian Knowledge, 2004.

Barker, Margaret. The Gate of Heaven. London: SPCK, 1991

Barker, Margaret. The Great Angel: A Study of Israel's Second God. Louisville, Kentucky: Westminster John Knox Press, 1992.

Barker, Margaret. "Where Shall Wisdom be Found?" Department for External Church Relations of the Moscow Patriarchate, January 28, 2017, http://orthodoxeurope.org/page/11/1/7.aspx

Barker, Margaret. An Extraordinary Gathering of Angels. London: MQ Publications Ltd, 2004.

Barker, Margaret. The Lost Prophet. London: SPCK, 1988.

Blavatsky, H. P.. "The Life Principle." Theosophical Articles, Vol. II, April 12, 2020, https://www.blavatsky.net/index.php/life-principle.

Barber, Malcolm. The Trial of the Templars. Cambridge: Cambridge University Press, 2006.

Blavatsky, H.P.. The Secret Doctrine, Pasadena: Theosophical University Press, 1977.

Blavatsky, H.P.. The Inner Group Teachings of H.P. Blavatsky. San Diego, California: Point Loma Publications, Inc, 1985.

Blofeld, John. The Tantric Mysteries of Tibet. Boulder: Prajna Press, 1982.

Breeze, William. "De Harmonia Mundi." In Arcana V. edited by John Zorne, 11-29. New York: Hips Road, 2010.

Britannica Online Encyclopaedia. "Jnana (Indian religion)". Britannica.com. March 15, 2020

Churton, Tobias, "Aleister Crowley and the Yezidis." In Aleister Crowley and Western Esotericism. Edited by Henrik Bogdan, 181 – 207. New York: Oxford University Press, 2012.

_____Aleister Crowley The Biography. London: Watkins Publishing, 2011.

_____Occult Paris, Rochester, Vermont: Inner Traditions, 2016.

Crowley, Aleister. 777 and other Qabalistic Writings of Aleister Crowley. York Beach, Maine: Samuel Weiser, Inc, 1994.

Crowley, Aleister, Blavastsky, H.P., Fuller, J.F.C. and Stansfield Jones. Charles. Commentaries on the Holy Books and Other Papers. York Beach: Samuel Weiser, Inc, 1996.

Crowley, Aleister, Desti, Mary and Waddell, Leila. Magic. Book 4, Parts I-IV. York Beach, Maine: Samuel Weiser, Inc, 1997.

Crowley, Aleister. Magick in Theory and Practice. Paris: The Lecram Press, 1929.

Crowley, Aleister, Neuburg, Victor. B and Desti, Mary. The Vision & the Voice With Commentary and Other Papers: The Collected Diaries of Aleister Crowley, 1909-1914 E.V.. York Beach, Maine: Samuel Weiser, Inc, 1998.

Crowley, Aleister. The Book of Lies. York Beach: Samuel Weiser, Inc, 1995.

_____The Book of Thoth. York Beach, Maine: Samuel Weiser, Inc, 1993.

_____The Confessions of Aleister Crowley. London: Jonathan Cape, 1969.

_____The Heart of the Master. Tempe, AZ: New Falcon Publications, 1997.

_____The Holy Books of Thelema. York Beach, Maine: Samuel Weiser, Inc, 1988.

_____The Law is for All. Tempe, AZ: New Falcon Publications, 1996.

_____The Magical Record of the Beast 666. London: Duckworth, 1983.

Crowley, Aleister and Adams, Evangeline, The General Principles of Astrology. York Beach Maine: Red Wheel / Weiser, Inc, 2002 .

Ehrlich, Arnold. Mikra Ki-Pheshuto. New York: Ktav, 1969.

Fremantle, Francesca and Trungpa, Chogyam. The Tibetan Book of the Dead: The Great Liberation Through Hearing in the Bardo. Boulder & London: Shambala, 1975.

Guenther Herbert V and Trungpa, Chogyam The Dawn of Tantra. Boulder & London: Shambala, 1975.

Gunther , J. Daniel. The Angel and the Abyss. Lake Worth: Ibis Press, 2014.

_____Initiation in the Aeon of the Child. Lake Worth, FL: Ibis Books, 2009.

Ishaq, Ibin. The Life of Muhammad. Translated by Alfred Guillaume. Oxford: Oxford University Press, 1967.

Iyer, Raghavan. The Bhagavad Gita with the Uttara Gita. New York: The Pythagorean Sanga & Concord Grove Press, 1985.

Jung, C.G. The Archetypes of the Collective Unconscious. Translated by R.F.C. Hull. New York: Princeton University Press, 1980.

Kastner, L. E. "Gavaudan's Crusade Song." In The Modern Language Review26, no. 2 (1931): 142-150.

Klossowski, Pierre. The Baphomet. Translated by Sophie Hawkes and Stephen Sartarelli. Hygiene, Colorado: Eridanos Press, 1988.

Levi, Eliphas. Transcendental Magic. Translated by A.E. Waite. York Beach: Samuel Weiser, Inc, 1992.

_____The Book of Splendours. York Beach, Maine: Samuel Weiser Inc, 1984.

_____The Key of the Mysteries. Translated by Aleister Crowley. London: Rider & Company, 1959.

M. Pryse, James. The Apocalypse Unsealed: Being and Interpretation of the Initiation of Ioannes. London: John M. Watkins, 1910.

Neumann, Erich, Depth Psychology and a New Ethic. Boston & London: Shambala, 1990.

Ootake, Risuke. Katori Shintou-ryu: Warrior Tradition, New Jersey: Koryu Books, 2007

Pinker, Aron. "A Goat to Go to Azazel." Journal of Hebrew Scriptures, January 02, 2020, http://www.jhsonline.org/Articles/article_69.pdf

Raff, Jeffrey. Jung and the Alchemical Imagination. Berwick, Maine: Nicolas-Hays. Inc, 2000.

Regardie, Israel. The Complete Golden Dawn System of Magic. Tempe: New Falcon Publications, 1984.

Shconfield, Hugh. Essene Odyssey, Ringwood: Element Books Limited, 1998.

Shiva, Frater. Aspiring to the Holy Order, June 2011.

Spiegel, J. 42 Letter Name of God. University of Utah. Accessed   11   April,   2020. https://www.cs.utah.edu/~spiegel/kabbalah/jkm010.htm

Tay, C.N., "Kuan Yin: the Cult of Half Asia." History of Religion 16, no. 6 (1976): 147- 177.

Tola, Fernando and Dragoneti, Carmen. The Yogasutras of Patanjali: On Concentration of Mind. Translated by K.D. Prithipaul. Delhi: Motilal Banarsidass, 1987.

Valentine, Basil. The Triumphal Chariot of Antimony. Quoted in The Alchemical Tradition in the Late Twentieth Century. Berkeley: North Atlantic Books, 1983.

Wallis Budge, E.A.. The Book of the Dead. New York: Gramercy Books, 1960.

Wippler, Migene Gonzales. The Kabbalah and Magick of Angels. Woodbury, Minnesota: Llewellyn Publications, 2013.

Zalewski, Wojciech Maria. The Crucible of Religion. Eugene, Oregon: Wipf and Stock, 2012

CONTRIBUTOR BIOGRAPHIES

Fr. ΦΑΝΗΣ currently serves as National Grand Master General of the Italian section of O.T.O. and is an Aspirant to the A∴A∴.

Krzysztof Azarewicz has been studying and practicing Thelema for over 25 years. He is a founder and director of Lashtal Press specialising in the publishing of scholarly editions of Aleister Crowley in Polish. Krzysztof has also written several essays on Thelema, Magick, Tarot and Alchemy that were translated into English, French, Spanish, and Portuguese.

Frater V.I.A. has been an Aspirant to Thelema for over thirty years. He has regularly performed Liber XV since 1998 and has written about this and related subjects. Professionally, he serves as an educator and lives in central Texas with his wife, rabbits, and snake.

Cynthia Crosse – FSR New Zealand, an OTO initiate since the '80s, a Kriya Yoga practitioner, and grateful resident of paradise.

Shawn Gray has an academic background in Intercultural Religious Studies (BA) and Western Esotericism (MA dissertation on the evolution of Enochian magic). Having presented research papers on topics such as Renaissance magic and Thelema at academic conferences and as guest lecturer at Toyo University (Tokyo), his current interests include the migration of religious concepts and iconography across languages and cultures. Shawn is an avid practitioner of classical Japanese martial arts and lived for 17 years in Japan as a student of ninjutsu grandmaster Masaaki Hatsumi.

Frater Ιαω Σαβαω (Cosimo Salvatorelli) is a researcher on spirituality. He is an Elector of Italian Grand Lodge O.T.O. and an Aspirant to the A∴A∴. On Facebook he hosts Thelema Radio.

Michael Kolson joined the OTO in 1993 and soon after became an Aspirant of the A∴A∴. He was initiated in Buffalo, NY, on a snowy night when the actual building the temple was in caught fire from the neighbors upstairs — his cohort of initiates were subsequently called the Minervals of Fire and Ice. For a time, he served as Secretary of Pyramid Lodge, followed by serving an 11-year term on the Electoral College. When later became the third US Grand Lodge Ombudsman and Master of Horizon Lodge in Seattle.

Ian Drummond (Tau Nektarios) has been a member of the OTO since 1997, active in Sydney's Oceania Lodge and as a Deacon, Priest, and Bishop in the Ecclesia Gnostica Catholica. Ian was also a founding member of the Australian Grand Lodge Electoral College, completing his term of office in 2017.

Padraig MacIain lives in Western Australia with his son. He is an Initiate of the OTO, a Bishop of the EGC, and an Aspirant to the A∴A∴.

Marko Milenovic is a bookworm from cold Scandinavia. He has spent over a decade of his life exploring the system of the A∴A∴ and teachings of Aleister Crowley.

Frater O.I.P. (Joel Brady) has been an initiate of the O.T.O. since 1997, and is also an Aspirant to the A∴A∴. Currently serving as Grand Treasurer General of the Grand Lodge of Australia Frater O.I.P. has a special interest in the links between the two Orders and the wholeness that comes from their cooperation as intended by Aleister Crowley.

If you want
FREEDOM
You must fight for it

If you want
TO FIGHT
You must organise

If you want
TO ORGANISE
Join us

ORDO TEMPLI ORIENTIS
Grand Lodge of Australia

• SYDNEY • MELBOURNE • BRISBANE • CANBERRA •
• HOBART • PERTH • ADELAIDE • BALLARAT •

www.otoaustralia.org.au

ORDO TEMPLI ORIENTIS
International Contact

www.oto.org

The OTO does not include the A∴A∴ with which body it is, however, in close alliance. While the curricula of A∴A∴ and OTO interpenetrate at points, this is more by nature than design, and the exception, not the rule. The respective systems and their methods are distinct. One follows the Path in Eternity. The other, the Path of the Great Return. The Grand Lodge of Australia openly supports the work of the Great Order by providing resources to its Outer College, hosting lecture tours to Australia by its senior instructors, and collaborating on joint projects and learning events.

Those of you whose will is to communicate with the A∴A∴ should apply by letter to the Cancellarius of the A∴A∴

www.outercol.org

secretary@outercol.org

CPSIA information can be obtained
at www.ICGtesting.com
Printed in the USA
LVHW051223300321
682937LV00021B/1695